FIT TO BE TIED

The Granny Series

FIT TO BE TIED
Book Two ~ The Granny Series
Kelsey Browning and Nancy Naigle

Crossroads Publishing House

www.CrossroadsPublishingHouse.com

Fit To Be Tied

Copyright © 2014, Kelsey Browning and Nancy Naigle
Trade Paperback ISBN: 978-0991127221
Large Print ISBN: 978-0991127238

Granny Designs by Michelle Preast
Cover Art by Keith Sarna

Release, October 2014

Crossroads Publishing House
P.O. Box 55
Pfafftown, NC 27040

*For all the women who plan
to beat Father Time at his own game.*

*To heck with growing old gracefully, let's
do it with style.*

FIT TO BE TIED

Book Two

The **Granny** *Series*

Kelsey Browning and Nancy Naigle

Chapter One

Maggie glared down at her feet, currently sinking into greenish muck in Summer Haven's front yard. She wiggled her toes, but her bright orange toenail polish was barely visible beneath the brackish water tickling them. Worse, the unusually warm fall day was already beginning to make it smell.

Why she'd started wearing these dollar store flip-flips Sera loved so doggoned much, she didn't know. Back in her day, they'd called them thongs. Now that term was used for something that would leave her hind parts looking as pudgy as her toes. Today her winter galoshes would've been a much better choice.

Maggie pinched her nose, trying to tone down the odor because the squishy hole she was standing in could only be described as *eau de toilette*. Wasn't it enough that she'd replaced the huge house's upstairs commode after it crashed through the water-rotted boards between the first and second floors?

Apparently not, because now her best friend's family estate had septic system problems as well. And seeing as Lil was still on that extended *vacation* at Walter Stiles Federal Prison Camp, the potty problems were all Maggie's.

She heaved a sigh, but the girls didn't jiggle quite as much as they had a few months ago. A bonus. Taking care of Summer Haven, chasing bad guys, and wrangling both her life and Lil's had slimmed Maggie down a smidgen.

Good thing because she had a pile of poop to wrangle today.

"Maggie," Serendipity, Sera to her friends, called from the gazebo across the yard where she was contorted into one of her million yoga positions, "come practice your halasana."

Maggie did a quick translation in her head. The plough. Oh Lord, she preferred the vrksasana. The tree pose was easy enough and she'd gone from wobbling sprig to strong oak tree. Well, at least in her mind. True, she wasn't in love with poses that put her fanny in all sorts of vulnerable places, but she'd given in and begun doing yoga with Sera a few times a week anyway.

Their roommate Abby Ruth, on the other hand, was still holding out, insisting she got enough exercise by running her mouth and toting her guns.

Maggie glanced down again. Thrusting her derriere up in the air sounded like a pretty darn good alternative to standing here. Then again, when had she ever met a honey-do task she couldn't master?

"Can't right now," she called back. "We've got potty problems."

Sera's graceful, yoga-toned stride had her at Maggie's side in a flash. "What kind of problems?"

"Sticky, oozy, stinky ones. The septic system is being overworked or worse."

"I wondered what that stench was." Sera's nose wrinkled. "I'm as much a fan of natural fertilization as any self-respecting Californian, but this might be taking it to the extreme. Will it be expensive to fix?"

Here at Summer Haven, they were always watching their pennies. The Greek Revival house and surrounding land might be dignified, but it was a money pit from Hades. Didn't matter, though, because Maggie had promised she'd keep the place from falling down while Lil was away. "Not if I do it myself."

A tiny line bisected Sera's strawberry blond eyebrows. With her long hair and toned body, she looked about thirty years old at first glance. But when she frowned, it was more apparent she was in the fifty-something range. "Don't you think some things should be left to the experts?"

Maggie jammed her hands onto her hips and widened her feet. But her indignant pose was ruined when her ankle twisted, tweaking her knee and weakening her stance. Sera grabbed Maggie's arm just before she toppled into the sloppy mess.

Once Maggie was steady again, she said, "Don't you think owning a hardware store for decades makes *me* an expert?"

"This sinkhole looks too complicated for a DIY project, especially for a couple of girls over fifty."

Over fifty. That was polite. Sera was barely that age, but Maggie and Lil had greeted seventy a birthday or two ago. "Aren't you always saying age is just a state of mind?"

"Yes, but—"

"Well, this is one helluva mess." Abby Ruth strode up but kept the toes of her blistering red cowboy boots on the edge of the septic sinkhole.

For a fraction of a second, Maggie wanted to lash out. Abby Ruth was handy to have around—especially with her native Texan knowledge of guns and take-no-prisoners attitude—but every once in a while, she still rubbed Maggie wrong.

Maggie took what Sera referred to as a cleansing breath, and let it out for a five-count before responding. "I'll get this mess fixed, but until I do, we have to ration our flushes."

"Ration?" Abby Ruth's icy gray eyes lowered to narrow slits. "What do you mean, ration?"

"Well, there's no need to flush every time you pee."

"Are you telling me I'm gonna have to head down to the sheriff's office to take a proper shit?"

This woman was so inappropriate at times, and Sera's tinkling laughter didn't help the situation any. It just encouraged Abby Ruth.

"Poops rank a flush," Maggie clarified. "Pees don't."

"I knew I should've converted that damned horse trailer," Abby Ruth muttered, referring to the white behemoth where she stored her arsenal of guns, collection of cowboy boots, and other worldly possessions. "Fine. Let's fix this thing. I'll get the shovels."

Maggie checked her watch. One o'clock. She'd promised Lil she'd come for visiting hours today, and it was an hour and a half drive to the prison camp. "This'll just have to hold until tomorrow. I'm due at the prison in two hours, and I obviously need a shower before I can get on the road."

"Oh, no." Sera's lips were rolled in, a sure sign of distress. "You've forgotten, haven't you?"

That sinking feeling Maggie got every time she ate too much funnel cake plunked down in her stomach. What had she forgotten? "Um..."

Abby Ruth shook her head. She was the only person Maggie had ever known who could display so much disgust with a simple left-right movement. "Angelina Broussard and her trumped-up inspection committee are due out here for a pre-inspection walkabout this afternoon."

"That's today?" The heaviness of that funnel-cake-binge felt as though it had been topped with a double shake of seaweed powder instead of sugar. She *had* forgotten. That was what she got for failing to check her list. Dang it.

There wasn't enough air in the entire town of Summer Shoals, Georgia, for all the cleansing breaths Maggie needed right now. Still, she sucked in a double lungful. Another quick peek at her watch told her they had less than thirty minutes until Angelina and her Historical Preservation committee pulled into Summer Haven's circular driveway.

Maggie backed out of the goo. "There isn't much time to shield this whole mess from Angelina's raptor-like gaze."

"So about those shovels?" Abby Ruth said.

"Believe me," Maggie said, "we don't have time to dig this thing out. Even if we did, it would be the biggest pothole you've ever laid eyes on. No way Angelina could miss that."

"She's right," Sera agreed. "We need another plan."

"We can use that hay Sherman Harrison stashed out in the old barn to sop up the mess," Maggie decided.

"That'll work," Sera said. "Hay is super absorbent. Especially when it's dried out like that old stuff. Plus, we'll clear out the barn at the same time."

Maggie trotted toward the barn, so proud when her breathing remained even. There was something to all that yoga.

With Sera and Abby Ruth right on her heels, Maggie pulled open the sliding barn door. Good thing she'd remembered to gas up the little tractor. "Abby Ruth, can you hitch up the trailer?"

"Sure thing."

"Ever moved bales of hay?" she asked Sera.

"No, but I'm game." That was what Maggie loved about the sunny gal who'd recently dropped into her life. She never hesitated to pull her weight, change courses, and go with the flow when needed.

Which was pretty often lately.

Maggie tossed Sera a pair of work gloves. "You'll need these." Thank goodness hobby farmer Harrison preferred the small rectangular bales. If they'd been storing huge round bales, Maggie's scheme wouldn't have worked.

"Trailer's all hooked up," Abby Ruth said.

Maggie did a quick mental calculation. "I figure we'll need twenty-four bales total."

Within ten minutes, they had a full load of fifteen bales on the little cargo trailer. That meant two trips. Maggie checked her watch again. "We need to hurry. Abby Ruth, you drive. Sera and I will meet you there."

Maggie's breath came faster on the jog back to the pit of doom, but she still had plenty of energy to drag bales off the trailer and lay a wall of hay around the mess. Rather than stack the last bale, Maggie snipped the twine with a pair of clippers.

"Sera, while Abby Ruth and I grab the

rest of the hay, I need you to do some window dressing." Sera could make a silk purse out of a sow's ear.

"I'm on it!" Sera went to work.

Maggie hopped on the trailer for the ride back to the barn, and Abby Ruth gunned the small tractor, bumping across the driveway and grass. If NASCAR ever started a farm equipment series, Maggie would sponsor Abby Ruth. They'd be flush with prize money in no time.

They didn't waste time or energy on talk, just loaded the trailer again as though they hauled hay every darned day. When the trailer was full, Abby Ruth shoved at one bale, making a tiny opening. "Hop on."

Maggie eyed it. That space would hold approximately one half of her rear end.

What the heck, you only live once.

She wiggled into place and Abby Ruth took off.

By the time they made it back, Sera had part of the problem area blocked by a couple of scarecrow people she'd fashioned from hay. One had rounded hips and breasts. Thank the good Lord she hadn't added any protruding details on the other. "You are going to put clothes on them, aren't you?" Maggie asked.

Sera nodded absently and kept shaping

her artwork.

Abby Ruth nudged Maggie with her elbow. "What? You have something against Adam and Eve?"

"Of course not, but you know Angelina as well as I do. She'll take one look at those naked straw people and decide we're peddling porn." She turned back to the trailer. "Let's get the rest of this hay stacked up."

They lifted, pushed and tugged, but when they'd put the last bale in place, there was still a gaping hole around the muck. All the work and huffing and puffing and Angelina would still be able to see the septic swamp plain as day. Maggie's insides felt about as mucky as the hole they were trying to gussy up.

Abby Ruth took a step back and stared at the pit. "Well, dammit."

Maggie's thoughts exactly. "We'll never get this hidden in time."

Abby Ruth scratched an eyebrow and cast a considering look toward Sera. "Gimme a minute. I think I have an answer to the problem." Then she hightailed it toward the back of the house.

A couple of minutes later, Sera's VW van came chugging across the lawn with Abby Ruth bouncing in the driver's seat. She barreled through the rough terrain and then, just as pretty as you please, that woman angled the van's flat nose toward the gap in the hay bales.

Before Maggie could protest or Sera could look up from where she was looping the scarecrow man's waist with a knotted belt from the leftover hay bale twine, Abby Ruth maneuvered the van inside the circle of hay, and rocked it to a stop, barely making the bales shift.

That woman could drive, and they had a suitable camouflage, but Abby Ruth had just dumped several thousand pounds of vehicle right onto Maggie's problem.

Not a good long-term solution.

Abby Ruth's spiky gray hair popped up over the hay wall, and she was grinning like a lunatic. She vaulted over the whole thing and landed on her feet. Just like a cat with nine lives.

Something told Maggie that Abby Ruth was luckier than any cat.

And as dicey as moving that van might be later, Maggie couldn't give Abby Ruth grief because Angelina's car was coming up the driveway right this second.

Still, Maggie had to ask, "Why didn't you park your dually over it instead?"

"Sugar," Abby Ruth drawled, "because

Abby Ruth Cady doesn't ever take the wet spot."

Chapter Two

Lillian sat at the blue table in the otherwise colorless visiting room of Walter Stiles Prison Camp wondering where the heck Maggie was. If Fitz, Lil's favorite guard, hadn't been on duty, Lil and her so-called friend Big Martha wouldn't have been allowed to sit here for the past twenty minutes without a visitor at their table.

Four o'clock was speeding toward them, and Lillian desperately wanted an update on her precious Summer Haven.

"I think your little granny friend is blowing you off." Martha pushed her freshly washed dark hair behind the shoulder of her khaki prison-issued shirt. "That starts happening after you've been here a while."

It wasn't like Maggie to be late, but Martha had that all-knowing look on her face. The one that gnawed at Lil on a regular basis.

Lillian had only been a guest—as the warden liked to say—for a few months, and if there was one thing she knew about Maggie Rawls, it was she'd always be by her side. They'd been best friends since their William and Mary college days. No ma'am. Maggie wouldn't *blow her off* even if she was incarcerated for years.

But the warden had mentioned Lillian's sentence could be reduced by months if she was a model prisoner. And Lillian Summer Fairview knew a thing or two about behaving like a lady.

"She'll be here."

Martha's eyebrow lifted. "Whatever you say, Miss H&M."

When she first arrived at Walter Stiles, Lillian had made the mistake of ending up on Big Martha's bad side. And although they had a tenuous friendship now, Martha hadn't dropped the less than complimentary nickname, Miss High & Mighty.

"If you want to go back to your bunk," Lil said, "you don't have to wait here with me." She really preferred to visit with Maggie alone, but she couldn't be more forthright about Martha leaving. She didn't want to make the woman mad. Not over something like this on a day when Martha had no visitors of her own.

"Nah, I've got nothing better to do."

A few minutes later, when Maggie finally hurried through the door and plopped down at the table, Lillian flashed a told-you-so smile in Martha's direction.

"Sorry I'm late." Maggie swiped the back of her hand across her forehead. Something wiggled free from her hair and drifted to the table.

Lillian leaned forward to follow its downward glide. Was that...*hay?* And what the heck was that stench?

Maggie's normal scent wasn't flowery, more the sharp tang of duct-tape adhesive and the sweet scent of WD-40, but pleasant nonetheless. Today she smelled of nothing sweet but gave off the pungent odor of something awful. What in the world?

In addition, Maggie's sheep-appliquéd shirt was askew, with the collar flipped up.

Maggie must have caught Lil's stare because she suddenly reached for her collar and adjusted it. That was when Lillian spotted the sweat stain under Maggie's arm.

"Is everything okay at Summer Haven?" Lillian tried to keep her tone casual, but Maggie had obviously been fighting more than traffic today.

Maggie's smile was slightly forced. "You'll be glad to know we made it through

Angelina   Broussard's   pre-inspection inspection this afternoon."

Angelina's name alone was enough to make Lillian pucker up. "Summer Haven has to pass the inspection to be included in the annual Christmas Candlelight Tour of Homes. It's always been the shining star on that tour."

"I know, I know," Maggie said on a sigh. "It's critical to keep up appearances."

Lil's friends and neighbors in Summer Shoals had no idea she'd been sent up the river for Social Security fraud, and she had every intention of it staying that way. "Now tell me why you have hay-speckled hair and are wearing less than palatable perfume."

Maggie reached down to the bedazzled tape holder she always wore on her belt and stroked her duct tape the way she did when she needed to soothe herself. "We're having a little trouble with the septic system, that's all. But I have it under control."

"For heaven's sake, Harlan had that system installed the same year we married. That makes it over fifty years old. Besides, that's too big a project for you, Maggie. Better to hire someone."

Maggie leaned forward, bracing her elbows on the table. "Tell me, Lil, how do you want me to pay for that? Maybe sell some more furniture? There's not much left in the way of big ticket items other than the Tucker Torpedo." The words were sharp, but then her voice softened. "Or Sera, Abby Ruth and I could pay a little rent since we're living at Summer Haven for free."

The thought of selling her daddy's car, the one she'd made a deathbed promise to keep in the family, made Lil's heart contract. So she simply ignored Maggie's comment about it. "No rent. The house would be sitting empty if not for the three of you. And you know empty houses deteriorate quickly. Or worse, someone might vandalize the place."

"If I can't fix the septic system myself, it'll cost us the world. How do you expect we'll pay for it? With your prison income? Come on, Lil."

"I might be able to help you." Martha's head was cocked to the right, and her mouth was curved in a smug smile befitting the self-professed inmate queen of Walter Stiles. And when the queen offered her subjects something, it meant she wanted something in return. "You need a new septic system. Well, I've got a guy."

"A guy?"

"So happens that my uncle's third cousin owns Roto-Ready—"

"I couldn't possibly take charity from your family," Lil said, "any more than I'll take money from Maggie."

"No charity." Martha clucked her tongue against her teeth, producing a sound as if she was pulling back the trigger on a gun. "Barter. I've got this little problem that I think your grannies could help *me* with. After all, they fixed your guy up something good, didn't they?"

After Maggie, Sera and Abby Ruth had caught and corralled the greedy man behind the Social Security fraud that had landed her in prison, she'd boasted to Martha about what great sleuths her girls were. But that had been months ago, and she really didn't want to drag her friends into something dangerous again. "I don't know—"

"I can handle this," Maggie said to Martha.

"Maggie, now hold on. Let's hear her out." Lil knew better than to disrespect Martha in public. A newbie had done that recently, and Martha'd had her girls confiscate all the woman's underwear. And these uniforms were made from rough fabric. Lil didn't want her panty drawer robbed.

"I've got a niece who's like a daughter to me," Martha said. "Her biological clock is ticking so loud that men can hear her coming a mile away. I told her not to do it, but she signed up for one of those stupid online dating services called ThePerfectFit.com. One guy's spent over a month messaging her back and forth on the site. But she's never met him in all that time."

"What's the problem with that?" Lillian asked. Didn't seem so bad to her. Sounded as if the suitor was taking his time, getting to know the girl. Young people rushed into so many things these days. When Harlan was courting her, he'd spent a good four months simply visiting with her on the front porch before he'd ever tried to hold her hand or asked her out for a Sunday drive.

"He's finally asked her on a date, and can you guess what he wants to do?" Martha's fingers thrummed the table like a drum solo. "That weirdo is taking her to play...paintball."

Maggie leaned toward Martha. Now this was interesting.

"Paintball?" At least it was an outdoorsy activity. Certainly better than sitting in a dark theater watching a movie. She didn't know a thing about Martha's niece, but paintball sounded like a perfect date for someone like Abby Ruth. Then again, Abby Ruth wasn't exactly a normal woman.

"Yeah," Martha huffed. "My niece said he's taking her to an outdoor course, one where the NPPL people compete. Can you imagine, grown men getting paid to splat each other with paint? What a racket. The girl's so desperate she thinks it's an exciting and romantic date. I swear she's gone off her rocker."

Dating was a foreign concept to Maggie these days. With George gone well over a year now, she thought about men occasionally. But she thought about them in the same way she thought about being a hundred and twenty pounds again. Nostalgia mixed with the certainty that her dating again was about like a seventy-to-one long shot winning the Triple Crown.

"It's just entertainment. Like mini-golf or bowling. What's the big deal?" Normally when Martha joined Lil at their table for a visit, Maggie tried to edge the other woman out of the conversation. After all, what Maggie discussed with Lil really had nothing to do with Martha. Plus, the woman was obviously in prison camp because she'd broken the law. It was hard to trust someone like that.

Martha's mouth drew tight, and her

lowered eyebrows made her look as though she might jump across the table and tear into Maggie. "You don't think it's the least bit screwed up that he wants to take my niece to a place where they wear face paint, helmets and camo? He can't be normal if his idea of romance is shooting at her with paint bullets on their first date."

"I don't know what *we* can do to help. Are Sera, Abby Ruth and I supposed to crash your niece's date and take this guy out on the paintball course?" Maggie's tone came out snippy even to her own ears.

Martha pounded on the table, prompting one of the guards to give them a sharp-eyed look. With a clenched fist still on the table, Martha lowered her voice. "This guy's screen name is OnceUponATom, and he told her his real name is Tom Thumb. Seriously, what man's momma names him after a fairy-tale midget? If I had to guess, he's probably a peeping Tom. That name's a fake. Has to be."

"That *does* seem a bit unrealistic," Lil piped in.

"I obviously can't do any snooping around—" Martha blew out a big breath, "—since the powers that be watch everything I do on the computer. I need your help."

Maggie knew Martha was in for

something related to computers, and didn't really want to help the likes of her. "Neither Abby Ruth, Sera nor I know enough about computers to hack into stuff," Maggie said, even though Sera was becoming more of a whiz every day.

"It could be as easy as a Google search and a little stakeout work," Martha explained. "If you girls would be willing to track down this guy and report back, I'll set up that septic system repair for you...on my dime. It could work out for everyone."

"A little quid pro quo." Lil nodded thoughtfully. "That seems fair enough."

"Didn't you hear a thing I said?" Maggie said. "We don't need any quid pro quo. And if you ask me, Martha is overreacting. The guy is taking her niece on a date in a public place. No harm there. And, Lil, I've handled everything else at Summer Haven to this point, and goodness knows, that house demands a lot of attention. I'll handle this situation too."

"But why when there's another option?" Lil lifted her chin and gave Maggie her I'm-the-homecoming-queen-and-you're-the-lowly-court look. "Finding this man would be so much easier than fixing the septic system. And if you're so convinced he's on the up-and-up, the search shouldn't pose any of the danger you three got yourselves into a few months ago."

That was entirely different. That had been for Lil, not Martha. At the memory, satisfaction bloomed in Maggie's chest. Searching for the guy who'd set up Lil and had preyed on innocent senior citizens had made her feel alive. Powerful. And besides, she'd learned on YouTube how to pick a lock like a pro. Why subscribe to all those DIY Improvement magazines when a gal could get free instructions off the internet?

But something about doing little favors for Lil's prison BFF crawled all over Maggie. If she gave in now, the next time she came to visit, Lil would probably ask her to spruce up the Azalea Room with clean sheets for Martha.

Although the guards frowned upon it, Lil reached across the table, gripped Maggie's hand in hers. "Think clearly, Mags. Angelina and her crew will be there in a little over a week for the inspection. Surely, finding this man will take less time than digging up the septic tank. Could you do this one favor for Summer Haven? For me?"

One? More like Lil had asked a hundred of Maggie since she'd moved to Summer Haven. Heck of it was, she'd never been able to deny her best friend a favor.

Chapter Three

Saturday morning, Maggie stared down into the sunken area in the front yard. She'd hoped reducing flushes and the hot sunny weather might begin to dry out the septic field. But the situation was even worse, with soggy, stinking hay mixed in and the wheels of Sera's van dipping below sea level. If they didn't move that VW off the wet spot, they'd be down a vehicle and still unable to flush.

Lil's house was beautiful with its wide front veranda and stately columns, but it was like an aging woman. Lots of creaks and pops requiring daily maintenance. And more and more spackle needed to cover up her sagging facade. Sometimes Summer Haven was simply more than Maggie could handle alone, and this was one of those times. But she elbowed aside the nagging exhaustion living inside her because that wouldn't help her get the job done.

And the job was fixing the septic, not wasting precious time trying to find OnceUponATom. If she made Martha's priority her own, Maggie would be up shit creek quite literally, and she couldn't take that chance this close to Angelina's inspection.

Ten days and counting.

With Abby Ruth off watching a Little League game, it would be up to Maggie and Sera to handle the VW van removal.

Since Sera was meditating down by the creek, Maggie couldn't do anything with the van or the exterior septic system at the moment. Maybe she could help the situation from inside the house by pouring one of those biological additives down the drains and toilets. With all the natural stuff Serendipity had introduced to their diets, the good and bad bacteria were probably waging a war inside the pipes. Looked like the bad guys were currently edging out the good. Not surprising since Maggie had often wondered if she'd survive Sera's food herself.

A quick trip down to Darrell Holloway's hardware store and Maggie was back sprinkling septic additive like fairy dust in every sink and potty in the house when Sera came back from her cross-legged session.

Maggie said, "I need some help moving the van so I can dig."

"Should we wait until Abby Ruth gets home?"

"No telling when that'll be. We can handle it." Maggie led the way outside, pulling on a pair of work gloves as she walked. She had a feeling that van wouldn't glide over the grass. "Best to do it now. Help me toss a few of these hay bales out of the way."

They hefted the soggy bales, which weighed twice as much since they'd sucked up water. Still, Maggie tossed them aside one after the other. Her muscles might have seven decades on them, but they worked, by God. Better and better every day.

"You take the wheel," Maggie told Sera, "and I'll help guide you out. Gotta be careful not to run over the pipes or the tank itself."

Sera wiggled along their makeshift wall to get to the van. Another reason Maggie was serving as guide rather than driver. She might be slimmer than she'd been a few months ago, but she couldn't have squeezed herself through that tight space.

Maggie stood before the van like one of those guys who waved planes into the airport gates. All she needed was a bright vest and a flashlight. She raised her hands slowly, encouraging Sera to pull forward with caution.

The VW's engine revved and a rooster tail of brown muck shot from behind the bumper. That van wasn't moving an inch under its own steam. Maggie waved her arms in a frantic crisscross motion for a good thirty seconds before Sera caught on. Finally, she rolled down her window and called, "What now?"

"Gimme a sec to get into position behind the van." Maggie trotted around, took a closer look at the back tires. They were even more sunken than the front. Their quick fix for Angelina's visit had landed them in even deeper doo-doo.

Bad joke, Maggie.

"Make sure the van's in park," she hollered at Sera. "I need to get some leverage back here." It took a few minutes to wrangle hay out of a stray bale and stuff straw under each tire.

"You ready?" Sera called.

"Shift into drive and give the van a little gas. Be sure not to gun—"

Sera punched the gas like a teenaged street racer, and Maggie's last word was buried in an arc of water, mud and sludge. Her "Stop!" came out sounding like *Stahb!* She hunched over and spit the muddy goop out of her mouth.

Sera's engine went from roar to whine, and Maggie wiped at her tongue with her sleeve. Why was it she always ended up with something yucky in her mouth when she was around Sera? The knees of Maggie's khaki pants were muck-stained, and her paisley-printed shirt would never be the same so she didn't worry about wiping her gloves on it.

Her friend popped her head out the driver's side window as far as the hay would allow. "Oh, Maggie, I'm so sorry."

"Septic work is messy business. Don't worry about it." But it was clear the hay wasn't hacking it. "I need a couple of boards from the garage."

She was able to find a couple of sawed off two-by-sixes and hauled them to the front yard. Sera was standing at the back of the van, studying the sunken tires and flattened hay. "What a mess."

"I'm up to my ears in messes."

"What do you mean?"

"Lil's volunteered us for a completely different mess." Maggie mentally slapped her forehead for bringing up Lil's request. She hadn't yet decided what to do about Martha's tit-for-tat suggestion. Then again, Sera was a good sounding board. "Lil asked me to do her pal—" oh, calling Martha that tasted as bad as the mud in her mouth, "—Martha a favor. In return, Martha offered to have a someone in her branchy family tree fix the septic system."

Sera eyed the sunken van. "That might not be a bad deal. What's the favor?"

"Martha's niece met a guy on a dating site called The Perfect Fit, and even though she has absolutely no proof, Martha's convinced he's some kind of fairy tale Ted Bundy."

Sera got that faraway look she did sometimes before she said something strangely insightful. "Intuition is a powerful thing. What's got her all worked up?"

"They're finally going on their first date, and he's taking her to play paintball."

"That's the most violent first date I've ever heard of."

Maggie shrugged. Maybe she was the only one who didn't think it was a big deal. But then she'd bet a roll of designer duct tape that Abby Ruth would agree.

"You sound like you don't want to help Martha or her niece. Why?"

Well, and didn't that make Maggie feel like an old sourpuss? But seriously, that Martha woman was a criminal. Who was to say she wasn't planning a heist and using Summer Haven's potty problems to stake out the place? Not on Maggie's watch. No sirree. "We have things to do around here. If Summer Haven doesn't pass that inspection, we'll be off the register and the Christmas Candlelight Tour of Homes. If that happens, it'll just about kill Lillian."

Sera's eyes sparkled with mischief. "C'mon, we rocked that last little adventure, how hard could it be to find this guy?" She bounced on her toes, making the little bells on her ankle tinkle. "We're good at tracking down shady characters."

They were at that, and it was easy to get caught up in Sera's wide-eyed enthusiasm. "It was exciting." But the whole thing with Martha burrowed under Maggie's skin. "No. We need to make progress on Summer Haven, or we'll be sunk deeper than your tires. Let's get the van unstuck."

"At least think about it," Sera said with a hopeful smile. "Please?" She leapt to Maggie's aid, wedging a board behind each back tire. Once they had leverage, she ran back to the driver's side and hopped behind the wheel. "Ready?"

"Slowly this time," Maggie instructed.

Sera let the VW engine gradually amp up and thankfully the tires caught traction, allowing her to inch the van forward.

"A little at a time," Maggie called. "Keep going."

The once-yellow van slowly eased out of the muck, looking like an entry at the local 4x4 Mud Bog. They hadn't even needed the help of Abby Ruth or her monster truck, which cheered Maggie. In fact, she was feeling so optimistic, she was sure she could whip this septic system into shape and get Martha off her back.

Chapter Four

Abby Ruth sat on slightly sticky bleachers overlooking the Little League field. She'd forgotten the pleasure of watching fall ball— cooler temperatures, the scent of burnt popcorn and the ping of sunflower seeds as they hit the metal below her feet. Only now, the seeds came in new flavors like jalapeño, ranch and barbecue. She popped a handful of pickle-flavored ones into her mouth, and her eyes crossed from the sharp dill flavor dancing on her tongue.

Good...but they triggered an all-over body shiver.

The volunteer coaches, Deputy Barnes and Sheriff Teague Castro—Tadpole to her— were shouting encouragement to the boys. Teague's family had lived next door to Abby Ruth and her daughter Jenny back in Houston. That snaggletoothed little daredevil sure had grown into a handsome man. Over six feet tall with a muscular build, dark hair and a still-mischievous smile.

Damn, she loved that boy like he was her own son.

And he would've been her son-in-law if not for the nasty breakup between Jenny and him years ago. Those two should've settled their differences and pumped out a couple of ankle biters by now.

Abby Ruth's grandson Grayson was a hoot and a half, but she never would've guessed Jenny would marry into old Boston money and give birth to a kid who was as likely to wear starched khakis and a bow tie as he was jeans and cowboy boots.

Damned shame, that.

On the field, Teague's four-foot-nothing pitcher winged one perfectly over the plate. Nice, but too nice. Hit the strike zone right on, and the kid in the batter's box took advantage, whacking the crap outta the ball.

Snappy shortstop jumped straight up, and the ball smacked into his glove as though they both had magnets attached to them. Third out.

In celebration, Abby Ruth tucked her fingers into her mouth and let out a whistle that could probably be heard a county over.

Teague had always been a lucky one.

Except when it came to Jenny.

His team galloped into the dugout, the field dust following them in rust-colored clouds.

Teague's first two batters made it on base, one with a fly ball between centerfield and right field, the other with a grounder the second baseman blew.

The third batter to the plate was a skinny little runt with "Broussard" embroidered across his bony shoulders.

Abby Ruth stopped mid-clap. Hell's bells, that had to be Angelina's kid. Too much lanky pinch-faced likeness to be otherwise. The fact that the team's uniforms were emblazoned with "Broussard B&B" told her all she needed to know about that situation.

And she'd thought Teague was lucky? More like a poor bastard.

Abby Ruth leaned over and tapped the shoulder of the man sitting on the bench below her. "Doesn't the batter's momma come to the games?"

"Always over there." He hitched his head to the right, indicating where Angelina had set up a folding chair between the stands and the announcer's box. But she wasn't sitting. Instead, her entire body was plastered against the fence, probably pressing hash marks from the chain link into her face.

When the third batter approached the box, Angelina yelled, "You can do it, Booger. Hit it out of the park."

Booger? That kid was going to need a therapy fund.

Sure enough, the boy's shoulders hunched toward his ears, so high they skimmed his batting helmet.

First pitch was a nice one, but he was too wound-up to get a swing off in time.

Second one came in tight, and he shied away, stepping out of the box.

Third one was outside, and he reached for it. Swung so hard that he lost his balance, turned a circle and ended up on his knees in the dust.

"That happen a lot?" Abby Ruth asked the man.

"Every single time he's at bat."

Poor Teague and poor kid.

The boy plodded back to the dugout, and Teague stepped out of the third-base coach's box to give him a consolation pat on the back. The sympathetic gesture only made the kid's head hang lower. Obviously, the Broussard boy needed help.

Teague was a patient sort and likely worked with the kid every chance he had. But with a she-wolf momma like Angelina hovering, Teague probably wasn't able to make much headway. Problem was, both Teague and Angelina had skin in the game.

Abby Ruth, however, did not.

She scooted down the bench toward the dugout. While Teague's other assistant, a high school-aged kid, was helping the next batter with his helmet, Abby Ruth stage-whispered, "Psst. Hey, Broussard. C'mere."

Kid turned around, and his face could've made even the most hardhearted person shed a tear. Bottom lip turned down like a rodeo clown's. Dark eyebrows low over his eyes. And a tiny trail of snot below his nose that said he'd already been crying.

He wiped his nose on his shirt sleeve. "What d'you want?"

"You want to learn how to hit that ball?"

He shuffled a couple of steps closer. "Yeah, but I don't know you. Mom says even in a small town like Summer Shoals there's stranger danger. Kids get nabbed by scary folks all the time."

Hell, she'd better stuff a twenty in the kid's bat bag for that therapy fund.

"Do I look like a kid nabber?"

His shrewd gaze ranged over her, from the top of her choppy gray hair to the roach-killer toes of her custom cowboy boots. "You look like a cowgirl."

"I've ridden a...horse...a time or two."

"What's a cowgirl know about baseball?"

"I know just about all there is to know about sports," she bragged. "I even know Red Jensen."

The kids eyes lit up. "He was the best hitter in the history of pro baseball! You really know him?"

This kid was too easily impressed. Putty in her hands. He probably *should* be worried about kid nabbers. She edged off the bleachers to the ground. "Nolan Ryan too."

That brought him a little closer. "For reals?"

"Cross my heart and hope to die." She grabbed his elbow and hustled him out of the dugout and toward the batting cages flanking another field.

"Hey, hey," he squawked. "I still don't know you."

"I'm Abby Ruth, Coach Teague's aunt." Wasn't technically true, but she'd known Teague since he was knee-high to a flea. "So I'm not really a stranger."

She urged him under the batting cage net. "You practice batting much?"

"All the time," he said miserably. "My mom helps me."

God have mercy on them all. "Sometimes, if you practice wrong, then it means you can't play right. Stand over here, and I'll show you the proper stance." She rotated his shoulders and turned his back toward her.

He said, "I'll have to tell someone if you touch my privates."

She wanted to laugh, but baseball was serious business and this kid needed help with a capital H. "Last time I checked, the only thing you need to do with your privates while playing baseball is stuff a cup down your sliding shorts."

"Just sayin'."

"Elbows up and shoulders down. Feet apart so you're balanced." Abby Ruth worked with him until he looked perfect. "Great. Remember that."

"This is boring," he whined. "I want to hit home runs."

"You dang well can't hit a home run when you're not even hitting the ball. Stick with me, and I promise you'll be connecting with the ball in no time."

A few minutes later, a cheer went up from the crowd, and Abby Ruth glanced over at the scoreboard to find Teague's team had lost by two. If this kid could hit, it might've ended up differently. What was done, was done. But the future—it was wide open.

"Give me that stance again," she told him, "and a swing this time."

The Broussard kid raised his bat and assumed the position. He glanced her way for reassurance and she gave him a nod.

He slashed the bat in a wobbly swing.

"Okay, when you swing, your head is swiveling around like an owl." She dug a penny from the pocket of her jeans and placed it on the ground near the corner of the cage's home plate. "I want you to keep your eye on this."

"But what about watching the ball—"

"Booger!" Angelina rushed inside the batting cage.

Abby Ruth was three-quarters tempted to aim a fastball at her head, but that probably wouldn't encourage her to be fair during Summer Haven's inspection.

"What in the world are you doing over here with this woman?" Her glare would've petrified a lesser gal, but it just warmed the cockles of Abby Ruth's heart. Whatever the hell cockles were.

"She's teaching me how to bat," the kid said.

"Wh—why would you need that?" Angelina snatched the bat from her son's hand, then wrestled his helmet off his head. "I already taught you."

Not very well, sugar.

"But...but Abby Ruth knows—"

"We do *not* call adults by just their first names, young man."

Abby Ruth couldn't fault her for that. Too many parents let their kids run around willy-nilly these days saying stuff like "yeah" instead of "yes, ma'am." Manners could make you or break you in this world.

"Miz Abby Ruth said she can teach me so good that I might be able to hit a home run."

"First off, it's well, not good," Angelina told her son. "Second, Ms. Abby Ruth is not your coach. And you directly disobeyed my rule about going off with a stranger."

"She's Coach Teague's aunt."

Angelina whirled around, fixed her stare on Abby Ruth. "You're no more Teague Castro's aunt than...than..."

"Than you know how to teach a boy how to play baseball?"

"I don't think Lillian knows what kind of person she has staying at her home. I fully intend to let her know." Angelina's face went as purple as if she'd fallen face first into a barrel of crushed grapes. Probably the reason that last Cabernet Abby Ruth had sampled had been so sour. It'd had Angelina Broussard's face in it. "And don't think you can keep me from telling her."

"I'm afraid you'll have to just hold that nice little thought until Lillian gets back.

She's on vacation." Abby Ruth imposed an iron control over her face rather than let loose the sneer she wanted to direct at Angelina. That woman had no chance in hell of telling Lillian Summer Fairview anything for a long time, but if she found out that Lil wasn't really just traveling...well, that would be a problem.

Deputy Barnes hustled into the batting cage and threw his body between Angelina and Abby Ruth, using his arms to put some distance between them. As tall as Abby Ruth was, Barnes still had a few inches on her. She liked a tall man, but this one had better get his hind parts out of this fight before she sent him running off with a boot to the butt.

Angelina grabbed her son by the shirt and shook her fist toward Deputy Barnes. "And you better be careful where your loyalties lie too." Angelina dragged the kid out from under the protective netting and turned back to Abby Ruth. "You think you're something else, being from Texas and all that. You think you can just run around doing all of Lillian Summer Fairview's bidding for her. You're just a big blow of hot air. A...a...Texas tornado."

"Why, thank you," Abby Ruth said with a wide grin that only seemed to spin Angelina up.

The woman made a sound that was a cross between a growl and an oink. "Teague Castro serves as sheriff at the pleasure of the Bartell County voters, of which you are not! So don't be so sure he'll always be in your corner in a fight. If you haven't noticed, this county is in the great state of Georgia. Your Texas street *cred* doesn't mean a thing around here."

Abby Ruth had to give it to the woman, she had a quick wit about her. Something she could almost admire if Angelina wasn't a massive boil on her backside.

Chapter Five

From the corner of his eye, Teague glanced over the team mom's shoulder to see Abby Ruth—Aunt Bibi to him—and Angelina Broussard still going after it. When he'd ordered Barnes to head over there and break up that catfight, he probably should've given his deputy a warning too.

Because honestly, he might as well have handed a lamb over to two lions with tapeworms. He loved Abby Ruth as much as he loved his own momma, but that woman could test the patience of Job.

Because he was so busy watching the ruckus in the batting cage, he hadn't heard a word the mom was saying to him.

"Ma'am, I'm sorry," he said, glancing at her for a half-second. "But there's a situation in the batting cage needing my attention."

She followed his line of sight and

immediately stepped aside. "I'd say there is."

Most people around these parts didn't know Abby Ruth all that well yet. But Angelina's reputation as a troublemaker was solid. Give Aunt Bibi a couple more months and all of Bartell County would know exactly who she was too.

County residents would be throwing those two women together and placing bigger bets than Teague had confiscated at illegal cockfights.

He hustled over in time to hear Angelina screech, "I should file a complaint."

If she did, it would surely mess up the takeout pizza, ESPN and six-pack of Terrapin Hopsecutioner IPA he had on tap for tonight. He was officially off duty, but he couldn't, in all good conscience, haul these two women in and then leave his deputies to deal with them.

Abby Ruth stood in the middle of the batting cage, chin a million miles in the air and elbows stuck out aggressively. "You just go ahead and do whatever you think you have to. But it won't change the fact your boy—" she speared the kid with a look, "— what's your real name, anyway?"

"Benjamin."

"That Ben here couldn't hit a beach ball thrown at the speed of a turtle fart."

Shit. She was right, but did she have to say it aloud? Kids could be scarred by that kind of thing.

Instead, Ben was doubled over with a terminal case of the giggles. "Did you hear that, she said *turtle fart*. And she's an old lady. Old ladies ain't supposed to talk that way."

"Aren't," Angelina snapped.

Abby Ruth came in right behind her with, "And I'm not an old lady."

If he didn't jump in pronto, this little spat would blow up faster than a handful of bottle rockets. "Ladies." He slid between them in case one decided to go for the other's throat. "I'm sure there's just been a mis—"

"I want to press charges," Angelina said. "She kidnapped my son."

This was proof. God had some kind of grudge against him. His momma would say it was because he'd slept through Sunday school too many times when he was a kid. "Angelina—" he sidled up and took her arm, trying to pull her off the battlefield, "—it's not really kidnapping if she didn't take him anywhere. Besides, she was only trying to help."

Her lips flattened, so tightly pursed that she looked a little like a platypus. "Teaching my child values and skills is a parent's job—

mine. She has no right to interfere."

Teague had tried working with Ben every chance he had, but it wasn't nearly enough with fifteen kids on the team. He'd even—gently—mentioned to Angelina that she might consider a finding Ben a private batting coach.

Apparently, she'd hired herself.

"I think if you both drop it now, we can put all this behind us." He pitched his voice low, the same tone he used on the out-of-control drunks they sometimes hauled in on the weekends. Hell, he'd been known to croon a lullaby or two to settle them down.

Somehow, he didn't think "Rock-a-bye, Baby" would work on these two.

Angelina's eyes narrowed to slits. "Have you noticed all the trouble in Summer Shoals since this woman—" she jabbed a finger in Abby Ruth's direction, "—hit town?"

"Sugar," Abby Ruth drawled, "that's the nicest thing anyone's said to me today."

Trouble did follow Abby Ruth Cady like a pack of dogs chasing after a meaty bone. Hell, *it* chased *her?* Sometimes it seemed she pursued trouble as easily as her dually tires could crush a beer can.

"Seriously, Teague," Angelina huffed. "Have you checked into her past? Do you know anything about her background?"

He'd bet he knew a few things about Abby Ruth even her daughter Jenny didn't have a clue about. In fact, a few years ago he'd gotten his hands on a secret that, if revealed, could put a rift a mile wide in their mother-daughter relationship. Not that he'd ever do anything with that sensitive information. "Look, she's outrageous. And more often than not, she acts before she thinks." He paused, raising a hand to keep Abby Ruth silenced. "But her heart's in the right place. She didn't mean any harm and Ben doesn't look the worse for the wear."

"Humph." Angelina tossed another glare toward Abby Ruth. "Don't think I won't remember all this come election and historical preservation inspection time."

The only way to describe Angelina's departure was all-out Southern female flounce.

Turning toward Abby Ruth, Teague pulled off his coach's cap and rubbed the back of his sweaty neck.

Abby Ruth cocked her hip and braced her hands on her hips. "That woman could give a headache to a wheelbarrow full of BC Powder." She whacked Teague on the back. "You up for a beer, Tadpole?"

"Dammit, Aunt Bibi, you can't just go

around doing whatever the heck you please. Summer Shoals is a small town. You may not like Angelina, but she does have influence. I wouldn't underestimate her." He slid his sunglasses down to pin Abby Ruth with what he hoped came across as an I'm-a-full-fledged-adult-and-a-cop-to-boot stare. "I asked you to come to town to check into what was happening at Summer Haven. Not stir up more trouble."

"What are you saying?" Abby Ruth limboed under the batting cage netting. "That it's time for me to move on?" She strode forward with the aggression he normally admired. When it wasn't aimed at him. The toes of her boots bumped his tennis shoes. "Think you don't need ole Abby Ruth anymore after I narced on Maggie and Sera about that Social Security hullabaloo a few months ago?"

"It's not narcing when you change teams in the middle of the game." Besides, Abby Ruth still hadn't come clean about Lil being in prison. If he had to guess, she planned to keep that secret. "That's not what I'm saying and you know—"

Her nails were short, but pain was still involved when she poked him in the chest. Five times had that effect. "It's all fine and dandy for me to do your spying and dirty work when it's convenient for you. But when it causes your ass to ache a little, you're not so interested. I'll have you know that in a couple of sessions I could have that kid consistently getting base hits."

"I know you have his best interests at heart," Teague told her, "but you picked the wrong kid to take under your wing."

"Yeah—" her glare reminded him so much of the one Jenny had given him the last time they'd seen one another that it made his knees lock, "—this wouldn't be the first time I backed the wrong contender."

When she walked into Summer Haven's kitchen, Abby Ruth was still muttering compound curses made of every four-letter word she'd ever learned, and a couple five-letter ones for good measure. And she'd been in the roughest locker rooms in professional sports, so her vocabulary was as long as the distance between two goalposts.

"Whoa," Sera said from her perch at the desk tucked into the room's back corner. "I knew you were a journalist, but I had no idea how truly creative you were. Are any of those in Webster's?"

"If *muleturd* isn't, it damn well should be." Abby Ruth tried for a grumpy tone but couldn't pull it off. Something about Sera, their middle-aged flower child, tended to soften Abby Ruth's caustic edges.

"It's got visual punch, I'll give you that." Sera grinned. "Probably smells like our front yard."

That was when Abby Ruth noticed what was sitting on Sera's nose. A pair of tie-dyed cheaters. Only Sera would buy hippy-style old-lady glasses. "I knew you were too good to be true."

"What's that supposed to mean?"

Abby Ruth pointed a pistol finger at Sera's face. "You're getting old just like the rest of us. The proof is sitting right there on your nose."

"Oh." With a quick flick, Sera slipped them off. "They're only for close-up work."

And that refocused Abby Ruth's attention to the computer screen in front of Sera. *What in the world?* She stepped closer, bent to get a better look because—truth be told— she needed a little help on close-up work too. "Why are you looking up fraud and dating sites on the internet? What's ThePerfectFit.com? And why in heaven's name are you looking for someone named Tom Thumb?"

"Keep it down." Sera pushed her chair to the side and shot a glance over Abby Ruth's shoulder. Then she nestled closer. "Just wanted to make sure Maggie wasn't within hearing distance."

Oh, this day just kept getting better. If Sera was doing something Maggie wouldn't like, it would probably be a helluva lot of fun. Abby Ruth grabbed a chair from the farm table in the middle of the room and scooted it close to Sera. "Spill it, sister."

"Lillian wants us check out this guy her prison friend's niece met on a dating site. A favor for that Martha woman."

"Why?"

"Maggie says Martha's convinced there's something about the guy that's not on the up and up."

"Then why are we hiding it from Maggie?"

"She doesn't want to help Martha."

"Oh. The guy's name is Tom Thumb? What's with people and naming their kids? No wonder everyone is in therapy these days. What else you got?"

"Just the dating site name and his screen name. OnceUponATom."

"No way." Tracking down this bozo was right up Abby Ruth's alley. She rubbed her hands together, eager to get in on the fun. "What have you found?"

"That's the problem," Sera said. "I've been searching for the past hour, and I've got nothing."

"What about social media?"

"The only thing on Twitter or Facebook under that name is a grocery store chain."

"Hmm," she mused. "That's a little shifty." It was actually too easy to find people online these days. Not like way back when she'd started her journalism career. Back then, tracking people down took walking the streets and honest sweat. Now, a gal's fingers could do all the work. And what fun was that?

Even though hunting up dirt on folks online wasn't as enjoyable as old-fashioned sneak and peeks, a good Google search and a waltz through social media were the right tactics. So no Facebook profile said big, fat fraud to her. "And why are we hiding this little look-see from Maggie, exactly?"

"Martha proposed a trade." Sera continued to click on links. "We find this guy, and she'll have someone fix Summer Haven's septic system."

"Why would Maggie have a problem with that? Sounds like a win-win to me." Lord knew, mucking around in some guy's muddy past was a whole lot more fun than slogging through the crap bubbling up in Summer Haven's front yard.

"I think it hurt her pride that Lil didn't

think she could handle the latest house problem herself. Maggie told me to leave the dating site research alone."

Abby Ruth elbowed Sera. "And look at you, being the rebel. Wouldn't have dreamed it." Actually, she wouldn't have dreamed Sera was so experienced with technology. She was the strangest combination of airhead and brainiac. Problem was, you never knew which Sera would show up on which day.

"But I've hit a dead-end. And I don't like it."

"Have you really? Or have you just struck out—" and didn't that make her wince; if Maggie was on edge now, she would teeter over when she caught wind of what had transpired between Abby Ruth and Angelina at the ball field...so better to keep that close to her chest, "—on the easy stuff?"

"If he's not online, he doesn't exist."

"No, that identity doesn't exist, but you can bet your hot buttered buns there's a real person behind the fake. I'm sure half the people on that The Perfect Fit match website are lying about one thing or another."

"That's not a good way to start a relationship."

"Oh, Sera, if everyone were as honest and kindhearted as you, it'd be a different world." Abby Ruth laced her fingers and cracked her knuckles. "But they're not. If this guy is doing something under the table, I'll catch him in it. Did I tell you about the time I discovered the Super Bowl-winning QB was dating the ref's wife? Made the ball player 'fess up to it too. If I can pull that off, this OnceUponATom is a piece of red velvet cake."

Chapter Six

During lunch hour on his next off-duty day, Teague sat in an Atlanta restaurant at a teensy two-topper table that couldn't have been any bigger than a kindergartner's desk. Suddenly, someone shouted above the milling crowd, "And time. Three minutes, ladies, three minutes."

What had to be a hundred women shot in every direction, scurrying toward tables as if the music was about to stop at the county fair cakewalk. When a woman dove into the chair opposite him, it skidded across the floor with a tooth-tingling screech.

Her hair was bleached blond with bright pink ends, which clashed with her red lipstick. "Hi, I'm Heidi," she rushed out.

"Teague."

"What's your favorite position?"

"Second base."

Heidi reached over and slapped his hand. "I do love a man with a sense of humor. Sexual position, silly."

Teague squeezed his eyes closed. Why had he thought coming to a speed-dating session was an even remotely good idea? Probably because Abby Ruth had thrown his mistakes with Jenny in his face. "I...uh..."

"You do like sex, don't you?"

He shot a glance at the bar. Alcohol was against the speed-dating rules, at least until the so-called dates were over. But damned if he couldn't use a double shot of Crown about now. "Tell me something about yourself, Heidi."

"Well, I'm not much into missionary, but I can get behind some doggy—"

"Whoa!" He hit a traffic cop pose with his hand to stop her flow of words. "Know what? I don't think this is going to work out."

"But we still have a minute left."

Which would be the longest sixty seconds of his life if he had to hear this woman quote the *Kama Sutra*. "I'm impotent."

"Bye, then!" She sprang out of the chair as if he'd pushed an eject button.

He rubbed a palm across his eyes. As ideas went, this had been a bad one. But before he could stand and walk out, the shout came again. "And switch!"

This time, a tall, stacked redhead sat down across from him and held out her hand. "Alissa."

"Teague."

"Well, Teague the Miserable. What brought you here?"

Good thing he'd never aspired to be an actor because he wasn't fooling this one. "I just wanted... I'm just..."

She smiled. It was pretty as smiles went, but it wasn't a Jenny Cady blow-your-socks-off smile. "We all get lonely. It's nothing to be embarrassed about. But this doesn't seem like your kind of scene."

"My first time."

"I can always spot a virgin."

He winced. "No more sex talk, please." Hell, no sex was better than putting himself through this to find a date.

Her laughter was low and soothing. "Not everyone is cut out for these face-to-face deals. Have you ever thought about online dating?"

God, he was pathetic. "You know what? This whole thing has been a huge mistake. I've been in love with the same woman since I was—" Probably even more pathetic to admit he'd been in love with Jenny since he was ten years old. When would he accept he'd ruined their chances years ago and finally move on? Regardless, this micro-dating wasn't going to work for him.

The redhead reached into her purse, then pressed a card into his hand. "This is a new dating site I just heard about. You don't have to do much work. The system even picks matches for you." She leaned on the table and whispered, "If you want to duck out, I'll cover for you. If you don't get out now, you'll be covered up the entire hour. The girls were fighting over you before the rounds even started."

"Thanks," he said, and bolted from the table. When he made it to the door, he turned and gave her a little salute.

Alissa waved back and, when the organizer called out again, she headed for her next date.

Outside, Teague sucked in a lungful of air. That was the worst experience he'd had in...forever. How did guys do that? He glanced down at the card in his hand.

Just throw it away. But he couldn't resist and turned it over.

ThePerfectFit.com.

Monday morning meetings with the warden never amounted to good. Everyone in this terrible place knew that, but still Lil had hoped the summons would yield happy news. Like early release news.

Lillian left Warden Proctor's office on legs heavy with disappointment. No such luck.

So far, there was no news of an early release. Instead of promising Lillian she'd go before the parole board, the warden had assigned her a new project. But once again, the warden had softened her *request* by dangling the early-release carrot. Lil was beginning to believe the warden's garden was full of veggies she never harvested or served.

When she walked back into the pod she shared with her bunkmate, Dixie asked, "Everything okay?"

"Oh, it's fine." Although she felt deflated inside, Lillian gave Dixie a smile. "The warden just asked me to spearhead another project. That's good, right?"

"That's not good. That's awesome." The redhead's face lit up. "The more you do for her, the more she'll do for you. At this rate, you'll be out of here before me."

That was a huge stretch, and they both knew it. Her roomie's stint was up tomorrow, and Lillian hated to think what things would be like around here without Dixie at her side, guiding her through all the ins and outs of prison life. The girl had saved her hide a few times. Lillian settled on the bunk bed's bottom mattress. "I'll miss you when you get out."

Dixie dropped down beside Lillian and leaned back against the bed's metal frame. "So, what's the new project?"

"A couple of initiatives, including an interviewing and dress-for-success session specifically geared toward the ladies about to be released."

"I sure could've used that," Dixie said. "It's hard to find work on the outside once you've been on the inside. No one wants to hire someone who's been in jail. Even if you were in for something minor, people out in the real world treat you like you murdered someone."

Lillian worried about Dixie's ability to land work. She didn't have many skills, and full-time employment was part of her early release criteria. "I think it will be a beneficial program, but I'm worried about the timeline. I only have a week to get it all in place."

"That's not much time," Dixie agreed. "Why the hurry?"

The reason was supposed to be kept quiet, but she could trust Dixie. "You can't tell anyone."

Dixie crossed her heart.

"A Bureau of Prisons team is visiting the smaller prisons because they need to close a few. It's a budget thing. If Walter Stiles ends up on their closure list, Warden Proctor and the others who work here would have to move or they'd be out of jobs. She doesn't want to let that happen on her watch."

"Too bad for them."

"It could be devastating for the inmates too." Lil picked at a loose thread on her pillowcase, accidentally unraveling a good portion of the seam. "If they shut down this facility, we'd all be relocated. The next closest facility is five hours away."

"Oohh." Dixie blew out a breath that made her lips sputter. "Your friends wouldn't be able to visit as often if you're that far away."

"Exactly," Lil said. "And in addition to the interviewing session, she charged me with a beautification project. How I'll get all that done in a week, I have no idea."

"What exactly is a beautification project?" Dixie's face turned mulish. "What's wrong with the way we look?"

"It's not about the way *we* look, although you have to admit the uniforms are more than a little tired. I have to get the grounds and buildings spiffied up—paint, plants. You name it, she wants it. And Lord knows that's like slapping lipstick on a pig."

"This is not good." Dixie shook her head as if she were watching a ping-pong match. "Not good at all."

"I know it's only a week, but hopefully the warden will be happy with the little I can do in the time I have. Besides, she's right. The grounds could use some color, and the buildings themselves could benefit from a fresh coat of paint. It's just so much to accomplish in such a short time." Lillian felt exhausted just thinking about it. This was not a job for someone her age.

Dixie bit her lip. "Lil, gussying up the place isn't the warden's idea. The brain behind the whole paintin' and plantin' thing is Big Martha."

Lillian paused the slideshow in her mind of robin's-egg-blue walls, pansies in the courtyard and immaculately dressed mock interview candidates. "What are you saying?"

"While I was waiting for my exit interview, I heard Big Martha pitch the whole idea to the warden. Pretty much word for word what you just told me." She gnawed on her cuticle, caught Lil's raised brows, and stuffed her hands into her lap. "Trust me, Martha was angling to run it herself. She considers herself quite the green thumb.

She'll flip when she finds out the warden picked you to pull off *her* idea."

Lillian's stomach gave such a lurch her breakfast rolled. Probably not unlike the septic mess bubbling up at Summer Haven. Because when Martha heard Lillian had once again stepped on her toes, she would say *adios* to their deal to have Summer Haven's septic system fixed.

Dixie jumped up and paced around the tiny pod. "For once, I sure am glad I'm not you."

"I wish I weren't me right now too." Dang the warden. Her ideas and requests always seemed to drive a wedge between Lillian and Martha. And Big Martha's bad side was the last place Lil wanted to be.

She hopped up and made for the open doorway between the cinderblocks surrounding their little space.

"Where are you off to so fast?" Dixie's voice rang with panic.

Lil spun around and bracketed her hands on her hips. "I'm going to tell Martha. No sense her finding out from someone other than me."

"You be careful," Dixie called after her.

Lillian marched straight to Martha's cottage. Although it was clear across the prison yard, she made the trip in short time.

The prison's required daily exercise time had upped her stamina, a small plus in an otherwise depressing situation.

Lillian climbed the steps to the porch, but one of Big Martha's girls blocked the cottage's doorway in front of her and snapped, "She doesn't want to see you right now."

Just as Lillian began to argue her case, a crash and a guttural growl filled the air.

"Maybe I should rephrase that," the girl said, glancing over her shoulder. When something hit the door behind her, she flinched, then lowered her voice. "Old girl, *you* do not want to see *her* right now."

Martha had definitely received the news about the project.

"Skedaddle. Get on outta here before she throws you next. Go, granny, go!"

Lillian didn't need to be warned twice. She spun as fast as a skater on thin ice and high-tailed it back to her unit, never looking back.

Everyone else in the block was out in the courtyard. She was thankful to be alone, because her brain was about to explode. Overwhelmed just thinking about the mess she was in, Lil crawled into bed and pulled the covers over her head.

What could've been minutes or hours

later, Dixie nudged her awake. "It's dinnertime."

"I'm not hungry."

"You know that don't matter. You still have to come."

Lil knew it all too well. She pushed back the covers and pulled herself together. "You go on ahead."

"You sure? Might be easier if I'm with you."

"Being with me would just get you in trouble. I'll be fine by myself." Lonely, but fine.

Dixie hesitated, and Lord knew Lil would've loved to have her at her side. But hanging around with her could put Dixie's release at risk if Martha had a mind to make trouble. As angry as she was over this beautification project, Martha wouldn't hesitate to use Dixie to hit Lil where it really hurt.

Lil scooted into the cafeteria just before headcount. She grabbed a tray and slid it across the metal rail. She held her thumb and forefinger up indicating that she only wanted a little of what looked like meatloaf smothered in a vat of tomato sauce. The girls behind the counter were generous with Lil's portions, a fact underscored by the snug fit of Lil's pants, but today her tummy wasn't up to a full meal. Just enough food to keep the guards from suspecting something was up. Any hint of a problem and they'd be all over it.

She carried her half-empty tray to a table populated with inmates she recognized but had never dined with. They all stared up at her, not hostile exactly, but not friendly either. "Do you mind?"

"Suit yourself."

She sat and tried to keep her head down, pushing food around on her plate.

"I heard Big Martha is in a mood and a half," the woman next to Lil said.

The woman across the table flicked a panicked look over Lil's left shoulder. "Shh!"

Just then, something bumped that same shoulder. Felt like a shark warning its prey of imminent attack. Lil didn't even have to look behind her to know exactly who the shark was.

"I let you into my circle," Martha said, "and this is the thanks I get? I guess where you come from, hoity-toity society ladies steal ideas from each other all the time. Maybe they even steal each other's jewelry and shit."

Lil let her fork clatter to her tray, stood and turned to face Martha. "I did not steal anything from you."

"What do you call it when you swipe someone else's idea?"

Although Lil's insides were now a tight coil of fear, she couldn't give in to Martha's bullying. She took a pause for effect, and to steady her voice. "It's not as if I waltzed into the warden's office begging for another project. She came to me, asking for my help."

"You didn't have to say yes," Martha said.

"Well, at the time, I didn't have any idea beautifying Walter Stiles was *your* idea. And seriously, if the warden started talking early release to you, what would you have done?"

"Maybe," Martha said in a low tone that reminded Lil of the slow warning dance of a King cobra, "I would've wondered why a woman like Warden Proctor, a woman with a limited number of good ideas, was having a great one."

"I suppose I'm not a suspicious sort like you are. When someone tells me something, I tend to believe them."

"Well, I'm telling you this, Miss H&M. It would be in your best interest to stay away from me unless you have some news I'm interested in hearing."

Which meant she had no interest in honoring the deal they'd made about Summer Haven's septic system.

Chapter Seven

Maggie held the cushy-handled drain spade in one hand and rested her foot on its shiny blade as she surveyed Summer Haven's front yard. The matted grass looked as though a merry band of possums, moles and armadillos had staged a hoedown—or maybe a throw down. She'd dug holes all around the septic tank looking for the distribution box and the source of the effluent breakdown, and things were looking worse rather than better, but she couldn't stop until she found the source of the problem.

She took in a breath and lifted her drain spade. Then she chopped downward and—*holy hotdogs!*—what she hit wasn't soft dirt but rather her own foot. "Yeeeow!"

She dropped the spade and hopped around on one foot, holding the one she'd sliced tight between her palms. Blood seeped out of the thin canvas of her tennis shoe to ooze between her fingers and drip to the soggy grass. She darn well knew better than to work in those lightweight shoes. She pulled off the bright red one and dropped the ruined thing to the ground.

Her awkward hops took her to the edge of the mucky part of the yard before she allowed herself to collapse to the ground.

She shot a glance toward the driveway to check for Sera's and Abby Ruth's cars. Now, they'd give her three kinds of heck for insisting on working on the septic herself.

Yep, and there was the dually and the VW.

Shoot, shoot, shoot.

How in Pete's name would Maggie make it past them to get her hands on a first aid kit?

She stretched out the hem of her T-shirt and mopped at the blood on her foot. Yeah, that was a long flap of skin she'd sliced. She scrounged around in her fanny pack. Three assorted finger bandages, but that was all. Where was a butterfly bandage when a gal needed one?

Well, if duct tape could patch the fuselage of a 747, it could patch a slice of skin.

Maggie reached to her hip for the duct

tape tucked into the blinged-out holder she wore on her belt. She ripped off a long strip of pumpkin-patterned tape and wrapped it twice around her instep, trying not to think of how it would feel to peel the super-sticky stuff off her skin. Because doing that made her stomach twirl. A glass or two of special iced tea would definitely be required for the ripping.

Pushing to her feet was an awkward affair, with a lot of grunting, wincing and waving her butt in the air. Finally, she was upright and hobbling toward the house. Lots of weight on her right foot and baby tiptoes on the left. Hobble, schlump. Hobble, schlump. Hobble, schlump. The front porch stairs seemed like Mount Everest, but Maggie gripped the handrail and muscled on.

She eased open the front door and peeked inside. A rumble of voices came from the back of the house. Dang, hitting the kitchen for bandages was obviously out. Instead, she shuffled toward the stairs, then took a few seconds to pause and give them the once-over. Exactly fourteen steps. Fourteen Quasimodo hobble-schlumps.

A deep breath, and Maggie grabbed the balustrade. She pulled herself to the first step, then caught actual words streaming from the kitchen.

"Well, I don't care what Maggie wants," Abby Ruth said. "She might be Summer Haven's caretaker while Lil's in the clinker, but we all live here."

Excuse me? Just when Maggie thought she and Abby Ruth were coming to some type of peaceful cohabitation, the woman's real colors bled through again. That one didn't do well with being second in command. And that was certainly as high as she would ever climb on the Summer Haven ship.

"I don't know," Sera responded. "I don't feel quite right about going behind her back."

"We're not doing anything," Abby Ruth said.

Not doing anything? That usually meant *something*. And Maggie had caught Abby Ruth's unspoken word. *Yet*. We're not doing anything *yet*. She had a mind to stomp into that kitchen—okay, maybe not stomp because right now belly-slithering was her best option for moving fast—and give Abby Ruth what-for about whatever. If those two were hiding something from her, it meant they didn't respect her or her authority over Summer Haven. Was that the thanks she got for sharing Lil's home with them?

But with a warm puddle forming under her foot, she couldn't deal with her so-called friends' treason right now.

Lord, the fatigue from the pressure of caring for Summer Haven, keeping Lillian's secret and overseeing those two women in the kitchen swamped Maggie. The oak steps suddenly looked like a soft, comfy place to collapse and rest her face in her hands. She would've done it too, if she thought she could ever get up again.

She gathered her wits and gained another step. Then another. She was a third of the way up the staircase when Sera's and Abby Ruth's voices came closer.

Maggie tried to increase her speed, doing a hop-shuffle up two stairs. On the third, however, her technique failed her. She stumbled, cracking her right shin against a step, and if it weren't for her quick reflexes and death grip on the rail, she'd have bumped back down the stairs to the foyer. She twisted to sit on the step above her and tried to look casual as Sera and Abby Ruth came into sight.

Sera's eyes narrowed immediately. "Maggie, why are you sitting on the stairs? I thought you were outside working on the septic system."

That girl was just a little too bright at the

most inconvenient times. "I...uh...did you know there's a nice view of the gazebo out the transom window over the front door?"

"You're sitting up there—" Abby's Ruth craned her head back as though to peer out the transom herself, "—looking at the gazebo?"

"It does a body good to slow down and take in her surroundings every now and again."

"Normally, that's something a body does from one of the rocking chairs on the front porch," Abby Ruth replied.

"Neat. I love a great view," Sera said, rounding the newel post at the bottom of the stairs.

Maggie glanced down to find bloody footprints trailing up the steps. Sera didn't miss that tiny detail either. Lil would have a hissy fit if she could see the mess Maggie was making.

"Maggie," Sera gasped, scampering up the steps two at a time in a way that had Maggie clenching her teeth in envious pain. "What have you done to yourself?"

"It's nothing."

Abby Ruth climbed up behind Sera. "Bleeding like a stuck hog doesn't look like nothing to me."

Sera crouched at Maggie's foot. "You hurt

yourself."

She wiggled her toes, which were already so swollen that they looked like pink baby mice. "It was just a little slice with the shovel."

"Around that cesspool? Who knows what kind of flesh-eating bacteria might already be invading your body!" Sera scolded. "You put duct tape on it? Maggie, why didn't you call for one of us? We would've come out to help you."

"I don't need help." Even to her own ears, Maggie sounded sullen. "I fix things."

"You need stitches." Abby Ruth stepped over Sera in one long-legged stride. She clomped her way to the top of the stairs and disappeared into the upstairs bathroom.

"A butterfly bandage will fix me right up," Maggie called.

"I don't know—" Sera continued to study Maggie's foot, "—your foot's turning purple below the tape."

Abby Ruth came back down with a towel and shoved it into Maggie's hands. "Probably cut off the circulation by wrapping it so tight."

"Maybe we should take you to the clinic," Sera said. "Let Dr. Broussard take a look."

Lord, that was the last thing in the world she wanted to do today. "I'll pass. Cuts always look worse before they've been cleaned up. I'll just make my way upstairs and then—"

Abby Ruth turned to Maggie and drawled in the annoying way that insinuated she knew better than you, "Tell me, Mags, when was the last time you had a tetanus shot?"

Maggie clenched a fist but resisted banging it against her leg. That woman was insufferable when she was right.

"Umm-hmm," Abby Ruth said, winking in Sera's direction. "Looks like a trip to the clinic is just what the doctor ordered."

They wouldn't let Maggie drive herself to the clinic. She'd never been one of those girls who needed an entourage to visit the ladies room, and this little expedition felt a lot like a group primp and pee session. Which reminded her she should've hit the potty before they left the house. Abby Ruth insisted they take her monstrous truck. Made no sense seeing as Maggie almost took off her other foot trying to climb up into the thing. Then again, the shag carpet in Sera's van would've wicked up the blood still trickling from Maggie's foot, and that certainly wasn't sanitary.

"I have to say—" Abby Ruth glanced toward Maggie huddled against the passenger side door, "—sulking isn't really your color."

"My foot would've been fine if you two hadn't gone all mother hen on me. There's almost nothing in the world that a butterfly bandage can't fix."

"Yeah." Abby Ruth's tone was dry. "Every case of lockjaw ever documented was cured with a Band-Aid."

Dang it. This was time better spent in the yard whipping that septic system into shape. If Maggie couldn't report some progress by the time she visited Lil again, she'd be forced to fight off Martha's charity. Why in the world Lil would trust that woman over her, she couldn't figure. Yes, they'd both made new friends since Lil got herself locked up, but no one would ever replace Lil in Maggie's heart.

Maybe Lil was a touch more fickle.

Maggie rocked her forehead against the window, smashing her bangs. She should be ashamed of herself. She and Lil were not twelve-year-olds with friendship jealousy issues. No doubt, Lil had to do whatever she could to stay sane in that federal prison camp, even if it meant hanging out with the kind of people she never would've cottoned to before.

"Besides," Abby Ruth said, "this gives us

the perfect opportunity to pump Dr. Broussard for information. Maybe dig up a little dirt."

"Why would we want to find dirt on the doctor?" Sera said from the backseat.

"Not the doctor." Abby Ruth looked as if she'd like to bonk Sera on the noggin. "His cranky, historic-preservation-committee wife."

"Ooohh." Sera propped her arms on the front seat and leaned in. "That makes a lot more sense."

"So my mangled foot is just an excuse to get cozy with the enemy?" Maggie said.

Abby Ruth cut her a look that could've lasered the whiskers off a cat's chin from a hundred yards. "Look, sugar, you can't have this both ways. First, you don't want to go, and now you're all down-in-the-mouth because you think this doctor's visit isn't all about you."

"Yeah, Maggie," Sera said, "this isn't like you. What's wrong?"

What was wrong? It was wrong that she was a little scared this septic mess was too big for her just like everyone kept telling her. She'd promised Lil she'd take care of Summer Haven, and she was already falling down on the job. "Just a little stress."

Sera reached over, rubbed Maggie's

shoulder. "Wouldn't hurt to have the nurse check your blood pressure. In fact, why don't you get a complete physical while we're there?"

"What?" Maggie squawked. "I have a cut on my foot, that's all."

"It wouldn't hurt for *all* of us—" Sera sent a wide-eyed look toward Abby Ruth, who met it in the rearview mirror, "—to get a physical."

"Wha—"

Sera's elbow hit Abby Ruth in the shoulder. "Oops, sorry about that. Lost my balance around that curve in the road."

Maggie peered out the windshield. They were driving straight down Main Street. Good Lord, was everyone conspiring against her in some way? Then again, it was nice having friends who cared enough to look out for her.

"You're right." Abby Ruth nodded so vigorously that her hair stuck up in back like a bird's tail feathers. "Wouldn't hurt for the doctor to give each of us the once over." She flexed her biceps. "Gotta keep this fine machine in fighting shape."

She was right. Maggie couldn't afford to ignore her health either, not at her age. Besides, she'd made such progress over the past few months, dropping a handful of pounds, toning her muscles and shedding a little back fat. It would be a shame to backslide now just because of a little cut. "Well, I have to admit that I like the efficiency of it."

Sera clapped her hands in a funky little rhythm. "Perfect. It's all settled then."

Abby Ruth pulled up in front of the clinic and parked her dually in two spots. At Maggie's narrow look, she said, "Hey, there are three of us. I could've taken one more parking spot if I'd wanted."

This woman made the most convoluted, yet rational, arguments Maggie'd ever heard.

Sera hopped out and raced to open Maggie's door to help her down. They almost made it to the clinic's front door when out sashayed Angelina Broussard. *Dang it to heck and back.*

Maggie could all but hear Abby Ruth's teeth grinding down to nubs so she slapped on her best customer service smile and beamed it toward Angelina. "Fancy seeing you here."

Angelina's over-plucked eyebrows rose. "Why wouldn't I be here? After all, my husband—" she said the word as though she meant *slave,* "—does own this clinic."

"Oh." Sera fluttered her hands. "We just figured you'd be out and about doing historic preservation committee business."

Maggie forced herself not to close her eyes and wince. One topic of conversation she did *not* want to stir up with Angelina was that committee and Summer Haven's tenuous place on the register.

"Well," Angelina drawled, "you'll be very happy to know I've filled the third committee position."

Oh, yay. "You don't say."

"The illustrious Hollis Dooley."

Was she serious? By the self-satisfied smile on her face, it appeared she was. Hollis was less illustrious and more inert. Good Lord, they'd need to install an elevator for the man to arrive at Summer Haven's second floor in time for next year's inspection. "Interesting choice."

Angelina's back went straight and stiff. "He is a pillar of this community."

Maggie imagined porcupine quills popping out all over Angelina's body. The picture made a giggle tickle the back of Maggie's throat, and she just couldn't keep the sound contained so she tried to cover it with a fake cough.

"Why did you say you were at the clinic today?" Angelina skipped back until the door stopped her retreat.

"Oh—" Abby Ruth stepped forward until

she was invading Angelina's personal space, then pointed toward Maggie, "—we think she has mono."

"The kissing disease? At her age?"

"Now wait just one darn minute," Maggie said. Was Angelina saying she was too old for a man to want to kiss her?

Abby Ruth's expression closed down, went mean in a way that would make grown men wet themselves. Dang, as much as Maggie hated having Abby Ruth against her, she loved it when the woman was on her side.

"I think—" Abby Ruth's voice was low and whiskey smooth. Oh Lordy, Maggie wanted to shout, "Run, Angelina, run!" but she kept her lips zipped, "—that you should never, ever underestimate an older woman, Ms. Broussard. We've experienced things you've only dreamed of. We have knowledge and resources, and we know where all the bodies are buried. Might've even buried a few ourselves."

"I...I didn't," Angelina stuttered. "I just meant that seems an unlikely complaint." She pointed toward the ground. "Besides, her foot is bleeding."

"Because she just finished kicking some smart aleck's ass."

That had Angelina lifting her chin. "I

don't suppose you told your friends that you kidnapped my son?"

"What?" Sera yelped.

Good Lord, give me a break, Abby Ruth, would you?

Abby Ruth waved Sera back and advanced closer to Angelina. "This woman is touched in the head. I try to teach her kid how to hold a bat instead of striking out every time he's up at the damned plate, and she thinks I'm some kind of bad guy. She should be thanking me."

"That'll be the day." Angelina lifted her chin to meet Abby Ruth stare for stare.

Lord have mercy, they would never get in Angelina's good graces this way. If the strained relationship only impacted Maggie, she'd be more than tempted to tell the woman to put her uppity self in a pipe and smoke it. But this wasn't about her. It was about Lil.

Maggie hobbled forward enough to lay a hand on Angelina's skinny forearm. "If you don't want Abby Ruth teaching...ah..."

"Booger," Angelina supplied.

Maggie glanced at Abby Ruth, who raised her brows as though to say *And you think I'm in the wrong here?* "If you don't want Abby Ruth teaching Booger anything about baseball, I completely understand. Why don't we just call it water under the bridge and move on? One little mistake doesn't have to affect anything else."

A smug smile crept across Angelina's face. "Worried about how this might impact my assessment of Summer Haven?"

By the clench of Maggie's own jaw, it was obvious both she and Abby Ruth would need major dental care after dealing with Angelina. "I don't see why one should have anything to do with the other."

Angelina hitched her sparkly silver-and-purple purse over her shoulder. "Well, in a small town, *everything* has to do with everything else." Then she pranced toward the parking lot, her narrow little behind swaying in jeans decorated with more sparkles.

"I swear," Abby Ruth said, "that woman just gave me a headache. In my ass."

Maggie had one, too, but it was throbbing in her foot.

"I just don't understand why she has to be so disagreeable," Sera said. "I always heard people in the South were hospitable. Downright nice. She must be a transplant."

Downright nasty was more along Angelina's lines. "All I can tell you," Maggie said, hobbling closer to the clinic's door, "is that down here, we don't hide our crazy. We parade it right down Main Street."

"And sometimes even throw a big ole parade for it," Abby Ruth added.

Sera reached past Maggie to push open the door. "Angelina would probably love a parade in her honor."

The clinic's lobby smelled of antiseptic, latex and cherry lollipops. Behind a sliding glass window sat the receptionist, her hair a bird's nest secured with Bic pens and tooth-marked pencils. When Maggie printed her name on the sign-in sheet, the girl glanced up, panic clear in her gaze. "Do you have an appointment?"

"No, but this is a walk-in clinic, right?" And there wasn't another darn name on the paper.

"Do you have an emergency?"

"Well..."

Abby Ruth elbowed around Maggie. "This woman darn near cut her foot off a half hour ago. She needs to see a doctor. Now."

"Oh," the receptionist said, "then you should probably take her to the emergency room."

Maggie spotted the full manicure kit sitting in front of the girl. Not just polish but all those doodads and glittery-looking stuff. By the way the receptionist held her fingers arched up, it was clear that her nails were freshly painted and still wet.

"I don't think so," Maggie piped up. "Besides, my friends also need full physicals. Probably a few shots too." She swept an arm around the waiting area. "Doesn't look like you're too busy to handle that."

"Fine," manicure girl huffed. "Take a seat."

Maggie hurriedly scrawled Sera's and Abby Ruth's names on the list and tried not to think of all the time she was wasting today.

While they waited, Abby Ruth played with a children's puzzle made of wooden beads and curving, intertwined wires. It took her a good ten minutes to maneuver all the beads to the left side of the thing. Maybe she wasn't quite as smart or quick as Maggie thought. Maggie reached for the puzzle. Maybe she would just—

"Margaret Evelyn Stuart Rawls?" A nurse called from the doorway leading to the examination rooms.

Sera stood. "Want me to come with you, Maggie?"

"No, but thanks." God knows, she didn't want Sera to see her with her drawers down if she had to take that tetanus shot to the behind.

"Ladies," the nurse said to Sera and Abby

Ruth, "the doctor is running a little behind today, but the good news is October is Breast Health Month. All three of you are eligible for a free mammogram while you're here. Our radiology tech can fit you right in."

Such a lovely day, one where I get to bare both my behind and boobs. All thanks to that darned septic system.

Chapter Eight

"We don't need mammograms." Abby Ruth told the nurse. She'd never been a fan of the breast press. Because hugging a big piece of cold metal while wearing nothing but your pants had to look ridiculous.

"Oh, no." Maggie whirled around and jabbed a finger at her. "When's the last time either of you had a mammogram?"

Both Abby Ruth and Sera were conspicuously silent.

"Uh-huh. That's what I thought. So you *will* get one while we are here." Maggie's wicked grin hinted that her mood was on the mend. "Sera already insisted on physicals for all of us. Why not get the full meal deal?"

"No, thank you," Abby Ruth said firmly.

"It wasn't a question. It was a statement." Maggie turned to the nurse. "Book them."

Dang that girl was getting some *cojones*

on her. Maybe Abby Ruth should schedule Maggie for one of those turn-your-head-and-cough exams.

"Excellent." The nurse smiled as if she earned bonus miles for each set of boobs she recruited.

Abby Ruth shot a round of eyeball hollow points at Maggie. "Make that all three of us."

Maggie shrugged and followed the nurse. "All you IBT girls whine about getting your boobs pinched. They can smush my girls all they want. It's worth my peace of mind."

Sera called after them, "IBT?"

"Itty-bitty-titty."

Even the nurse was chuckling as she pulled the door closed behind Maggie.

Sera plopped into the chair beside Abby Ruth. "Maggie comes out with a zinger now and again."

"Yeah, she's a regular Jeff Foxworthy. But what's all this about us all getting a physical?"

"I looked further into that dating site, and you have to submit a clean bill of health to register."

"Seems like overkill if you ask me." Abby Ruth flipped through a couple of magazines, but unfortunately Dr. Broussard didn't stock *Guns & Ammo* in his waiting room. Finally, she tossed aside one with a cover promising to teach her how to please her man, in bed and out. She leaned close to Sera. "That vain little receptionist isn't paying a bit of attention. Bet we can slip back to the doctor's office and take a poke around."

"What if the nurse comes back for us?"

"She'll think we skipped out on our mammograms."

"What do you think we're going to find back there?"

"I don't know. That's the beauty of the whole thing. It's like when you have an itch between your shoulder blades but you don't know what's causing it. You just have to keep hunting until you find something juicy. Something no one else has found."

"Like taking your chances on Nordstrom's sale rack, you mean?"

Abby Ruth drew back. She did like to look good, but mall shopping appealed to her about as much as taking a club to the back of the head. "Probably." Another out-of-the-corner-of-her-eye glance at the nail-obsessed receptionist, and she confirmed the girl was no more watching them than she was filing all that paperwork piled up on her desk. "Let's make a break for it."

Before Abby Ruth could say another word, Sera was out of her chair, crouched over and doing a speed-duck-walk toward the door connecting the waiting room with the exam rooms. *Dang, that girl's getting good.* Sera's gauzy skirt flowed behind her like a bride's train. Abby Ruth followed, a big grin stretching her facial muscles. She waved Sera to one side of the door. "When I open it, you check for anyone in the hallway."

Abby Ruth yanked open the door a few inches, careful to stay behind it.

"We're clear," Sera whispered, slipping through the opening.

Abby Ruth followed, her heart pumping in a perfect *hell-yeah* rhythm. Was there a better way to spend an afternoon than snooping around where you didn't belong? Well, maybe spending it in bed with the right man, but that wasn't something she'd focused on since she moved to Summer Shoals. In fact, she'd had a mighty nostalgia for Jenny's daddy lately. And she hadn't been in touch with that man in thirty years.

"Abby Ruth," Sera hissed from halfway down the hall, "what are you doing?"

Shoot, she was out in the open like a fat dove sitting on a telephone wire. *Idiot, get your head in the game.* She lowered herself to half-height, hunched over and galloped down the hall like some kind of lame horse. Smooth it wasn't, but it got the job done.

Sera was crouched down with her back against a door and pointed to the sign above her head. *Dr. Benjamin K. Broussard.* "I think this is it."

Yep, this gal was a keeper.

When she heard the rumble of a male voice from one of the nearby exam rooms, Abby Ruth gave a sharp nod. "Let's go."

This time, they barreled through the door and closed it quickly behind them with a quiet *snick*.

By the looks of the dark wood desk the length of a mid-sized car, the matching bookshelves, and the cozy grouping of hair-on-hide chairs, Dr. Broussard's little clinic was banking.

"Should we hit the filing cabinets first?" Sera stage-whispered.

Abby Ruth found that most folks didn't keep their most important secrets under lock and key. They were more likely to stuff them in their underwear drawer or conceal them in cereal boxes. Still, she said, "Sure, but they're probably locked."

As soon as Abby Ruth spit out the last word, one drawer slid open, and Sera turned to her with a sheepishly prideful grin. "Maggie's been teaching me to pick locks."

The gals Abby Ruth had started out thinking were a couple of duds a few months ago were turning out to be a damned good investigative posse. Maybe it was time to take inventory of all the skills they had at their disposal. If they were missing something critical, one of them could take a class at the Georgia Community College. Satellite classes were offered right here in Bartell County. Then again, when they'd needed those lock-picking skills in the past, Maggie'd gotten everything she needed to get the job done right off YouTube for free.

Abby Ruth headed toward the floor-to-ceiling bookshelves because people sometimes stashed goodies in their sleep-inducing nonfiction. She slid books in and out, revealing nothing behind or between. She avoided anything directly in her line of sight. Too obvious.

The sound of shuffling file folders accompanied Sera's search through the doctor's drawers. "I just found a file on Angelina's medical history. Did you know she's had a face lift, two tummy tucks, and gets Botox every third Thursday of the month?"

"Doubt seriously those bullet-point boobs are natural either. Don't know if that's scandalous enough to bribe her with, though."

When the door suddenly swung open to

reveal the nurse, Sera and Abby Ruth froze. "You're not supposed to be back here," the nurse protested.

Sera, with her head down and her hair hanging forward like droopy ears, looked guiltier than a mud-streaked hound at a poodle convention.

Abby Ruth walked right over to the woman and stood a couple inches too close. "My friend is so nervous about the mammogram. I was trying to find a cup of water and a quiet place to reassure her the process doesn't hurt."

The nurse relaxed and held a hand out to Sera. "You've never had a mammogram?"

Sera shot Abby Ruth a sideways glance. "No?"

Abby Ruth steamed forward to cover up Sera's questionable answer. "You know these tree-hugger types. They never trust machines when they can do things on their own. She uses her breast self-checks as foreplay. Go figure."

The nurse reddened, a sure sign Abby Ruth had successfully changed the subject.

"Who's going first?" the nurse asked.

Sera whirled and pointed at Abby Ruth. "She is!"

Abby Ruth grabbed Sera's arm and strode forward. "We'll go together."

They followed the nurse down the stark white hall and into a compact room. "Sorry, but we're a small clinic and only have one dressing room. Do you mind?"

"Not at all," Sera answered.

"You'll strip to the waist, then slip on the gown. Open in the front." She picked one up and demonstrated, slipping it on over her scrubs. "After you've changed, the radiology technician will be right with you."

Once the nurse left, Sera held the paper gown up to her chest. "Seriously? Why bother?"

Abby Ruth turned her back to Sera and stripped out of her shirt and bra, then pulled on the paper gown, tying it like her favorite Wrangler shirt at the bottom to hold it together.

Sera pushed her arms up through the draped neckline of her sweater as if she was executing a swan dive, then let the fabric land to rest at her hips. She wrestled with the paper for a second, finally slinging the make-do gown over her shoulders like a cape. "You couldn't smuggle anything in these outfits."

A quick knock on the door and the radiology tech ambled through the door. "Oh, there are two of you. We normally do this one at a time."

"We're sisters. We do everything together." Sera waltzed through the door and across the hall.

Whatever. Wasn't as if Sera hadn't already flashed Abby Ruth. So she and the tech followed.

"We'll go in alphabetical order." The tech consulted her computer screen. "Okay, Mrs. Cady, you're up first."

"Ms."

"I'm sorry?"

"It's Ms. It's never been Mrs."

"Well, step over here, Ms. Cady, and we'll get you set up." The woman guided Abby Ruth to the huge shiny machine. "You've had this done before, right?"

"Several times."

"Great, makes it much easier for me." The tech led Abby Ruth through a follow-the-leader game of up, back, down and scooch. Then positioned her with one arm in the air and pushed her shoulder back.

She stepped behind the barrier and studied Abby Ruth as if she were a piece of experimental art. "Lean toward me."

Abby Ruth craned her neck to look at Sera, waiting on the opposite side of the glass wall separating the machine and the tech's computer station, and said to her, "This ought to be a cake-walk for you. I think

I've seen you in this pose before."

The tech tugged Abby Ruth forward a little more. "This will be slightly uncomfortable."

"Bring it on."

She ruthlessly cranked the upper tray into place, and a screech clawed its way out of Abby Ruth's throat. "Lord Jesus, this thing is like ice! My girls in Texas always put a heating pad on this sucker."

"Great idea," the tech said. "Never thought of warming it up."

"Clearly. Careful now. Cold as that metal is, I could poke an eye out."

Sera snickered. "At least you'll warm it up for me."

"You're welcome," Abby Ruth said.

The tech zipped behind the half-wall to press the magic boob portrait button. "Don't move."

"Like I can," Abby Ruth complained.

"Hold your breath. Good. Now, other side." When she returned, the tech released the tray.

Abby Ruth glanced down at her left breast, sure it would be the thickness of a stingy flapjack.

The tech spun Abby Ruth around, then arranged her like she might a Barbie doll. One arm here, one arm there, back arched, one foot pointed, one foot flat. "Hmm. Can you tippy-toe a little? Yes. Perfect."

Abby Ruth was a holding a position that defied all gravity while the tech wedged her tiny breast between the two plates. "Suckers look big when you squish 'em all out like that."

Sera patted her bare chest. "I'm not even sure I have enough to fill a mammogram sandwich."

"Hold your breath," the tech told Abby Ruth and hustled back to her place next to Sera. "Hold it." She pressed the clicker. "Good."

She didn't rush back, however. Instead, she hovered over her computer clicking her mouse. "Let me take a quick look at these pictures to make sure I have what we need."

"Nothing like hanging by a nipple to put you in a mood," Abby Ruth said, her tone sour.

"Maybe I don't really need to get one done," Sera said. "I'm not as old—"

"Oh no," Abby Ruth cut her off. "We're *all* getting one."

Click. Click. Click. Was that tech looking at Abby Ruth's boob shots or playing spider solitaire? Finally, she said, "I need to get another picture, Ms. Cady." From her scrubs pocket, she whipped out two tiny circles printed in a pink leopard-skin pattern. In the center of each was a protruding BB. Put tassels on them and they'd make for some fancy pasties.

"You running a gentlemen's club here too?" Abby Ruth asked.

"I need to pinpoint your nipples and do this again." She squinted at Abby Ruth's boobs and stuck the circles on with precision.

Abby Ruth turned toward Sera and gave her a BB-boobed shimmy.

"Cute." Sera stepped closer to poke at Abby Ruth's BBs. "They look like those silver cupcake decorations."

"If you lick my nipple, I'm going to—"

"Ma'am." The tech waved Sera back. "I need you to stay behind the barrier."

Sera obediently stepped back.

Abby Ruth followed the awkward version of Simon Says meets Twister. She even obediently held her breath for the five-count in that godforsaken Panini maker.

Finally, Abby Ruth was done and it was Sera's turn to tango with the machine. That ought to quiet her snickers.

As they swapped spots, Abby Ruth leaned in and whispered to Sera, "You take your time, and stall her. I'm going back to do more digging."

Sera gave Abby Ruth a wink. "I've got this." She tossed the paper gown to the floor, then strolled over to the machine for her turn and struck a pose that would've done Beyoncé proud. The nurse shot Abby Ruth a panicked look, as if she didn't know what to make of Sera.

The gal was on her own because no doubt Sera would chat her ear off while Abby Ruth rushed back to dig up more dirt on Angelina.

Chapter Nine

After her own mammogram, a few stitches and a lovely painkiller, Maggie lay sprawled out in the back seat of Abby Ruth's dually with her foot propped up on an ammo box. Outside her window, the trees were such a mellow green and the flowering crepe myrtles danced like pastel-colored ballerinas. Summer Shoals was just so *pretty* today.

"Cute move with the mammograms," Abby Ruth said over her shoulder.

Maggie snickered. Then giggled. Then snorted at her own snicker-giggles. "For our own goods."

"Yeah, right. Regardless, I don't think your little butterfly bandage plan would've done the job on a cut that took five stitches, girl."

Sera turned and leaned over the seat.

"Maggie, you can't be schlepping around in that septic mess with an open wound. You'll end up with an infection. Or worse, worms."

"The worms crawl in. The worms crawl out," Maggie sang, drifting off into a fit of giggles. "I'll wear my rubber boots," she slurred. "It'll be fine."

"Those rubber boots will make your feet sweat and then those stitches might dissolve too fast. I think we should let the professionals handle that situation," Sera said. "It won't be hard to snoop for Martha. Besides we'd be helping her niece. Good works bring good karma, and we sure could use some of that around Summer Haven right now."

"She has a point," Abby Ruth said.

"Did you find anything else when you went snooping in the clinic?" Sera asked Abby Ruth.

"Nothing that would give us leverage with Sparklelina on that inspection," Abby Ruth said, her voice full of disappointment. "Maggie, that yard won't fix itself. We need that Martha woman to come through."

Sera nodded, and Maggie watched as they talked, but most of it sounded like one of those Charlie Brown scenes with the teacher. *Muaw muaw muaw muaw muaw.*

When they pulled up in front of the

house, Abby Ruth hit the brake with her normal zeal, pitching her passengers forward.

Maggie braced herself to keep from landing in the floorboard. Somehow, her arm had turned into a piece of cooked fettuccine so her forehead skimmed the back of the driver's seat. "No. No Martha snooping. Not happening 'cause I can f...fi...fix stuff." Maggie fumbled with the door handle. Why had the factory put that thing on upside down? Abby Ruth would be madder than a chipmunk with chapped lips if she found out.

Sera opened the door, and Maggie slid out into her waiting hold. "We know you can fix it, but—"

"No buts. Sera's got a toned butt. Maggie's got a fat butt. Abby Ruth's got a flat butt."

"She's three sheets to the wind," Abby Ruth commented, striding ahead to the front porch.

"I'm glad she's not feeling any pain," Sera said. "At least we don't have to worry about her traipsing around in sewage today."

"Summer Haven is falling down, falling down, falling down," Maggie crooned.

Abby Ruth pushed open the front door and just as quickly danced back. "Did y'all hear that?"

"Hear what?"

"I opened the door and I swear this house just burped at me." She waved a hand in front of her nose. "Worse than a beer belch."

Maggie pushed past her, only stumbling a little. There it was. A distinct *gurgle-swoosh-bwuuurp.*

Sera winced. "That can't be good."

"I got this." Maggie followed the demonic sounds to the first floor bathroom. "Pro'ly just a clog." She leaned over the toilet, watching the water bubble and dance. Like *Swan Lake.* She reached for the plunger she kept stashed behind the potty, only for her unreliable hand to land on a lush roll of triple-ply quilted paper hanging on the roll.

She wrestled the toilet paper off the holder and tried to stomp out to the foyer, but it came off as more of a mummy shuffle. Still, she shook the TP above her head. "Who in blazes bought thish? Thish stuff is bad, bad, bad."

Abby Ruth thrust a foot forward, angling her hip aggressively toward Maggie. "My rear feels as red as an orangutan's ass after using that newsprint you bought."

"Mine is sep...sep...septic-safe and bio-de-something-or-other," Maggie said.

Sera slinked off toward the kitchen.

"I'll take my business elsewhere then," Abby Ruth said. "My Texas tush can't abide by that sandpaper."

"Fine. But take this with you." Maggie tried to hurl the plush paper at Abby Ruth, but ended up doing a sort of side-arm pitch instead. To her credit, the roll bounced off the side of Abby Ruth's head and unrolled across the keyboard of the parlor's piano with a haughty twang.

With what she could salvage of her super-soft TP after Maggie winged it at her, Abby Ruth strolled into the kitchen. "Maggie has gone nuts!" she said to Sera. "She bounced this right off my head."

"Is that what I heard?" Sera didn't look up from the laptop she was tapping on at the kitchen desk.

"Yeah, I swear she's losing it."

"Where is she?"

"In the bathroom fussing at the toilet."

"Think she's okay to leave alone?"

"Her aim was good," Abby Ruth said, "so I think she's fine."

"That's a relief."

Abby Ruth wandered closer to Sera. "What are you up to?"

"Registering for ThePerfectFit.com." Sera held up a hand. "Look, I'm sorry, but we don't have time for you to poke around trying to find OnceUponATom using your sources any longer. We have to get inside this thing. Maggie won't admit she needs help, so I have to do something or Martha won't have our septic system fixed."

"Can't you just hack into the thing and dig up Tom's deets?"

"It's not that easy. These sites have security on them, and I'm still learning how to do all this backdoor computer stuff. Better to go through the front door. And apparently, the system doesn't allow you to search. It generates automatic matches instead. So we could create a profile that will attract Tom based on what we know about him."

"Which is that he likes paintball. That's not a lot to go on."

"We have to start somewhere. Besides, I can do this with Maggie none the wiser. Once I find OnceUponATom, then we can bring her in on it. She can't say no then."

"If one profile is good—" Abby Ruth tapped her chin, "—then three are better."

"We can't register Maggie without telling her."

"Sure we can. Type M-A-G-G-I-E. It's that simple."

"Abby Ruth! We shouldn't—"

"Waste a good opportunity. C'mon, we'll register her first. For practice." Abby Ruth pointed at the keyboard. "Then we'll know the questions and can answer them differently on our profiles. That'll cast us a wider net so we can snag this guy."

"Fine, you win." Sera clicked on a blank box at the top of the registration form and started filling in Maggie's information. "What's Maggie's middle initial?"

"Evelyn, so E, I guess, or maybe it would be R for Rawls. Who cares? Just make one up." Abby Ruth peered over Sera's shoulder. "Doesn't have to be the absolute truth, you know. It's not like any of us plan to kick up our heels with one of these online losers."

"They're not losers, but the average demographic might be a little younger than we are." Sera backspaced and took a few years off Maggie's age. "We'll need old pictures."

"I have my 1990s byline picture from the paper. That should do. Do you have one?"

"On my hard drive, and I saw some of Maggie in Lil's scrapbooks. I'll snap a picture of one of those and upload it." Sera continued to type, and three pages into the registration, a screen popped up requiring a credit card. "A hundred dollars?" Her mouth hung open. She turned to Abby Ruth. "We can't spend that much money on dating profiles we don't even plan to use for ourselves."

"We have to," Abby Ruth said. "That muck outside isn't going to cure itself, and Maggie has done some amazingly handy things around here, but there has to be a limit. I figure three hundred bucks is a bargain for a septic system. I'll pay for it."

"That'll just make Maggie madder."

"Hell, that's less than the KOA fees I paid while I was on the road. But I'll ask Maggie to reimburse me from the house account once we get this OnceUponATom guy pinned down."

"Then I need a credit card."

Abby Ruth rattled off her VISA account number.

"Now for Maggie's screen name." Sera twirled her hair around her finger. "How about...something with DIY or Virginia?"

"DIY Diva." After all, Maggie had been acting like a bit of one lately.

"Oh, no. Maggie can't be a diva. How about a darling? Everyone loves a darling."

Abby Ruth had never met a man yet who didn't like calling a woman darlin'. "DIYDarling. That'll work."

They worked nonstop to set up the profiles. Sera picked SunnyOutlook for her screen name, and then it was Abby Ruth's turn to create her account.

"You finish yours." Sera stood and executed a yoga stretch holding one foot over her head in a way that reminded Abby Ruth of those *Cirque du Soleil* shows. "I need a potty break."

"Better go outside or Maggie might start throwing more than toilet paper." Abby Ruth scooted over to take Sera's place at the computer and read the first question aloud. "What's worse? A starving puppy or a starving child?"

Sera quickly dropped her grip on her leg. "I don't want to be present while you answer that." And off she darted.

Abby Ruth typed, *No reason for either to starve as long as you can hunt.* Satisfied with the answer, she moved on to the next one.

::What would be your chosen superpower? Would you use it for good or evil?
X-ray vision. And hell, boy, if you don't know what I'd use it for, then I'm not interested in dating you.

::Do you have a nickname? If so, what's the story behind it?
Bibi. And let's just say that I could get a job as the stripping cowgirl at a gentleman's club.

::If you were a stalker, would you be really good at it?
Put down the remote, the beer and the bag of BBQ chips. Now, look out your window. Does that answer your question?

After another sixteen painful questions, she finally made it to the screen name. Nearly done. She thought about it for a second, then typed in *TexasTough*.

Just as Abby Ruth hit ENTER, Maggie's rain boots squeaked against the hardwoods.

Crap on a cracker. Abby Ruth typed faster, but she couldn't close down the page before the credit card processed.

Maggie, looking more sober, stopped right inside the doorway, and leaned against the jamb. "Disaster averted."

Abby Ruth stood and turned, using her butt as a screen saver. Her smile was fake, but it was wide. "Excellent. Great job."

About that time, Sera walked in and

quickly scoped out the situation. She dodged between Maggie and Abby Ruth, providing another layer of concealment. She rubbed her chest in an exaggerated circle. "Anyone else's boobs still feel like they haven't regained their natural shape? Mine may never be the same."

Maggie popped to her tiptoes. When Sera followed her movement, Maggie poked her head to the side. "What are y'all up to?"

"Nothing." Both Sera and Abby Ruth said the word at the same time, and even Abby Ruth knew there'd be no dodging the accusation this time.

She pushed away from the computer. "Look. We signed up for that dating site." No sense pussyfooting around. What was done was done.

"ThePerfectFit.com?"   Shoulders drooping, Maggie stared at Sera. "Why? I'm handling Summer Haven's problems. You two don't have to...to...pimp yourselves out."

Sera grabbed her in a hug. "I know, but just in case."

Maggie looked as if she'd just eaten a bucket of worms. "Well, I'm not doing it. No one will pick me when they could have the likes of y'all. Sera, even on one of your bloaty days, you look like Bo Derek in that movie *10*." Maggie peered at Abby Ruth over Sera's shoulder. "And Abby Ruth, you rock a pair of skinny jeans better than college girls on those reality TV shows. Me? On my best day, I look like a marshmallow Peeps version of the Michelin man."

Abby Ruth's heart clenched a little for her friend. Maggie had that pass-the-funnel-cake look on her face. She had no idea just how attractive a woman she was. All she ever focused on was her weight. But she was talented with any kind of power tool. She was loyal and generous. And she was obviously forgiving. "You have tons to offer a man."

"No, all I have to offer is love handles...and those haven't been handled in years."

The tears in Maggie's eyes made Abby Ruth want to bolt to another room. She'd never been good at that girlie emotion stuff. "You shouldn't feel that way about yourself, Mags."

"Well, I do, and you can't change it. I can fix that septic problem. My gifts aren't in the good looks department."

Sera held out her hand to Maggie. "That's not true. Your aura is so colorful and you're a beautiful soul."

"Yeah," Maggie said with an air of defeat. "But that stuff is all on the inside."

Chapter Ten

Teague's computer monitor was filled with a yellow-and-black-themed website with two interlocked metal hearts and the words *register now!* splashed all over it. Looked more like a Steelers fan site than a dating site. Then again, what the hell did he know about this stuff?

Since that speed-dating fiasco, he'd pulled this page up a dozen times but could never quite pull the trigger. It just seemed a little desperate. And when it came to his thoughts of Jenny Cady, registering for ThePerfectFit felt more than a little disloyal.

What's it gonna be, Castro?

He could either sit around for the rest of his life pining for a woman he'd done wrong or get on with things and find someone who was less than perfect.

"Sheriff—" the department's secretary

stuck her head inside the door, "—got someone here who wants to talk to you."

Teague fumbled with his computer mouse, clicking like an idiot to close down that dating site. "Give me a sec, and then send them in."

Maybe the interruption was a sign. Maybe he'd been saved from making another mistake that would cost him the woman he loved. He sat there for a minute with his head in his hands. When he heard footsteps outside his office, he took a deep breath and looked up.

And groaned silently.

His visitor was Sue Ellen, a young waitress from the Atlanta Highway Diner who had a habit of flashing her brightly colored bras at him anytime he went in for a blue plate special. So he put on his best serious sheriff expression and said, "What can I help you with today?"

Sue Ellen plopped down in a chair in front of his desk, and no surprise, an eye-blinding yellow bra strapped peeked out from her shirt. "Someone is charging stuff to my credit card."

Credit card? Shouldn't there be a law against someone this young running around with plastic money? "Have you called your credit card company?"

"Seriously?" She rolled her eyes dramatically. "It's one of those automated things. I spent ten minutes trying to talk to a robot voice. I did finally manage to dispute the charges, but it said to contact my local law enforcement. That's you, right?"

"Sure is." Teague scooted his chair back and focused on Sue Ellen's left eyebrow. "I can get someone to take the report for you."

She smiled and fluttered her lashes. "Can't you do it for me?"

She'd been uncomfortably attentive to him at the diner, which made this a little awkward. Unfortunately, Barnes was busy filing the monthly reports for him. "I'll need all the accounts and banks involved."

"Well, I've only used that card on two things in the past six months, and it's the only credit card I have." She waved an envelope in his direction.

Fine, he'd hear her out. "Let me see what you've got." Teague reached across his desk for the copy of her bill, which was a mishmash of bright pink highlighter streaks. He took the statement and flipped through it. "These charges in pink? They're the ones in question?"

"Yes," she said, leaning on his desk and providing a clear view down her shirt.

"Several of these are local. Love 'Em or

Leave 'Em Florist and the farmers market. Are you sure you didn't just buy something and forget about it?"

"Positive," she said, folding her arms across her chest, making even more cleavage. "I only use this card for emergencies and very important stuff. I know exactly what I've used it on."

Almost everything on the paper was highlighted in fluorescent pink. Would have been easier if she'd have highlighted just the two things she'd charged. "And which are your two charges?"

"A tooth-whitening session from my dentist, Dr. Evans," she said, "and creating a profile at ThePerfectFit.com."

Emergencies? If the dating site was as successful as that tooth whitening had been, the girl would be married before he figured out who had charged her card. Most of the charges were just a few dollars each. "I'll make a copy of these for the report, then I'll poke around and see if there are any similar complaints."

Well, hell. Looked like Teague had a good reason to register for that dating site after all.

Lillian watched her bunkmate fuss with her bed corners, pulling them taut and straight. Probably the best job Dixie had done on that sheet the entire time Lil had been at Walter Stiles. Finally, Dixie said, "I'll miss you, Miss Lillian."

Lil stepped forward and hugged her. Not a pat-on-the-back hug, but a real Southern hug. "I'll miss you too, dear. You be good out there, and don't you let anyone stand between you and your dreams."

"I won't."

"And when I get out of here, I want you to come visit me in Summer Shoals. You'll love Summer Haven. I'll serve us tea—"

"And I can use all that etiquette stuff you taught me."

"You most certainly will," Lil said. Dixie was squirming a little in her hold, but it was hard saying goodbye to the first person who'd taken her under their wing. Because when she was getting settled into prison camp politics, Dixie had been the only one willing to stick her neck out for her. "You'll do great things, so keep me posted on all those."

"I will." Dixie moved out of Lil's embrace, but she seemed reluctant. "I want you to promise me you'll keep a safe distance from Martha. She's like a feral cat. Just when you think you can trust her, she'll bite you. And you know her so-called friendship comes at a cost."

"Don't worry about me."

A guard slapped the cinderblocks that surrounded their pod and told Dixie, "Time to go."

"Bye, Miss Lillian."

With a silent wave, Lil let Dixie pass. Lord, part of her felt as if she was losing the only friend she had in this place.

The guard lifted her chin toward Lil. "Warden wants to see you."

"Yes, ma'am." Lil was beginning to dread these little visits with the warden. Martha's volatile reaction to the whole beautification project was proof the warden was working her own agenda and didn't care if it put Lil in a bad position.

Lil took her time making her way across the camp. At a hallway window outside the warden's office, she paused to gaze across the courtyard. Stalling a little, but also looking for Dixie since this window provided a sliver of a view to the parking lot. She stood there until she saw her former bunkmate walk out with someone and get into a car. A moment later, the car left the protected area.

Dixie was free.

Tears tickled Lil's lashes. How she longed for that feeling again.

A sudden shroud of loneliness weighed on her. But rather than wallow in what she couldn't change, she pressed the button, requesting entry to the warden's office.

Someone on the other side pressed the buzzer, and the lock disengaged with a clunk. Lil pulled open the heavy steel door and stepped inside.

"She's expecting you," the warden's assistant said.

Warden Proctor motioned Lil into her office. "How're the projects coming along?"

"Doing the best we can." As if she'd had time to do more than make a list of all that needed to be done. A very long list.

"I need on target and on time. No wiggle room on this one."

Lil wanted to just sink to the floor and cry. Why couldn't the warden have picked one of the young girls who had so much energy they were always in trouble? "I won't let you down."

Her mother's words drifted through her mind. *Good girls don't tell lies, Lillian.*

Well, Momma, good girls don't go to prison either.

"I know you won't, and that's why I have a wonderful surprise for you," she said.

No more surprises. Because the warden's surprises were less reward and more penalty.

"With Dixie's departure, along with several others over the past few weeks, I'm shuffling people around in the dormitories and cottages," the warden said, breaking into a warm smile. "You're among the relocations."

Worry squirmed inside Lil. She liked where she was. Yes, it would be lonely without Dixie, but Lil had gotten used to the other women, the sounds and smells, and her little corner of the unit.

The warden handed her a unit transfer form.

Lil glanced at the familiar abbreviation and gulped.

"You'll now be sharing quarters with Martha Davilo," the warden said.

"Oh, no." Panic flowed through Lil like porcupines on parade.

"You don't have to thank me. Think of your move to a cottage as a reward for the positive impact you've had through the etiquette classes. Oh, and a little advance bonus for helping Walter Stiles' doors stay open."

Thank her? The woman had just handed her a ticket to a hard time. "Warden, this is generous but not necessary."

"It's done." The handsome woman

squared her fullback-sized shoulders. "Besides, the cottage beds are better than the bunk beds."

Warden Proctor had taken a little pity on Lil from the time she entered prison camp, but this move wasn't a boon. "I...I'm not quite sure what to say."

She wasn't tongue-tied because she was so thankful for the warden's *generosity,* but because Lord have mercy, Martha would flat-out die when she found out about her new roommate.

"Take the relocation form to the guard station in your unit immediately," the warden told her.

"Right now?"

"Yes. You'll be all settled in before dinner." The warden smiled, looking so pleased with herself. "Now you have a wonderful day. Ciao."

Ciao? This delusion the warden had about casting herself as some kind of institutional cruise director was irritating.

Lillian plodded out of the warden's office with the pressure of this newest disaster on her shoulders. Every time things started leveling out for her, something went wonky here or at Summer Haven. As tired as she was, this was the kind of day that made Lil wonder if she'd live long enough to get out of

Walter Stiles. And even if she did survive, would Summer Haven survive her absence?

An hour later, Lil hand-trucked her belongings across the courtyard toward Martha's abode. Hers was a much nicer section of the prison camp, dotted with small cottages. Lil should feel excited, but instead she was reluctant to put one foot in front of the other. Because Martha would be surprised when Lil walked in, and it wouldn't be a happy kind of surprise. And by darned, she was tired of constantly having to smooth that woman's ruffled feathers.

When Lil thumped the hand-truck up the cottage steps, one of Martha's girls stepped out of the shadows with her arms folded to block the way. "What do you think you're doing here, granny?"

"Moving in."

The woman scoffed. "Don't think so."

"Warden's orders."

"Like I care."

"This isn't your affair." Lil tried to edge around the woman, but she sidestepped to thwart her.

"You think it makes you all popular when you talk snooty like that?"

"I'm not here to win a prison popularity contest," Lil said calmly, trying to defuse the situation. "I was instructed to move locations, and that's what I'm doing."

"You may act like you're so smart, but granny, you're a total wing nut if you think I'm gonna let you cut in the long line to be one of Martha's girls." After an extended staring contest, the woman, smirk firmly in place, finally stepped aside and waved her arm as though allowing Lil entry to the queen's throne room.

Which in a way, Martha was the queen.

Lil wheeled her belongings inside the cottage and, at the look on Martha's face, stopped short, causing the hand-truck to ram her Achilles tendon. That was definitely not an expression of surprise. Murder, maybe. But not surprise.

Lil drew herself to her full height, which wasn't much to write home about since she'd shrunk to under the five-foot mark. "The move wasn't my idea."

"Never is." Martha's lips were stretched into such a tight line that Lil could barely see them.

Four of Martha's girls stepped inside, forming a line across Lil's only escape. If they'd held hands, the scenario would look like a game of Red Rover. But they weren't smiling or inviting Lil to come over. "I know you're not happy about this," she said to Martha.

Martha tugged on her greenish-beige shirt. "You think?"

"Martha, why can't we be friends?"

"You know, Miss H&M, I kinda thought we were there for a while, but then you stabbed me in the back."

The line of women snickered and mumbled, making the hair on the back Lil's neck stand on edge.

"I already told you that I don't know why the warden asked me to spearhead this project instead of you, but I promise it was not by my design."

"Promise? Yeah, you know promises don't mean much around here, case you hadn't noticed." Martha mumbled a few words under her breath that were not on Lil's approved etiquette class vocabulary, but she wasn't about to stir up that hornet's nest.

Instead, she sucked in a breath to power through the conversation. One thing she'd learned about Martha was not to show worry. Any sign of weakness, and she would take advantage of the chink in Lil's thin armor. "We're roommates now, and that isn't going to change so we can make the best of it or be miserable. I plan to make the best of it. And as for that beautification project of yours, you may as well resolve yourself to helping me with it. Otherwise, you'll be chewing on that bitter pill for the better part of this week and that'll only put frown lines on your forehead."

Martha raised her eyebrows as if to chase away those frown lines. "You want me to help you?" She laughed. One look from her to her posse and they also mustered up an audience laugh track.

The echoing laughs swirled around Lil as the other women formed a semicircle behind her. She'd never before suffered from claustrophobia, but now her nerves were jumping and her breath was hitching. *Stay in control.*

Lil raised her voice above their ruckus. "No, I want to be *your* assistant. This is too big for me to accomplish alone."

Martha snapped a finger and everyone went silent. "I'm listening."

Regardless, Lil's heart was still doing jumping jacks. "As I see it, there are two clear projects here. The people and the place. I'll lead the people part. The dress for success, the interviewing portion, and all the things that align with the etiquette class, and you help me."

She took a deep breath. Martha hadn't balked yet. Maybe. Just maybe this would work. "You lead the grounds beautification part, and I'll help you."

"Coming from you, Miss H&M, that's a big surprise."

"You know a lot more about what we can get accomplished in a quick hurry around here." She waved at Martha's manicure, which was always fresh and creatively designed. "Besides, you have a stylish flair. And you know how to pull it off with limited resources. Doing things like fashioning barrettes out of plastic paperclips and toilet paper takes skill and talent. That should translate nicely to the grounds. I figure you already have a hundred ideas to improve the courtyard."

"I do," Martha agreed. "Too bad we can't fancy up the uniforms while we're at it. No matter how pretty the grounds look, these frumpy outfits still suck. Did the warden also mention my idea about using some old uniforms we found in the laundry locker room? Because that was mine too."

"No, nothing about that. Probably because she thinks the interviewing skills, camp beautification and old fashioned hospitality toward the BOP folks will make the biggest impression."

"You said yourself that good grooming makes a good first impression."

"True, but we're under a time crunch.

Maybe if we win over the BOP people, the uniforms will be the next project the warden throws our way."

"Humph," Martha grunted. "Your way, you mean."

Behind her, Martha's girls were whispering to one another. She prayed they weren't cooking up an ambush plan.

"No, we're in this together," Lil said. "Now that she's put us in the same cabin, she won't be able to so easily hoodwink me. So if the warden offers me another project, I'll insist she name you co-organizer."

Martha angled her head as if considering Lil's suggestion. "Co-organizer sounds like one of those ten-cent words that don't mean a thing. If you want me to have your back on this project, I need a little something in return, like full control over the flowerbeds and grounds improvement. What I say goes, period."

Lil drew in a quiet breath. She really had no evidence Martha could pull off the camp beautification, but what other choice did she have? "That sounds reasonable."

Finally, Martha nodded once and said, "Then I'm in."

When Martha's girls backed off, relief flooded over Lil. Sometimes manners could still win the day. "That's settled then."

"Oh," Martha said conversationally, "and don't forget your grannies have something I want. If you're even thinking about telling them to renege on the OnceUponATom deal, your septic system won't be the only thing that needs help."

"Are you threatening me?"

"No, I'm reminding you that a deal is a deal."

"My girls are still gathering information about your niece's predicament." Lil wanted to cross her fingers at the fib, but couldn't risk it with the toughs still in the room.

Martha shifted to the edge of her bed. "Really?"

"I can't give you any details yet, but rest assured they're making good progress on our side of that deal. So get your septic guy to clear his calendar."

"No worries on my end. My guy will come through as long as your girls get their shit together before something bad happens to my niece."

"Believe me, my gals aren't dragging their feet. They know your deal is no good to me if we've already failed the historic preservation inspection."

"Convenient timing," Martha commented. "A week to complete this BOP project you and the warden are taking my credit for, and six days for your shitters."

Lil knew what Martha was saying. Tit for tat. She wanted information from Maggie and the others. If she didn't get it, she wouldn't come through on the septic system, and she'd probably sabotage the warden's project to keep Walter Stiles open. And, with the support of her posse and the handful of guards in her pocket, an angry Martha could and would cook up something to keep Lil's hind parts in Walter Stiles for her entire sentence. She couldn't risk that.

"The timing is a coincidence, but I will make good on my promises—both to find information that will help your niece and to cut you in on the BOP project."

"That's what I like to hear." Martha grabbed a towel from the rack next to the curtain. "Now that we've settled everything, I'm grabbing a shower."

While Martha was showering, Lillian slipped out of the cottage to call Summer Haven. She had to confirm the girls were making progress. The last thing she needed was for Martha to figure out she'd stretched the truth. Fine. So she'd flat-out lied, but it had been necessary.

"Forgive me, Father, for I have sinned," Lil whispered as she stepped off the porch into the courtyard.

Heavy rain spit down on her head, and she glanced skyward. "Really? I'm in prison, what did you expect?"

Chapter Eleven

Maggie hobbled toward the ringing phone on Lil's desk, waving away Abby Ruth's attempt at help. Maggie's foot wasn't as sore as it had been, but she was still favoring her good foot in a way that had her loping around like a zombie. If she started hissing, she'd wonder if one of those flesh-eating bacteria Sera was worried about hadn't really taken hold. "Hello?"

"Mags, how are you?"

The familiar voice caught her off guard. She wasn't expecting to hear from Lillian. "Lil? Is everything okay?"

"Of course," Lil's voice was smooth and upbeat, but Maggie knew that Lil's phone privileges cost her a pretty penny so she wouldn't dare squander them just for a simple hello.

"What's going on?" Mixed feelings of pleasure and suspicion surged through her.

"I need an update on that man Martha's niece has been dating. Martha won't call her septic guy until we give her some...I think it's called intel. With the inspection coming up, it's time to make Martha happy."

Maggie felt her hackles rise. She tried to breathe through it, but they wouldn't be appeased and were still standing at attention.

Abby Ruth and Sera hovered close by.

She didn't want to snipe at Lil while the girls could hear. No sense in dividing the troops. So she limped out onto the back porch and closed the kitchen door behind her. "I'm on it, Lil." Not the boyfriend thing, but the septic. Sometimes being less specific was safer...even if it was a little white lie.

"Thank goodness." Lil let out a sigh. "I knew I could count on you. What have you got?"

Maggie's mind whirled. Okay, so this was where that white-lie thing became less convenient. She'd never been all that good at thinking on her feet, and with stitches in one of them, the painkillers were making it even harder to think fast. "Doing some digging. Going through some paper. A lot of it's a mess, but we'll get there." That was good!

"Maggie, I don't know what any of that means. I need something specific to tell Martha."

"Just tell her we're working on it. Sera's been on the computer for hours on end. It's coming together."

"Let me talk to her."

"To Sera?"

"No, to the computer," Lil snapped. "Of course, to Sera."

Maggie swallowed. "She's busy, but we'll be there to see you soon and we'll bring an update when we come."

"Put Sera on the phone, Maggie."

There was no fooling Lil. They'd known each other for too long, and that tone in Lil's voice told Maggie there was no use in trying to dodge her. Maggie dropped the receiver on a wrought iron table and called out to Sera, praying she'd already headed outside for a yoga session or a dip in the creek. Sometimes she slipped out to do that in the middle of the day—naked, of course. But no such luck. Maggie heard the slap of bare feet heading her way, and then the door swung open.

"Right here. What's up?"

Maggie picked up the phone reluctantly and shoved it in her direction. "It's Lil."

Sera's face brightened. "Cool." She took

the phone and spun around as she spoke. "Hi, Lil." Sera glanced in Maggie's direction, then hugged the phone close and walked around the corner of the porch.

Maggie took a step toward the edge to listen in.

"Yes, I know, Lil," Sera said. "I've been looking into it. I couldn't find one thing on Tom Thumb...Mmm-hmm...Oh, no. I went ahead and started searching from the other end. From inside the ThePerfectFit.com site. It connects you with your most promising matches so I set up profiles to see if we could find him that way."

Sera's laugh tinkled. "I know. Right? Oh, the profiles? Abby Ruth thought we'd have better luck that way if we all registered, so that's what we did. Yes, you can tell Martha that we're on the case and I'll have a better update by the end of the week. I mentioned paintball in my profile hoping to catch Tom's attention. With three profiles, we should get somewhere in no time."

Maggie's ears burned. *Three* profiles? Sera would never have put Maggie's profile up on that website without consulting her. Would she? Chilled with uncertainty, Maggie grabbed the wood siding and swung herself around the corner of the house.

Sera's eyes went wide. "Got to run, Lil.

We'll be in touch." She stabbed at the phone to end the call, and her gaze darted here and yon, like a trapped animal looking for an escape route. And her upper lip was beading with a sudden sweat. She wiped it away and fluttered around the porch, suddenly all smiles and rainbows and unicorns. "Lil sounded good."

"Sit," Maggie demanded, pointing to a yellow-backed metal chair that was now apparently all the retro rage. "Abby Ruth, get out here," she hollered into the house.

"Why are you so ups—" Sera started.

Abby Ruth strolled out onto the porch, glanced at Maggie, then stopped mid-stride.

Perfect. That meant Maggie's face showed just how hopping mad she was.

"Sit your behind down," Maggie said. "Right now. The three of us are about to have a little come-to-Jesus meeting."

Sera's mouth dropped open, and she plopped her butt into the chair. Understanding dawned in her eyes. "You overheard everything I told Lil, didn't you?"

"Did you really expect me to go back inside?"

"I thought the house would muffle my voice."

"These Georgians are well built, but even solid walls can't absorb secrets. Friends going behind other friends' backs. I expected more from you."

Lil had given Maggie the big brushoff by asking to talk with Sera. It seemed Lil was putting everyone and everything ahead of their five-decade friendship. Sera. Big Martha. Big Martha's niece, a woman Lil had never even met.

To check that steam wasn't actually escaping from her ears, Maggie stalked over to the little gilt mirror Lil had hung over an old sideboard, making the porch what she liked to call an "outdoor room." All she saw was a face filled with anger and sadness. Not only was Lil suddenly playing for the other side, but Sera and Abby Ruth had gone behind Maggie's back as well. "Both of you, stay right here."

She reached inside the back door and snatched up the laptop recharging on the desk.

Yes, she wanted Sera and Abby Ruth to be loyal to Lil, but what about loyalty to *her?* Shouldn't the women she lived with every blessed day have a little more allegiance to her than the woman currently too busy serving time in prison to take care of her own home?

Stop it, Maggie. Being hurt and angry rarely hurts those around you. It only stabs you in your own heart.

She clutched the laptop to her hole-ridden heart. Sera's and Abby Ruth's priorities might not be clear, but Maggie's sure were. The one and only thing on her priority list was the still-soggy septic system.

Abby Ruth opened her mouth as though to speak, but Maggie slashed her flattened palm in front of her face to ward her off. "I told you both that I didn't want to register for that silly dating site, yet you disregarded my wishes and did it anyway. Why does it take three profiles to look for one man?"

"Maggie, we're sorry, but—"

"I don't want apologies, Sera. I want action." Maggie slapped the computer's case, causing it to vibrate against her chest. "Now, log in to that site and do whatever it is you have to do to take down my profile. Right now."

She handed the laptop to Sera and stood behind her to watch the screen. A shame when a gal couldn't trust her friends to do what they said they would. But Maggie wouldn't be hornswoggled again.

Sera slowly lifted the computer lid, and the screen flickered to life.

"Why are you so darned against this dating site?" Abby Ruth waved a hand at the computer, which displayed a black-and-yellow login screen decorated with two intertwined hearts that looked as though they'd been crafted from scrap metal. Interesting logo for love.

"Because...because..." Because how humiliating would it be when Sera and Abby Ruth got all kinds of interest and invitations and Maggie received none? Because they would no doubt want to share every little tidbit and Maggie wasn't sure she could bear it. Yes, George had loved her to distraction, but Maggie had never been the most sought-after girl on the William and Mary campus. She was what gals these days would call the pretty girls' ugly friend.

Whereas Lillian had always been the belle of the ball.

Old resentments, old insecurities. They had no place in her new and improved life.

"For one thing, I don't appreciate you two going against my wishes and putting my personal information online. I mean, who in the world knows what could happen to it? It's like my details are floating out there in the mist for anyone to come along and snatch up. It could lead people to my bank accounts and Social Security number. It's just not a good idea."

Sera pulled her multi-hued cheaters from her head to settle them on her nose and peered up at Maggie. "These sites have security measures in place. Believe me, they're just as concerned about hackers as you are."

Maggie knew her arguments weren't holding much weight, but she just couldn't help herself. "How much did it cost to register—ten dollars? Twenty?"

Sera's eyes scrunched closed behind the lenses. Kind of an if-I-can't-see-you-then-you-can't-see-me response she sometimes had when she wanted to avoid conflict.

"'Fess up, right this minute," Maggie demanded.

"A hundred," Abby Ruth said.

"Total?"

"Each," Sera squeaked.

Maggie pressed her hands to her ears to try to contain the steam now billowing out of her brain like pollution from an industrial smoke stack. "Three hundred dollars. I cannot justify spending that kind of money on some silly goose chase when we could use that on repairs."

"Thought you said the septic system would be fine once the ground dried out," Abby Ruth said.

"Well, I'm not so sure anymore," Maggie said. "I was looking for the darned distribution box when I about chopped off my foot. But all this dating nonsense is just taking up time that could be better used on looking after Summer Haven. Besides, you knew how I felt about helping Martha, and you deliberately went against my wishes."

Abby Ruth looked at Maggie from the corner of her eye and lifted one eyebrow. Finally, she sighed and said, "She's right, Sera. We overstepped some boundaries here."

With Abby Ruth's admission, surprise zigzagged through Maggie.

"Fine." Sera typed in a login and password quick as a flash. That girl's fingers could fly over a keyboard. "I'll take down Maggie's profile."

She clickety-clacked over the keys and pressed the mouse pad in the center of the keyboard several times. After a couple of minutes, she pulled down her glasses and stuck her face closer to the screen. "Oh. Oh, no."

Maggie didn't like the sound of that. "Oh no, what?"

Sera pushed the glasses on top of her head again and sat back. "I'm sorry, but I can't delete your profile."

"Why not?"

Sera's mouth lifted in a smile. "Because once you have a hit on your profile, the registration fee is no longer refundable."

Maggie leaned over Sera's shoulder, squinting at the screen. "A hit? What does that mean?"

"It means," Abby Ruth drawled, "that someone has the hots for you."

Maggie stumbled back a step and held out a hand toward the computer screen as if she could hold off whatever was inside that website. "There must be some mistake."

Sera shook her head, her long hair waving across the chair back. "No. It shows the activity right here." She tapped the screen. "Your profile was accessed by DanOfYourDreams at 6:45 this morning."

"And, sugar," Abby Ruth said, "that's not all. Apparently, Maggie's beau is in love because he didn't just look her over once. He's accessed her profile every hour since."

"Let me see that." Maggie pushed closer to the screen. "DIYDarling? That's me?"

Sera bounced in her seat. "Isn't it perfect?"

She did rather like it, but she wasn't about to admit that now. Her attention flashed over to the profile picture on the upper right of the screen. "That picture is from fifteen years ago. How did—"

Abby Ruth quickly jumped in. "We all used younger pictures of ourselves. We found yours in one of Lil's photo albums."

"I didn't even remember she had a copy of that one." It was one of Maggie's favorites, taken on a sunset cruise she and George had splurged on when they were at a hardware convention up around the Great Lakes. Maggie was wearing a broad smile, and although she knew she'd been sweating like a sumo wrestler in summer, on the computer she looked as if she had a healthy glow. She'd thought she'd been fat her whole life, but what she'd give to be that size again. *Why is it we never appreciate the shape we're in at the time?*

She flicked a finger toward the gold icon decorating her profile picture. "What's that little star in the right-hand corner?"

Sera clicked over to the site's help page. "Hmm...it means your admirer has marked you as a favorite."

Abby Ruth's eyebrows went so high, they were completely covered by her hair. "From what I read, you can't just go around choosing as many favorite profiles as you want. Each registrant can only mark three profiles with one of those stars. Plus, once you mark a profile with that, you can't take it back. This guy really likes you, Mags."

Two things warmed Maggie's heart. One, that Abby Ruth had somehow picked up Lil's fond nickname for Maggie. And two, that she was someone's—anyone's—favorite.

"Let's see what he looks like," Sera said, taking control of the keyboard. A few clicks later, the man's picture popped up and Sera enlarged it to take up the whole screen. "He's hot."

The man was tall and fit, with blondish hair and a crooked smile. Arms crossed over his broad chest, he was lounging against a tree.

Abby Ruth's mouth dropped open, and Maggie couldn't hide her delight, letting out a tiny giggle. "He is *very* good looking." She floated on her snuggly little high for about three seconds. Because if she had one star, Abby Ruth and Sera's pictures were probably framed in sparkly little gold stars. "Check your profiles too."

Abby Ruth's brow went from the tenth floor to the basement, and Maggie knew immediately what that meant. She hurried to say, "Not that I think we'll get the registration money back on either of yours. That's for sure."

The tight expression on Abby Ruth's face eased a little. "She has a point. Sera, let's check them."

Sera typed TexasTough in the search box and hit enter. When Abby Ruth's profile popped up, Sera clicked on the link.

Surprise of all surprises, Abby Ruth's picture wasn't sporting a single gold star. Instead, one of those pop-up thingies flashed on the screen.

"What's that?" Abby Ruth demanded.

Sera said, "Apparently, the site wants you to answer some additional profile questions."

"The hell you say," Abby Ruth protested. "Those darn questionnaires were already a billion items long."

Sera glanced up at Maggie and rolled her eyes. "More like twenty, but you know she's patience challenged."

Maggie snagged her lip with her bottom teeth to keep from laughing aloud. But she wasn't about to pose the question that was racing through her mind. *Could* they get the money back on Abby Ruth's registration? Maggie would rather toss away a hundred bucks than deal with the fallout of asking that. Instead, she said, "We can come back to this later. Why don't you check your profile, Sera?"

Sera's login name was SunnyOutlook. When she opened her own profile, her picture was bare of even one sunny gold star as well. No pop-up questions though.

"See, Maggie," Sera said, her fingers

dancing over the keyboard to pull up Maggie's profile again. "We need you to get on board with this. We can't afford to pass up the opportunity to dig deeper into someone who's interested in you. He's not OnceUponATom, but maybe your Dan will get us closer to the truth. It's possible some of these guys know each other."

That deflated Maggie's momentary pleasure at being the popular girl. "Are you saying that he has to be a wacko just because he's interested in me?"

Sera popped straight out of her chair and wrapped her arms around Maggie. "Of course not. I just mean it will give us one more investigative avenue. A gift horse and all that."

"Fine," Maggie finally said. "Since I can't do a darned thing about yanking my profile now, you two can keep an eye on it. But no more secrets. If there's something I should know, you have to promise to tell me immediately. Even—" she shot a hard look at Abby Ruth, "—if you think I won't like whatever it is. Are we all in agreement?"

But rather than looking chagrined, Abby Ruth's face was lit with humor and possibly admiration. "You drive a hard bargain, Mags. Have I told you how much I love that in a gal?"

Chapter Twelve

Teague enjoyed the Indian summer warmth on his back as he hit one last fly ball to his Little League team. They were playing on Summer Haven's back forty, where Lillian had agreed to let him build a practice field. Only he'd forgotten Wednesday evening was when Sera held her big yoga class on the lawn. The class was well-attended, and a few of the baseball moms had been angry he hadn't coordinated practice time with the yoga class.

How the heck had he forgotten that half of coaching was handling parents? As a peace offering, he'd promised to finish practice by six.

The ball hit the sweet spot between the makeshift first and second bases and winged out to right field where Benjamin Broussard chased it down, got under it with his legs planted and his glove up. Kid made a textbook perfect catch, using his bare hand as insurance to keep the ball in the glove.

Teague's practice pinch runner was closing in on second base, scooting as fast as his legs would carry him. Broussard took one look at the situation, judged it, and rocketed the ball toward the second baseman. The runner knew he was cutting it close and went in for the slide. Didn't matter because the ball smacked into leather milliseconds before the runner's cleats slammed into the bag.

As Broussard's teammates mobbed him and pounded him on the head and back with their mitts, the bright look on the wiry kid's face would've outshone the sun. That was the kind of confidence money couldn't buy. Maybe it would carry over from the outfield to the batter's box.

A man could sure hope.

"All right, y'all," Teague hollered. "That's the kind of catch that deserves a reward. Thanks to Broussard, you can skip your five laps around the practice field this afternoon."

That instigated more good-natured jostling on the mob's run from the field to the area where they kept their equipment bags and the cooler of sports drinks.

What he wouldn't give to have his own kid on this team. Did Jenny's son, Grayson, play baseball? If Jenny would ever reward them all with a visit to Summer Shoals, maybe Teague could get to know her son a little better.

When he'd heard she was expecting Daniel Northcutt's baby nine years ago, he'd finally let go of his pipe dream that he and Jenny might get back together one day. He might lust after another man's wife, but he wouldn't lust after a kid's married mother. That night, he'd hit a Houston sports bar and slugged back cheap whiskey, one glass after another. His police department buddies had finally been forced to pour him into someone's backseat and drive him home.

That hangover in his head had lasted a week. The one in his heart was still throbbing to this day.

He tucked his bat under his arm and leaned down to pull home plate out of the ground. Barnes was already circling the infield, grabbing the base markers. They met back at the equipment pile and organized everything while the boys sloshed their sports drinks on each other.

Like clockwork, the parents in their SUVs

came trundling through Summer Haven's back pasture at exactly six o'clock. Teague had quickly learned that holding closed practices, the kind where parents couldn't stay around to badger their kids, was the only way to run a baseball team.

This evening, most of the parents remained in their cars while their kids shoved their bags and themselves inside. But the parent in the late model Cadillac SUV cut the engine and stepped out.

Barnes glanced up from the bag holding the catcher's equipment and said, "Oh, hell."

"You can say that again," Teague agreed. Barnes looked as if he was about to bolt, so Teague said, "Hey, if you stick around while she's here, I'll make sure there's some of Maggie's special tea in it for you."

Barnes' smile was more toothy than Teague thought even Maggie's tea warranted. But what the hell, the guy would deserve a whole pitcher of the stuff if he kept Teague from having to deal with Angelina Broussard by himself. Because she was, of course, picking her way directly toward him on silver high heels.

"Teague," she called, "can we have a word?"

"Sure," he said, but made no move toward her. In fact, his feet were planted more firmly than Angelina's son's had been when he made that spectacular catch.

Angelina's lipsticked mouth drew tight, but she continued her trek until she stood in front of him. She flicked a dismissive look at Barnes. "I need a word with the coach."

"As assistant coach," Teague said, "Barnes is in on all the parent communication. Isn't that right, Barnes?"

The guy's Adam's apple convulsed as though he'd just swallowed a rat. "If you say so."

Regardless, Angelina angled her body toward Teague, purposefully excluding his assistant coach. "I wanted to make sure we were clear on how my husband and I expect Booger to be coached, especially since the team is practicing here at Summer Haven."

Although he knew exactly what she was getting at, he asked, "What does our practice location have to do with my coaching ability?"

Angelina laid a hand on his forearm. "Everyone knows you're a great coach, Teague. I just don't want *that woman* thinking she can come out here and interfere with your team just because she's living on the Summer family estate."

He wouldn't pretend he didn't know who she was talking about. "Do you see Abby

Ruth out here anywhere?"

"Well, a parent can't be too careful. And she can be more than a little pushy. I really need to talk to Lillian about Abby Ruth Cady. She clearly has no idea how that woman is impacting folks' opinions of Summer Haven, possibly Lillian herself."

Good Lord, if Abby Ruth was the pushy pot, this woman was the damned kettle. And something about Angelina just got all over him today. "I don't think it's as bad as you make it sound. Abby Ruth Cady actually taught me how to play baseball when I was Benjamin's age."

"I'm sure that was—"

"I'm not one to brag," he continued, "but I was named Player of the Year in high school and earned a full college ride off my sinker."

"Your what?"

"It's a type of pitch," Barnes piped up.

Angelina waved it off. "That's nice and all, but a Georgia team needs to win the Little League World Series, and honestly, it's about time for Summer Shoals to push those Warner Robins kids out of the way."

"Angelina, we're Minor League so we're not even eligible for the World Series this year."

"Oh...well, it's a work in progress and I

want my Booger to be on a winning team."

Didn't matter if Teague was the best coach in the world. Little League in this town was for fun. It wasn't the same caliber as the leagues that groomed their kids from birth to make it to the prestigious World Series tournament. "I appreciate your concern about the team, but Barnes and I have everything under control. His nephew James is my other assistant coach. He's on the high school team here and bats over .500 so he'll be the one helping the boys with their hitting from now on."

"That'll be fine," Angelina declared as if she were the queen of baseball. She motioned to her son. "Let's go, Booger. We're having dinner with Nana Broussard tonight."

The kid dragged his feet, kicking up dirt and grass. He passed by Teague and muttered, "I'd rather stay here. Nana always smells like Ben-Gay and raw shrimp."

Teague and Barnes waited until Angelina backed out and headed toward Summer Haven's circle drive before they started laughing.

"You gotta feel sorry for that kid," Teague said.

"Feel sorry for him? What about his daddy?"

Teague elbowed his deputy in the ribs. "I bet Angelina has a sister somewhere who could help relieve you of your single status."

"Can you imagine me bringing home someone like that to my momma? She'd have a conniption fit. Besides, last time I checked, you weren't hitched either. Maybe you could date the sister."

"I've got other fish to fry." He'd signed up for that dating site to investigate Sue Ellen's complaint. Still, it made him uncomfortable, and he hadn't even taken the time to check his matches yet. Something about it felt disloyal. Like he was finally letting go of his dream to be with Jenny.

"Oh, really?" Barnes hitched up his elastic waist shorts. "You been seeing someone on the sly? The ladies down at the diner are gonna be mad when they find out."

"Why?"

"Last I heard from Momma, they were looking to set you up with Miss Gurtie's granddaughter."

"Not interested."

"You sure?" Barnes pulled off his baseball cap and swiped at his sweaty head. "Have you seen her? Now, she looks like a real woman. None of that skinny magazine crap. She has those grab-yourself-a-handful baby-making hips." He held his hands out in front of his chest as though he was cradling a couple of watermelons. "And some prime tatas."

Teague had admired a tata or two in his time, but he preferred his women on the tall, lean side. He punched Barnes in the arm. "Sounds like you should go after Miss Gurtie's granddaughter. But first, let's get this equipment in the truck and we'll stop at the big house for a glass of Maggie's tea."

Barnes looked over his shoulder and hollered at his nephew, "James, let's load up."

A few minutes later, the three of them were standing on Summer Haven's front porch. Teague knocked and waited.

When the door opened, the yoga-loving Sera stood in the threshold. "Are you here for this evening's session?"

Oh, no way in hell. "Not tonight." Or any other night.

"I'm so glad the weather held," Sera said. "When it rains, we move the party into the parlor."

Maggie had to love that. People tromping all over Miss Lillian's house. Then again, Maggie probably didn't tell Miss Lillian about everything that happened around Summer Haven these days. That was one reason Teague liked to stop in on occasion—

to check on the house itself. After Sera had fallen through the ceiling during the toilet incident, Teague figured he needed to keep his eye on things. Plus, it gave him a perfect excuse to make sure these mature ladies weren't up to the kind of trouble they'd almost gotten themselves into a few months ago.

"I'm up for yoga." Barnes' nephew was openly ogling Sera, who was wearing those tight below-the-knee legging things and an unzipped hoodie with a strappy workout tank top underneath.

Teague crowded the kid to the side, and said from the corner of his mouth, "She's old enough to be your grandmother."

"Seriously?" James looked her over again. "That's just wrong."

"Sera," Teague said, "we actually stopped by to see if Maggie had a little of her special iced tea available for Barnes and me. James here'll have to stick with lemonade. But we're mighty thirsty after baseball practice."

"I think she's been keeping Abby Ruth busy sorting memorabilia in the attic. Anything to keep her occupied while you were practicing."

"Appreciate that, especially since Angelina stopped by after practice to gripe about her."

"Anything that will help Summer Haven pass the committee's inspection," Sera said. "Once that's over, Maggie and I will both be tempted to let Abby Ruth loose on the woman."

"Don't forget the inspection is a yearly thing," he reminded her.

"There is that." Sera shook her head, then called over her shoulder. "Maggie, you have a gentleman caller."

Footsteps clattered inside, then Maggie was jerking the door from Sera's hold. Maggie's color was up and her breathing was shallower than made Teague comfortable. When Maggie caught sight of Teague, Barnes and James, her happy face deflated like a pricked balloon. Disappointment. Not normally the reaction Teague received from women of any age. "Oh," she said, stretching her mouth into a smile that didn't even make it to her cheeks. "It's so nice to have company."

"They're after some of your tea," Sera said.

"Give me two shakes of a lamb's tail," Maggie said, "and I'll bring some out to you."

Although Maggie seemed genuinely more cheerful than she had when she first spotted them, it was obvious something was going on here. So Teague said, "Why don't you come out and sit with us a spell?" He made a show of looking over her shoulder into the house. "Maybe Miss Lillian could join us, too, if she's around."

How in the world these women thought they were fooling him about Lillian's whereabouts, Teague had no idea.

"Oh, no, she's...well...she's in the city this week doing some...shopping. Christmas shopping."

"It's only October."

"She doesn't like the last-minute rush."

Each time Teague stopped at Summer Haven, Maggie came up with some new story about Lil being out or traveling for some reason or another. If he hadn't talked with Lillian about using her pasture for baseball practice before she went to prison camp, there was no way Maggie would've let him spend that much time at Summer Haven. Seeing as Lillian had made the promise, though, Maggie didn't fight it.

After Maggie scurried back into the house, Sera stepped outside and Teague led his crew to the porch's line of rocking chairs. Sera asked James, "Sure you wouldn't like to try the yoga?"

He shot a look at Teague. Teague just lifted a shoulder. He knew what it was like to question this woman's intentions. But over the past few months, Teague had come to realize what he'd once thought were cougar come-ons were just the way Sera displayed her open and honest personality.

In a volume no one else could hear, Teague said to James, "You're safe."

"By the way," Sera said, "did I happen to mention several of the high school cheerleaders attend my weekly class?"

James was off the porch and headed toward the white gazebo in one bounding leap.

Sera chuckled. "Men are so easily motivated." She followed James at a much slower, hip-swinging gait.

Rocking slowly in his chair, Barnes lowered his voice and said to Teague, "Got to give it to her. That gal is in shape, but she's not really my type."

"Mine either." Thank goodness Sera had quit talking about his sacral chakra. That stuff made him nervous, but he was learning to take her with a grain of salt, or sugar, as it seemed.

Teague rocked back in his chair, scanning the large group gathered for Sera's class. There had to be thirty people out there, including Billy Parr, who was so busy ogling Sera's behind that he toppled from one of those one-footed, stork-like poses.

Barnes cleared his throat. "So what do you think about older women?"

Jenny Cady was two months older than Teague, a fact she'd teased him about until he'd finally gotten his driver's license. "I feel favorably about them."

"What if there was a significant age difference between you and the woman?"

"Like over ten years, you mean?"

"Give or take."

The front door opened and they both turned their attention toward Maggie, who was balancing a huge pitcher and multiple glasses on a tray. Barnes jumped up from his rocking chair and rushed forward. "Let me help you with that."

With a smile, Maggie carefully passed him the tray. "It's so nice to have such polite young men around Summer Haven these days."

Barnes smiled broadly and set the tray on the table. Maggie filled the glasses and passed them around.

"So," Teague asked her, "what's with the straw wall out in the yard?"

She waved a casual hand. "Just getting a head start on the Halloween decorations."

"As a kid, I never forgot Aunt Bibi's birthday because it was so close to

Halloween. She used to tease that all those witch decorations were in her honor."

"Is that supposed to be a haunted house or a castle?" Barnes asked, gesturing toward the mound of hay.

Maggie bit her lip and stared at the crumbling structure. "Oh, you know Sera. She has to be artistic in her own way."

Teague leaned forward in his chair, trying to get a better look. "It has to be her version of a castle because it looks like it has a moat around it."

Maggie jumped out her chair and refilled all the glasses to the brim. "Did I mention we're having a birthday party for Abby Ruth Friday night?"

"This is the first I've heard of it," Teague said.

"Sorry about that. We wanted to keep it low key until we had the plans wrapped up. But it looks like it's a go. And Abby Ruth's daughter is even thinking about flying down for the party."

The excitement that bolted through Teague was so strong he barely registered the slight acid reflux expression Maggie wore. "Jenny's coming to Summer Shoals?"

"Well," Maggie drew out the word, "it's not a done deal yet. Of course, we want you to come to the party, and Deputy Barnes too."

"You can definitely count me in." Teague grinned and sat back to enjoy the best-tasting tea he'd put in his mouth in years. Forget all that ThePerfectFit.com crap. His perfect fit would be here this weekend.

After Sera finished up her yoga class, Teague and Deputy Barnes collected a starry-eyed James and headed out. Which meant it was time for Maggie to admit to the other girls that she'd committed them to a party she had no idea if they could pull off, especially the part about Jenny's visit. Why had she blurted that out? Stupid, but it sure had put a happy expression on Teague's face.

Maggie cleaned up the glasses and pitcher, then called out, "Girls, we need to chat. C'mon in here to the kitchen for a minute, would ya?"

Sera wandered in a minute later, still with the glowing sheen of yoga perspiration on her shoulders. Abby Ruth wasn't far behind. "Thank the sweet baby Jesus," she said. "I'd had about all of digging through Summer family heirlooms as I could stand. Do you know somebody in this place collected chocolate bar wrappers? Hershey's, Hershey's with almonds, Mr. Goodbar,

Nestle Crunch. You name the kind, there's a wrapper up there for it."

"That has Harlan Fairview's name written all over it. Guy was a hoarder in the biggest way." Maggie braced her hands on a ladderback chair. "But candy bar wrappers are the least of our concern right now. I kinda promised Teague something, and Abby Ruth, I'm not sure you're going to like it."

"As long as you didn't promise him I'd cook and clean for him, I figure it's fine."

"I told him we were throwing you a birthday party."

Abby Ruth thrust out her chest as if she might crow. "Well, hell, I'm all for that."

"But that's only one part of it. I may also have...hinted...that Jenny and Grayson were flying down for the festivities."

"Why would you do that?" Sera asked.

"Because he and Deputy Barnes were admiring your fall decorating handiwork out there by the septic system."

"So?" Sera angled her head to one side. "What does it matter if Teague knows we're having a few potty problems?"

"I wasn't so worried about Teague, but Deputy Barnes' momma is one of the biggest gossips in town. If he told her, and she told someone...well it would end up back to

Angelina, and I just couldn't risk it."

"I do love parties thrown in my honor," Abby Ruth said. "But that's barely two days away. If Jenny hasn't visited Summer Shoals in the months I've been here, I can't see her hopping on a plane with this short notice. Couldn't you think of something better?"

"Well, I'd like to see what you would've done if you were under that kind of pressure," Maggie said. "I had to come up with something quick. Teague mentioned your birthday, and I just ran with it."

"I can call her," Abby Ruth said. "But it's no secret that girl doesn't always listen to her momma."

Sera glanced up from where she was engrossed with the computer. "I'd be happy to call her, if you think that would help."

"Sure can't hurt to take a different approach." Abby Ruth craned her neck to look at Sera. "What are you doing over there?"

"Checking all our profiles." *Click, click, click.* "Oh my gosh!"

Maggie and Abby Ruth rushed to the desk to peer over Sera's shoulder. "Another favorite?"

"No. Maggie has a private message. DanOfMyDreams has asked her out on a date. A real live face-to-face date. And it's tomorrow."

Maggie's skin began tingling—excitement? Or maybe eczema brought on by nerves? She flicked a finger toward the computer screen. "Well, you just send him one back saying no, thank you."

Sera twisted around and goggled at her. "Why in the world would you say no?"

"Because we're looking for some man named Tom, not Dan."

"But what if they know one another?"

"How many men do you think are registered on that site—hundreds? Maybe thousands?" Maggie said. "What's the likelihood of Tom and Dan being friends?"

"We registered together. Maybe they did too. It's a long shot, but it's a shot," Abby Ruth said. "We can't afford to pass up this opportunity. You have to find out if Dan knows Tom. Besides, you'll get a free meal and maybe find true love."

Uh-huh. That was about as likely as that septic system out front fixing itself.

Chapter Thirteen

While Sera and Maggie were up in the Magnolia Room getting Maggie all gussied up for her date with DanOfYourDreams, Abby Ruth sat downstairs in the kitchen jabbing at the mouse on Sera's laptop. If she had to answer another round of those damn questions to get favorited by some online dating dude, she would do it. After all, Maggie had a gold star and a date.

There was a reason Abby Ruth had been a sports journalist. She thrived on the thrill of competition. And good-looking men.

She logged into her account and smiled at her screen name. TexasTough. Hmm...maybe the men on this site were intimidated by a woman who came out and told them right upfront she didn't need a man. It was one of the reasons she'd stayed

single all these years. It would take one
helluva man for her to consider bringing him
home, wherever the heck that was these
days. She'd never wanted to put Jenny
through all that step-daddy stuff some of her
friends had subjected their kids to. Sure, it
had just been Jenny and her most of the
time. But they'd done fine by themselves.

And she'd never, not even for a day,
regretted having her daughter. Even though
she had chosen to keep Jenny's daddy a
secret from her.

Sure would be nice to have a little
companionship now that she had plenty of
time on her hands. Nothing serious, of
course, but someone to kick up her heels
with, maybe take to the shooting range.

When she clicked into her profile, the
same pop-up box they'd encountered when
Sera tried to unregister Maggie flashed on
the screen.

Abby Ruth scrolled through the
questions. And scrolled. And scrolled. "For
the love of the sweet baby Jesus," she
muttered to herself.

Fifty. This damned thing wanted her to
answer fifty questions over and above the
twenty she'd filled out when she registered.

Both her competitive nature and the fact
that she didn't want Maggie and Sera out

there trolling these virtual dating waters by themselves made her plug along. Who knew what kind of sharks were online trolling back?

And as Abby Ruth was living in the Summer Haven money pit, she had a responsibility for its upkeep.

::What is your stance on cannibalism? For or against?

::Do you stir your coffee clockwise or counter clockwise?

::Why don't they make bulletproof pants?

Lord, these things were getting more and more absurd with every click. Well, except for the bulletproof pants question. That was actually pretty smart. Still, she needed some liquid fortification to get through them, so she hit the cabinet above the refrigerator for her good sipping whiskey. Not that she really had to worry about either Sera or Maggie raiding her stash, but it didn't hurt that she was the only one in the house tall enough to reach this spot. She poured herself two fingers, then held it up, considering. What the hell. She splashed in another half inch.

But before she could settle herself back in her chair, the front doorbell rang.

Unfortunately, no feet pitter-pattered down the staircase. Abby Ruth stuck her head into the hallway outside the kitchen and yelled, "Hey, gals. Someone's at the door."

"I'm in the middle of styling Maggie's hair," Sera called back. "Besides, is there something wrong with your legs?"

Those two gals were getting mouthier by the minute. It would piss off Abby Ruth if it didn't make her so happy. She strode for the front door and yanked it open. A delivery guy stood there, electronic clipboard in one hand and a small Styrofoam cooler in the other.

"Can I help you?" she asked.

He checked his clipboard. "Got a delivery for an Abby Ruth Cady."

"You found her."

"Sign here, please."

She scribbled *AR C~~~* on the screen, and the guy handed over the ice chest. He gave her a quick salute and bounded down the front stairs to his delivery truck.

What in the world? Maybe Jenny had sent her an early birthday gift. That girl was on the ball that way, never letting details like that slip through the cracks.

Not like Abby Ruth had done a few times over Jenny's growing up years.

But that was in the past. Now, she had the opportunity to develop a new relationship with her daughter and grandson.

She turned to take the package back to the kitchen when Sera and Maggie appeared at the top of the stairs. She froze in place when she got a good gander at Maggie. "Hot damn," Abby Ruth said.

Maggie touched the back of her hair. "Oh, no. If Abby Ruth doesn't like it, that's a sure sign it's too foofy."

Maggie's normal ponytail and mind-of-their-own bangs were subdued in some kind of classy updo that would've cost three hundred bucks at a Galleria salon in Houston. "If I had any hair—" she tugged at her short strands, "—I'd be begging Sera to fix me up next."

The smile that spread across Maggie's rounded face was pure pleasure. "I think that's a compliment, so I'm going to take it and run."

"You do that, sugar. You look really pretty."

Sera headed down the stairs and nodded toward the ice chest under Abby Ruth's arm. "What have you got there?"

"I'm not sure, but I suspect it's an early birthday present from Jenny."

"You're not planning to open it, are you?"

Sometimes Sera was three shades of loco. "Uh...yeah."

"But it's bad luck to open gifts early."

Abby Ruth patted the cooler. "Seeing as whatever this is probably needs to be refrigerated, I figure it would be worse luck to wait."

"She has a point." Maggie joined them at the bottom of the stairs. "We can cut those yellow straps with scissors in the kitchen."

They all trooped to the back of the house. Of course, Sera spied the open laptop in the kitchen right off. "Working on something?"

No reasonable reason to lie. "I decided it was time for me to answer those questions on the dating site."

"Made it very far?"

"Not nearly far enough. At this rate, I'll be jitterbugging down at Dogwood Ridge Assisted Living by the time I get through all these."

"Maybe I could help—"

"Presents first." Abby Ruth plopped the package in the middle of the table. "And dating later."

Maggie grabbed scissors from the desk she used to manage all the business—mainly repair business—at Summer Haven.

Bypassing the plastic encased card on top, Abby Ruth ruthlessly cut through the straps.

"Shouldn't you read the card first?" Sera asked.

"You know, for such a free spirit, you sure have a lot of rules about opening gifts. Haven't you ever heard that saying about eating dessert first? Well, same thing applies to presents and cards. Always get the goodie and then go back for the boring stuff."

Sera read the label and grimaced. "It's from McAdoo's Steaks. Your daughter sent you dead cow to celebrate the anniversary of your birth? Something is wrong with you people."

Jenny sending steaks? Wasn't like her, but maybe she'd finally figured out that Abby Ruth appreciated a good piece of beef more than all the pedicures in the world.

She popped the top and thumbed through six packages.

Maggie lifted one of the frosted packages from the dry ice and read the label. "Cube steak?"

"Jenny enjoys a good filet mignon as much as the next girl, but this isn't really her style." Abby Ruth flipped the lid over and wrestled with the plastic envelope. Inside, the card was printed in a calligraphy font.

> *Dear TexasTough,*
> *Thank you for registering with ThePerfectFit.com. However, it has come to our attention that you do not fit our site's demographic so your profile is being disabled. If you should choose to try online dating again in the future, we would recommend a site better suited to your unique needs.*
>
> *Our best wishes in your search for love.*
> *Sincerely,*
> *ThePerfectFit.com*

"Son of a bitch," Abby Ruth said.

"Not from Jenny then?" Maggie asked.

"Not by a long shot. It's from ThePerfectFit.com."

"Why would an online site send you—oh, they sent you a birthday gift." Sera clapped like a child who'd just been told she could eat candy for every meal.

"No, Sera," Abby Ruth said, "they sent me a kiss-off gift." That was when she remembered she's been in the middle of updating her profile. Maybe if she got back to it fast enough, she could—she lunged for the laptop. *Click. Click. Click.*

This time the pop-up box wasn't filled with idiotic questions like *Would you rather marry Donald Duck or Mickey Mouse?* Instead, it said *You've been successfully deleted from the ThePerfectFit.com website. Thank you for letting us be part of your journey to find the mate that fits you perfectly.*

"Oh my gosh," Sera exclaimed. "You've been blackballed from love."

Chapter Fourteen

Llewellyn Farm was twenty minutes outside Summer Shoals and as pretty a piece of land as Maggie had ever seen. Even though the fall air was cool enough to drive with the windows open this afternoon, she'd cranked up her truck's AC because Sera had worked so hard to make her hair look nice.

She parked near a bright red pole gate and slowly hiked toward the buzz of activity. With each step, she could feel the slight pull of her stitches. But darned if she'd let an annoyance like that impact her—as Sera had called it—*investidate*. In a huge corn maze, small children darted in and out of the stalks while their parents urged them to go through the maze properly. And although this area of Georgia wasn't known for its apple orchards like the towns north of Atlanta were, this farm had a small cluster of them. Probably gave them a great reason to serve apple cider and other apple goodies this time of year. Maybe she'd buy some apple butter to take back to the girls.

Traditional picnic tables were scattered everywhere. A couple of blondish men were sitting alone. Maybe the one wearing the red polo shirt was her date.

But while Maggie stood there ogling her potential blind date, a woman walked up to the table carrying two plates and sat next to the man.

Strike one.

Anyway, Dan had asked her to meet him at the little information booth. It would be hard to miss the purple-and-white-striped cabana sitting in the center of all the action.

Maggie took a steadying breath and approached the booth where a college-aged girl was handing out pick-your-own instructions and hints to the corn maze. "Excuse me," she said to the girl, "I'm supposed to meet a friend here. I don't suppose—"

"Are you Maggie?"

"How did you know?"

The girl gave her a cheeky grin. "I'm magic." Then she laughed. "Nah, the dude told me to look for a nice older lady with...uh..." The girl's gaze dropped to

Maggie's bosom.

"It's okay," Maggie told her. "In our family, we call them supersized muffins."

She shook her head. "To think yours probably came naturally, and I have friends paying thousands to supersize their muffins."

"These are definitely the ones God gave me." Well, that wasn't completely true. The boobs she'd been given sixty years ago were perky and bouncy. These were...not. A woman should be able to trade in for a new pair every three years. "Back to my friend. He's here?"

"Oh, he's been here for a while." She pointed to the west. "If you walk down that way, you'll find a small barn." A quick check of her watch, and she said, "You have about ten minutes until the next tour starts, so you probably want to get going."

"Tour? I didn't realize we were taking a tour." Darn it, her stomach was grumbling because she'd spent the morning frantically making invitation phone calls for Abby Ruth's birthday party and she'd been too nervous to eat. Besides, she'd been hoping for a fresh air picnic. "What exactly are we touring?"

The girl gave her another one of those we're-sharing-a-secret smiles. "The beekeeping operation."

Ten minutes later, Maggie was fighting a nervous sweat while a nice lady helped zip her into a pair of head-to-toe coveralls. She was so overheated that she almost regretted rejecting Sera's suggestion of wearing a thong under her Capri pants. Because her normal granny panties were sticking to her cheeks like an American cheese slice to bologna. She flapped her arms a little, trying to get some airflow, but it was useless with the thick weave of her canvas jumpsuit.

The woman grabbed a white bush hat from behind Maggie and plopped it onto her head. Then she fluffed the protective veil and tucked it into Maggie's collar before zipping her up the rest of the way. "You'll also need gloves."

Maggie held out both arms, and the woman worked elbow-length gloves over her fingers and wrists as if she were prepping Maggie to perform surgery. "Is this included in the romance package?"

The woman looked up, her head tilted to the side. "Excuse me?"

"On your website, I read about the romance package. You know, the custom picnic, a two-person hayride and a souvenir photo. Maybe the tour is an add-on?"

"Not that I've ever heard of."

"Do you know if my...friend...made a reservation for the romance package?"

"All I know is we booked a private tour through the beekeeping operation."

Well, that was sweet. He'd arranged for them to have a special experience together. That spoke well of him. "Did you help him dress too?" Because let's face it, Maggie was dying to know if he was half as handsome in person as he was in his profile picture.

"You know, he came with his own gear. We don't see that every day."

Well, dang it.

The woman grabbed a roll of plain gray duct tape and swept a length around Maggie's ankles and patted her legs. "That'll keep the bees out of your drawers."

"Another good use for duct tape." Maggie could just imagine what she'd look like if she got a bee up her pants leg. Probably like she was trying to pull off one of those hip-hop dances and failing miserably. "Thank you so much for all your help."

She pointed at a door opposite the one Maggie had come in. "Your tour guide will meet you right out there."

Maggie paused with her hand on the knob. When she opened this door, her life could change. She could meet a man who enjoyed her company. Who liked her for herself and didn't give a hoot about weight or age.

With a breath, she let out the nerves jittering inside her and opened the door. Outside stood, what she assumed by their height, two men. Both dressed in white like she was. One had his back to Maggie, but the other held a small binder and faced the other man. They almost looked like a groom and preacher.

Which was utterly ridiculous.

"Hi," she said, and the men's conversation stopped.

The groom turned slowly, and Maggie's heart was thumping in her chest. Was he handsome?

When he was facing her fully, her heart did a stutter-flop. Rather than the see-through veil like she wore, his was so dark and so tightly woven that she couldn't see through it. His jumpsuit was a bit fancier than hers too. Instead of duct tape wrapped around his cuffs and sleeves, they were secured with jute tied in a cool knot shaped like a heart.

"You're DIYDarling?" the man croaked. He shook his head, cleared his throat and reached out to take both of Maggie's hands in his. "I mean, I'm so glad you made it."

The way he said *darling* almost made her

swoon. And his hands. My, he had a nice grip. Firm yet gentle. "Margaret, really, but my friends call me Maggie."

"Do you consider me a friend?"

She raised a shaky hand to hide a nervous giggle. "I suppose so."

"I'm Dan." Something about his voice seemed familiar, but maybe that was just wishful thinking on her part. Because she would've remembered meeting any man as good-looking as Dan was in his picture. She pumped up her smile even though she felt a trickle of sweat roll down her spine and into an unmentionable spot. "Wouldn't miss this for the world."

The preacher—uh, tour guide—said, "Let's get started then."

He took them to the Observation Hive, a wall of approximately 50,000 bees. Although he assured them that the bees were safely secured behind glass, just watching them dance around the queen bee made Maggie itch all over.

For the next hour, the beekeeper showed Maggie and her date the hives, talked about the plight of the honeybee, and gave them the lowdown on the queens and their male harems. The whole thing was much more fascinating than Maggie would've imagined.

But she couldn't afford to be distracted by

bees or romanced by Dan. She was here on a mission, and she needed to keep that forefront in her mind.

"So, Dan," she said casually, "have you been on The Perfect Fit for long?" Lord, that sounded about as smooth as one of those you-come-here-often pickup lines.

"Just a few months."

"Are any of your friends registered too?"

He tilted his head, shook it slowly. "Why? Are you already looking to date someone else?"

The way he said it, with a small hint of hurt in his voice, made Maggie's stomach shrink. "No, no. It's not that. It's just that some of my friends and I joined at the same time and I thought men might do the same thing. One of my friends has a real thing for men named Tom," she ad-libbed. "And I just thought if you had a friend named Tom, you might—"

"Nope," he shot back, his words clipped. "Absolutely no friends named Tom. Have never known a Tom in my life."

That seemed a little unlikely based on the popularity of the name, but Maggie let the topic drop. He obviously wasn't their path to OnceUponATom.

Dan held her gloved hand through the entire tour. But since he kept bumping into things along the way, she wasn't sure if the handholding was a sign that he liked her or a result of his being unable to see what was three inches in front of his face.

"Can I answer any questions?" the tour guide asked.

Actually, Maggie had a couple. "So if I understand what you're saying, anyone can keep bees."

"Well, anyone who responsible and willing to learn and put in the effort needed to take care of some of the earth's most precious gifts."

Sounded right up Sera's alley. "Can you make your own honey bee boxes?"

"Most people order theirs from suppliers," he said, "but your friend here was telling me that you're quite handy. I've seen plans online for beehive frames."

How nice of DanOfYourDreams to remember that from her profile. "Do you mind if I look closer at their construction?"

"Be my guest."

Over the years, Maggie had become good at measuring distances just by using her arms and legs. She contorted over and around the glossy white boxes that were stacked five and six high, making note of the measurements and construction.

Her date said, "I like a woman who likes

to be outside and get a little dirty.”

That was Maggie’s natural element. “Most men like women who’re dainty and sweet-smelling.”

If she wasn’t mistaken, DanOfYourDreams leaned closed and sniffed her. “I’m more into the earth goddess type.”

Oh, no. That meant he was Sera’s type, not Maggie’s. “I’m more of the duct-tape goddess type.”

“I’m very attracted to a woman who can handle herself. Fix situations that need to be fixed. I’m not interested in someone who waits for a man to solve all her problems.”

Well, that definitely sounded more like the new and improved Maggie since she’d moved to Summer Haven. “I’m actually in the middle of a major home improvement project right now.” Okay, so that was a bit of a stretch. What she was in the middle of wasn’t so much improvement as it was necessary maintenance.

“You do a lot of DIY work?”

“There’s almost nothing I can’t fix.” Maggie pushed out her chest with pride and noticed that DanOfYourDreams’ head dipped for an instant. Her date was, in fact, a breast man. “Tell you what, why don’t we get out of these coveralls? I’d be happy to tell you all about my projects over a cup of apple cider."

He started fidgeting as though an entire frame of bees has just swarmed into his boxer shorts. "You know, as much as I'd love that, I have to...uh...be at work in an hour, and—"

"Oh? Where do you work?"

"Nowhere as interesting as this farm, that's for sure."

Talk about a runaround answer to her question. "Surely you have ten minutes to—"

"I almost forgot," he blurted out. "I bought the souvenir photo and the beekeeper was supposed to take that for us. Let me go get him." And off he dashed.

Well, he's gone, Maggie.

She plodded toward the changing area. She'd become so involved in the tour that she hadn't pumped her date for nearly enough information. That would be a big, fat fail when she got back to Summer Haven. And it was clear that he wasn't interested in her. Her cooler of steaks would probably be sitting on the front porch when she got home.

Oh, well. She'd tried.

Before she could slip inside and change her clothes, DanOfYourDreams came loping across the grass. "Wait," he hollered. "What about the picture?"

Sure enough, the preacher-tour guide-beekeeper was jogging her way as well.

DanOfYourDreams hadn't ducked out. He'd come back and he wanted to take a picture with her. *How thoughtful!*

Maybe this dating thing wasn't so bad after all.

Knowing she'd get no visitors today, Lillian moped around the cottage. Maggie had called to let her know a visit just wasn't in the schedule. With the deadline on this project looming—just four short days away—she shouldn't have cared so much about a visit from her girls. But the comment Martha had made—the longer you were in, the less your friends visited—weighed on Lillian.

Big Martha walked in and stared at her lying on her bunk gazing at the ceiling. "What's got you all down in the mouth?"

"I'm not getting visitors today."

"That sucks. May as well get used to it."

Lillian didn't even have the energy to reprimand Martha. She wanted to be considered a lady, but it would be a long road if she didn't clean up her language. Then again, Lil had picked up some colorful phrases over the past few months. She'd keep her stones to herself lest they boomerang into her glass house. "It does indeed."

"Well, why don't you come with me? My niece is visiting today. Supposed to tell me all about her date with Tom Thumb." She said it as if it she were spitting out a rotten plum.

"I don't want to horn in—"

Martha tugged on Lillian's shirtsleeve. "Get your bony old butt off that bunk and come to the visiting room. Last thing in the world I need is your sad face bringing me down later."

Lillian shoved her feet in her prison-issued shoes. "Fine."

"Let's go." Martha hurried her across the grounds. The door to the visitation area was just opening when Martha finessed her way past at least thirty other inmates to snag a place at the front of the line.

Lillian nodded apologetically, and Martha tugged her by the arm into line.

Everyone walked single file into the room, taking the next available table, except Martha. She stepped out of the khaki conga line and commandeered her normal spot.

Martha plopped down into one of the chairs, causing the legs to screech against the utilitarian tile. Lillian gently pulled out a chair and settled in next to her, crossing her legs.

The first person through the door was a woman with straight, dark hair. She beelined straight to Martha's table and bounced into a chair across from them.

Martha silently studied the woman's bright eyes and glowing skin. "Spill it, girl. You look like you have a secret that you're just busting to tell."

"Tom is amazing."

Martha's eyes narrowed. "OnceUponATom is amazing?"

"Yes! Our date was so romantic."

Times had certainly changed if shooting your date was considered romance. It was obvious this was the niece Martha was so worried about. Lil could see why now.

Martha made a come-on motion with her fingers. "Give it up. I want to hear everything about this whack-job."

"He's not a whack-job. He's my boyfriend." The niece thrust out her chin. "And I'm...I'm in love with him. Tom is my meant-to-be. My perfect fit. I just know it."

Oh, this was serious, and Martha looked mad enough to kick a kitten. "Start at the beginning and don't leave out a single detail. Where did he take you? How did he treat you? And did he pay for the whole thing?"

The girl sighed and sat back in her chair. "He thought of everything. Even had my favorite color paint pre-loaded in the gun when I got there."

"Do you mean to tell me he didn't even pick you up?"

Lillian didn't know why that upset Martha so much. She'd much rather not have the lunatic know where the clueless girl lived.

"Well, no, but that's because he had all those surprises for me." She rummaged in her purse. "Look." She pushed a picture across the table.

Martha edged it closer between she and Lil.

The cardboard picture frame held a picture of two people who, in camo outfits and bulky headgear, weren't even distinguishable as male or female. Both had big guns strapped across their bodies. Lil couldn't even imagine. "That looks—"

"Dangerous," Martha spat out.

The niece rolled her eyes. "You're an old fuddy-duddy." If Martha—in her forties—was old, then Lillian was an artifact. "It was sweet and fun."

"Sweet? Did he shoot you?" Martha asked.

"No, we were on the same team. I wasn't

much help, but with Tom shooting at the enemy, our team won easily. A man who's a great shot is hot."

"Did he try anything afterward?"

The girl visibly deflated. "Not for lack of my trying. But he claimed he was too dirty and sweaty. Wouldn't even take off his paintball helmet. How in the world is a girl supposed to get a little something-something when a guy won't even kiss her? He had great eyes, and bet his lips are totally kissable."

Martha's jaw pulsed. "What's that mean?"

"His profile picture showed him smiling, so it was hard to tell. Then, with him wearing a helmet during paintball, I just had to use my imagination."

"Are you telling me," Martha said slowly, "that you don't even know what this guy looks like?"

"Of course I do, silly. I told you I've seen his profile picture. He's about six feet tall. He has short hair. And his aim is the sexiest thing I've ever seen."

"Yeah," Martha muttered where only Lillian could hear her. "I don't like this guy's aim one damn bit." Then she increased her volume and asked, "Did you make another date? When are you planning to see him again?"

"I don't know yet, but just this morning I got a bushel of fresh roses. Those things had to cost fifty bucks if they cost a dollar."

At the end of their visiting time, Martha's niece was so high on paintball love, she floated out of the room.

Lillian and Martha headed out of the main building and across the camp without so much as one word until they returned to the cottage.

Martha shut the door behind them. "I don't like it one bit. That guy sounds like bad news." She paced, kicking at anything in her path. "He could be one of those social-paths. Gonna lure her in with paintball and flowers and then wham! He's gonna cut her up into hash-sized pieces."

"You have a bit of a gory side I didn't know anything about."

Martha whirled around, got in Lillian's face. "You have people you love more than you love anything else in this world, don't you?"

"Of course I do." Maggie's dear face— sewer grime and all—floated in Lillian's mind.

"Then you're willing to do any damn thing it takes to protect them, right?"

"Absolutely."

"Well, Miss H&M, we had a deal. You promised your granny girls would figure out who this weirdo is. They making any progress on that?"

"The last time I talked with Maggie, she hadn't yet tracked him—"

Martha took a half step closer, so close Lil spotted an almost invisible scar at the corner of her right eye, a reminder that she didn't know everything about this woman. "If they don't get on the stick, not only will I not call the plumbers in my family, but I *will* put in a call to the leg-breakers."

Chapter Fifteen

Maggie was surprised her little truck didn't sprout wings and glide home. That was how over the moon she was after her unconventional first date. Definitely not your normal dinner and a movie, but the guy had shown originality. That was worth a thousand dinners because he was the kind of man who would always keep a woman guessing. Not the kind of man who would lapse into the habit of plopping into his easy chair every evening to snore his way through a few TV shows.

This man would keep things fresh. Exciting.

When she pulled around Summer Haven's circle drive, Sera and Abby Ruth were both rocking on the front porch like parents worried about their daughter, making Maggie grin.

She hopped out of the truck, the door slamming behind her from the adrenaline still pumping through her. She couldn't help herself. She practically skipped up the steps. "Were you worried about me, girls?"

"No," Abby Ruth said quickly. "We just wanted to enjoy a little cool fall air."

And thank goodness for the cool air because after an hour in that beekeeping zoot suit, Maggie had been worried she was suffering from a nuclear meltdown hot flash. The sweat was still drying at the small of her back.

"How was your date?" Sera asked.

"It was...different."

"Different doesn't sound good." Abby Ruth rocked forward in her chair and pinned Maggie with her I-*will*-get-to-the-bottom-of-this stare. "Was he a freak? Ugly? Smell bad?"

"The date *was* good. No. I don't know. And no." In fact, he'd smelled of citrus and slightly of gun oil.

"How can you not know if a man is ugly?" Abby Ruth asked. "I mean I get that eye-of-the-beholder thing, but ugly is pretty easy to recognize."

"If he looked anything like his profile picture, he's certainly not ugly," Sera said.

"He did look like his picture, right?"

Maggie slowly shook her head. "Don't y'all care about anything besides the way he looked?"

"Of course we care." Sera leaned forward and grabbed Maggie's hands. "We want to hear every detail."

"Why don't we go inside so I can get a glass of iced tea, and I'll tell y'all all about it?"

"How about I bring some out?" Abby Ruth stood and offered Maggie her chair. Then she was gone.

Her mouth gaping, Maggie turned to Sera. "Did she...did she just volunteer to do something nice for us?"

"Sometimes you don't give her enough credit."

It was true that she should probably give Abby Ruth the benefit of the doubt more than she did. No one was all good or all bad. Before Maggie could give that any deeper thought, Abby Ruth stuck her head out the front door and said, "Holy high waters. Get in here, girls, because we're in deep shit."

Oh, no. Abby Ruth never minced words at the best of times, but her voice contained a hysterical note Maggie had never heard before. She and Sera shot out of their chairs and hit the front door at a jog.

When Maggie stepped inside, even she had to agree there were no better words to describe what they'd walked into. The downstairs toilet had erupted into a simmering mess that was oozing straight toward them like something out of a sci-fi movie.

All the good feelings Maggie's date had built up, the potty sludge chased away.

"It's time for Plan B," Abby Ruth sidestepped the muck and headed for the back porch. "I'll get your rubber boots, sugar."

To their credit, Abby Ruth and Sera did walk out to the septic line with Maggie and helped by shining flashlights on the swamp. Although she'd checked it before, Maggie went straight for the outlet tee. *Please, please let a layer of bacon fat have risen to the surface. That's easy enough to skim off.*

But when she checked, it was clear the outlet tee was still allowing water to pass through.

"Mags," Abby Ruth called, "I think you might want to see this."

Maggie carefully picked her way through the dark to see what she'd found. Didn't take long to get the lay of the land. Abby Ruth was straddling one of the VW van's tire tracks with her flashlight pointed toward the ground. Between her feet, a mangled terracotta-colored ceramic pipe protruded from the ground like a bleeding, fractured femur.

Maggie had thought Sera had moved her van without incident. But now it was clear the main sewer line to the house was a fatality.

"So, what exactly does this mess mean, Maggie?" Abby Ruth's brow was arched so high it looked almost like a question mark. "That we're back to that flush, no-flush zone again?"

Maggie sagged under the heavy weight of defeat. She knew what this meant. It meant she couldn't handle the septic mess alone. It meant she couldn't save Summer Haven without exhausting the better portion of their dwindling funds. It meant, worst of all, that she had to suck it up and play nice with Martha so the woman would come through on the septic deal.

Tears glazed her eyes, but she blinked them back. "It means our facilities are out of order. Completely."

"We can just go outside." Sera shrugged. "If animals can do it, so can we."

"I'm not an animal," Abby Ruth said. "I'm not doing my business outside."

Sometimes Abby Ruth was a bit mule-

204 Kelsey Browning and Nancy Naigle

headed, but this time she was right. They couldn't live without a proper septic system, and they couldn't be without toilets. "We can get a portable potty. The ones they used at the fair last year were clean and nice, and they were from a company just outside of town."

Sera and Abby Ruth both whirled around and gave Maggie a synchronized the-heck-you-say look.

"What?" Maggie shrugged. "Best we can do for now. I'll make an SOS call to Mrs. Potts and see if she can have a portable potty delivered right away." She'd pay for it out of her own funds. Lil needn't even know about it. Not only because of the cost, but because Lil would be beside herself if she knew a bright pink portable potty was sitting on Summer Haven's lawn.

"Oh, that ought to go over like gangbusters with the committee," Abby Ruth said, drawing air quotes around the word committee.

That danged committee would be the death of Maggie. "True, but we'll just say we're using the portable potties for Abby Ruth's birthday party tomorrow night. It'll be fine."

"Actually," Abby Ruth said, "that's a pretty good excuse."

Maggie took in a breath. "Thanks. I'll go ahead and get a washing station at the same time. You know, like they use at the petting zoo. That'll give us a sink to clean up in too."

"I am not bathing in a sink. I may just have to hitch my wagon and go to the nearest KOA campground."

"You can bathe in the creek with me," Sera said.

"Lord, girl," Abby Ruth said, "the creek is colder than that blessed mammogram machine. No, thank you."

Maggie and the girls plodded back to the house. "As soon as we sop up the overflow inside, we'll have to get the dirt on this guy for Martha pronto. We just hit the critical stage, and I hate to admit that I didn't find one helpful thing by going on that date."

"It's okay, Maggie. It was a long shot, but at least we took it."

That didn't make her feel much better. "Sera, can you get ThePerfectFit.com up on the computer so we can put our heads together?"

"Sure."

"Abby Ruth, you're on cleanup duty while I call about the porta-potty."

"Why don't I call the pot place and you deal with that toilet tornado?"

Maggie located the phone number for

Mrs. Potts Pots in the *Handy Shopper* newspaper she'd left on the kitchen desk. "Because I'm the one who's been dealing with the even bigger mess outside."

"Fine." Abby Ruth snatched a mop and bucket out of the pantry and stomped off toward the bathroom.

Although they were still up to their necks in problems, Maggie grinned as she called and placed the potty order. By eight o'clock in the morning they'd have the party package delivered—a sink with a three hundred gallon tank of water and three portable potties. At least they'd each have their own private bathroom.

A bit later, Maggie, Sera and Abby Ruth were all hunkered around the computer, staring at ThePerfectFit.com.

"I don't even understand what we're supposed to look for," Maggie admitted.

Sera absently twirled her hair around her ink pen. "We need to find out more about OnceUponATom, but the only way to do that is to get on his radar."

"Well, can't one of us just ask him out?" Maggie asked. Not that she was volunteering, but her first date had been quite a success.

"It doesn't work that way. I can get to his profile, but it's not allowing me to favorite him under either your account or mine," Sera said. "It's like the guys get that function, but the girls don't. This site has some gender inequality issues."

"I fought that crap my whole career," Abby Ruth said.

"And unfortunately, the private message function only works if your profiles were matched by the system or you've been favorited by a man."

"Apparently, whoever started this site has never heard of Sadie Hawkins Day," Maggie commented. "What's all this about matching?"

"The system makes recommended matches, probably through an algorithm based on our answers to the profile questions. And that means we each end up with access to different guys."

"Well, that's not fair," Abby Ruth complained. "I don't like having my choices limited."

But Maggie's interest piqued. What if the site had matched her with someone even better than DanOfYourDreams? A flush, the kind she hadn't felt since menopause, crawled up her chest. She took a step back to keep Abby Ruth and Sera from feeling the sudden heat pouring off her body.

"Well, let's take a closer look at y'all's

matches," Abby Ruth said.

Sera brought up her profile and clicked through the pictures one by one. Each man was more attractive than the last.

Abby Ruth crossed her legs and bounced a toe up and down. "Let me see Maggie's guys."

Sera's fingers danced across the keyboard, and a screen full of handsome men popped up.

Abby Ruth made a sound that reminded Maggie of the noise her cat used to make right before he hacked up a nasty glob onto her carpet. "This thing is obviously rigged," Abby Ruth said. "Sera got all the leading men types and Maggie's pulling in the hot lumberjacks."

"Well, if we change the answers to our profile questions, maybe the system will offer up new matches," Sera said.

"Me first!" Abby Ruth scooted her chair closer to the computer. "I want another chance at this game."

"You'll need a different email address," Sera said.

"Well, set that up. And this time, I want the screen name CowgirlFun."

"I like it." Sera clicked over to Gmail and created a new account. A quick logout from ThePerfectFit, and she began re-registering the new Abby Ruth. "You probably want to use something besides your real name since you were...asked to step down...the first time around."

"Fine," Abby Ruth snapped. "Whatever you think'll get the job done."

Sera typed in *Polly Golightly*.

"That's supposed to attract a guy who likes to bruise people with little blobs of paint?" Abby Ruth asked.

"He'll never see your real name. That's the reason for screen names, remember?"

"Good thing because I sure as hell wouldn't give anyone that name."

"The questions are the key," Sera told her. "Question one, what do you most often do in your spare time?"

"Clean my guns."

"Good Lord, you can't say that." Maggie flopped back in her chair and covered her eyes. "Is that how you answered it the first time?"

"Well, yeah. What was I supposed to say? Bake cookies?"

Maggie had her doubts any account Abby Ruth set up would pull in anything but the crazies. "You'll get matched with the serial killers, but then I guess that's the point."

"The guy plays paintball," Abby Ruth said, "so he obviously likes guns."

"Fine, we'll let that ride." Sera typed and clicked. "Question two, if you had to choose between living in an igloo or a teepee, which would you choose?"

"Why are some of these different questions than I answered the first time around?"

"This is actually a pretty sophisticated system," Sera said. "It seems to constantly adjust its input parameters."

Input parameters? If they didn't watch out, Sera would become a geek rather than a hippy Or maybe she could be both. A heek. Or a gippy.

After another eighteen questions with Abby Ruth arguing about every blasted one of them, Sera raised her pointer finger over the keyboard, then let it fall on the ENTER key.

The three of them watched the ThePerfectFit.com icon spin around as it processed Abby Ruth's new registration.

Abby Ruth's new CowgirlFun profile finally displayed on the screen.

"Push the button for the matches," Abby Ruth demanded.

Sera did as she asked and four rows of four men's screen names appeared.

"Yes!" Abby Ruth pumped a fist into the air. "Sixteen matches. These boys better not look like they came off the post office wall, or they'll wish they were wanted dead or alive."

"Where are the pictures?" Abby Ruth asked.

"Hang on. I'm still figuring this thing out." Sera chewed on her bottom lip as she clicked buttons on the screen. "Here we go. I think I've got it."

"You're supposed to pick based on more than looks," Maggie said. "Besides, the screen names give you a real sense of the person."

Abby Ruth traced a finger across the list on the screen. "Fine, but I'm sure not interested in HappilyEverAdam. Who picks this stuff?"

Sera clicked into the profile anyway.

"I think he sounds romantic," Maggie said, leaning forward to read some of the other details on that profile, until she got to part about Adam's desire to live in a nudist colony. Maybe he was more up Sera's alley.

"Go back to the list," Maggie said. She scanned the names. "How about LetsPlayBall?"

Abby Ruth lifted her chin, squinting slightly at the screen. "Yeah, click on that one, Sera."

"He's six foot three," Sera read from the

screen. "Loves to fish, plays baseball, very athletic. No felonies. Texas boy who loves small-town life."

"That guy sounds like my Tadpole," Abby Ruth said. "Which makes that match downright creepy. Next guy."

"Wait," Maggie said. "Scroll over to his picture. What if Teague is registered? I've wondered where he meets girls, because he sure doesn't date anyone around here."

Sera moved the mouse and there was Teague in all his handsome glory. He was out of uniform, wearing a casual T-shirt and a smile. No wonder Abby Ruth wanted Teague and Jenny to get back together. Their sheriff was, as the younger girls would say, a total hottie.

"Holy crap," Abby Ruth said. "Will he see these same matches from his side?"

"I'm not totally sure." Sera shook her head. "Every time I think I have this system figured out, it seems to change on me."

"Reject him," Abby Ruth ordered. "Immediately."

Sera clicked a big X and Teague's profile disappeared from Abby Ruth's page. "Fine. Here's another one. Retired athlete. Widowed two years ago. Over six feet tall. Sandy hair. Loves women who can handle things on their own and not afraid to take charge. Shoe shoppers need not apply, but boot girls are a shoe-in. That's so you, Abby Ruth."

She cut Sera a narrow look. "That man's looking for a dominatrix," she said, clucking her tongue against her teeth.

"He is not," Maggie said with a laugh.

"Handle things. Take Charge. Boots. Yeah, that's got BDSM written all over it."

Sera snickered. "I'm not so sure that still doesn't have *you* written all over it. And look, he's already favorited you! And his screen name is TexasBallPlayer. How perfect is that?"

"Lemme see his picture."

Sera scrolled over to reveal a sixty-something man with graying sandy hair.

The open, laughing expression on Abby Ruth's face closed down faster than a government office at five in the afternoon. "No. I'm not interested."

"Interest has nothing to do with it," Maggie said. "You were the one who said we needed to cast a wider net. I went on a date. You have to do your part too."

"I need to get to the ball field." Abby Ruth turned on her heel and walked out.

"Well, that was abrupt, even for Abby Ruth," Maggie said. "After all her jawing about wanting the handsome men and she walks away from him? That woman makes me crazy sometimes."

Sera scanned the rest of Abby Ruth's matches. "Do any of these pictures look familiar to you?"

"Teague's the only one I know."

"Hmm...I wonder..." Sera typed something, and a moment later the screen filled with dozens of handsome faces.

"Oh. My. Gosh." Maggie could barely breathe for all the good looks crowding the page. "Are those all on ThePerfectFit.com?"

"No. I just Googled *male models.*"

"How do you do all that?" Maggie needed to hone her computer skills to keep up with not only her grandkids but her friends too. She had a Facebook account, but that was only because her daughter had set it up so she could see pictures of the kids Pam posted.

"It's practice, just like you with those power tools." Sera pointed to one on the fourth row. "But, oh my goodness, look at this."

"What?"

She clicked again, bringing up Abby Ruth's match results, and pointed to the leftmost picture.

"Okay."

And back to the Google images. Sera

pulled her bare foot into the chair seat, waving at the screen full of images. "Several of these guys showed up on Abby Ruth's matches."

"Why?"

Sera slowly leaned away from Maggie, met her gaze head-on. "Because we're on to something. Some of these profiles. These pictures. They aren't real guys."

"Don't be silly." Maggie laughed. "Why would someone do that? I know my guy is real. DanOfYourDreams most definitely showed up for our date."

"We don't know if his real name is Dan, do we?"

"I didn't ask for identification, but why would he lie? I told him my real name."

"Let's see if we can Google up his picture."

Maggie felt a trickle of concern climb her spine. She didn't want Dan to show up on Sera's Google search screen. She so wanted him to be real. She needed him to be real. But before she could protest, Sera had already typed in a search for *handsome handymen*.

And the first picture on the first row was a guy who strongly resembled her DanOfYourDreams. The shot was from a distance, but it was clear Dan's profile picture had been cropped from it.

Sera studied it. "He's very attractive. Was he this good-looking in person?"

Maggie bit her lower lip. "You know, we were beekeeping. All that netting and the big hat and all. I'll admit I wondered if he may have fudged his picture a little, but honestly, I couldn't see his face." Why hadn't that bothered her more? Probably because she'd imagined him looking exactly like his profile picture. Which was ridiculous considering her photo was a bit of a misrepresentation.

Plus, he'd been so sweet. So thoughtful. So romantic. "Maybe there's an explanation."

"This picture is from a stock art site." Sera must have sensed her disappointment—heck, almost felt like a darn heartbreak—because she started rambling. "But maybe he models too."

"Doubtful." Maggie's heart stalled, and her mouth went dry. "We've been duped."

"No, honey." Sera reached out and wrapped an arm around Maggie's shoulders. "Martha's niece was duped. We're investigating."

I wasn't just investigating. I was invested.

Chapter Sixteen

The next morning, the sound of a backup alarm sent Maggie running outside with Sera right behind her. A bright yellow rollback truck was backing up the driveway, carrying three hot pink portable potties and a pink leopard print wash station.

"How fun," Sera yelled. She leapt from the porch and ran out to greet the truck driver.

Fun wasn't exactly how Maggie would describe this situation, but at least Abby Ruth's birthday party would be the perfect cover to give them *facilities* until the septic system was back in working order. That woman had griped up a storm when she'd had to do a squat-and-tinkle out behind the carriage house last night.

As for this birthday party, Maggie needed to start thinking a little faster on her feet when she was making up stuff, because whipping up a good party in two days was hard work. And now they were down to hours until people started showing up.

While the Mrs. Potts Pots driver set up the equipment, Maggie finalized the list of tasks and tore the sheet of paper into three parts.

Abby Ruth stepped out on the porch with a *clomp-clomp* of her boots and pointed toward the pink potties. "I'm still not using those things. I don't care if they're brand new."

"Suit yourself," Maggie said, handing her one of the lists. "But you get to drinking and I know you're not going to hop in your truck and drive clear across town just to use a real one."

"Says who?" Abby Ruth glanced at the list and crumpled it against her hip.

She was in a mood this morning. "What's wrong with you?" Maggie asked.

Abby Ruth stepped down on the second porch stair and plopped her blue-jeaned bottom on the top one. "I hoped Jenny and Grayson would come for the party. That's all."

"Of course they'll come. Sera talked to Jenny. Who can say no to Serendipity Johnson? No one. That's who."

Abby Ruth looked at her short nails and buffed them on her thigh. "My girl is so busy. And hard-headed."

"Wonder where she gets that?" Maggie smiled, but it hadn't really been a joke. "What's the matter?"

Abby Ruth shrugged. "I just wish she'd come. I haven't seen her in too long. Besides, it's time for her to get back in the man saddle, and I don't want her making a mistake like she did last time. She needs to give Teague another chance. Oh, Maggie, if you'd seen those two back in the day..."

Maggie sat down beside her. "You're getting all maternal on me." She'd never really seen this side of Abby Ruth, making her sorry she was always generalizing when it came to her friend.

"You would be all maternal too. Those two were perfect together. If I could get her here for my birthday party, maybe...just maybe...they might get a little ember sparkin' again."

Maggie knew what it was like to want your daughter to find a really good relationship. She'd had those worries before. "You know how Sera is always telling us not to let any negativity into our universe?"

Abby Ruth nodded.

"Well, let's just keep on working on these

tasks and plan on Jenny showing up. I bet the universe won't let us down."

"Maybe you're right." Still, Abby Ruth's shoulders remained slumped.

Maggie was reading through her task list when Sera walked up and Abby Ruth said, "Just in time. We're checking our list. Again."

Grinning like a barn cat after an all-you-can-eat mouse buffet, Sera draped herself over Maggie's shoulder. "That's great. I love lists."

"I don't know what you're on, but I need a tablespoon of it," Abby Ruth said.

Sera's response *was* a wee bit too happy. Abby Ruth was right about that because Sera wasn't a list-lover by a long shot. "What's going on? You're extra happy today."

"I got a date." The bells rang on Sera's ankle as she skipped around the porch. "I'll have to leave your party just a little early, Abby Ruth, but I can still help with all the before stuff."

"A date? It's my birthday," Abby Ruth huffed. "You'd think I'd get a damned date."

"Oh, don't be like that." Sera took her list from Maggie and waved it in front of Abby Ruth. "Come on. You can drive me to town to pick up supplies for the party."

Abby Ruth grabbed her keys from inside,

then she and Sera were off.

Maggie was climbing the stairs to get holiday lights out of the attic when a knock came at the door. Down she climbed again.

Deputy Barnes stood on the porch holding a bouquet of Dallas Cowboy themed balloons. "Sheriff asked me to drop these off for the party."

"Did you get those from the flower shop in town?"

"Sheriff did. Had me pick them up for him. I didn't know they even had balloons." There had to be two dozen blue and silver balloons and three mylars shaped like football helmets.

"Me either." There were so many helium balloons that it looked like enough to pull a lesser man right off the ground. Maggie laughed at the sight of the poor deputy holding them. "Nice of him. Why don't you come in?"

She took the balloons, not sure where they'd use them, but for now she just needed to be sure they didn't fly off. She struggled with the bouncing batch, trying to tie them to the newel post.

"Let me get that for you." Deputy Barnes swept the bright pink curling ribbons into one hand and then whipped them around in a flurry that produced a lovely knot.

"How pretty."

"It's called a stevedore knot. I was a Boy Scout. Eagle Scout actually," he said with a note of pride. "I can tie just about any kind of knot. Believe me, those balloons won't go anywhere until you want them to."

"Got it. Thanks." Maggie inspected the knot—four twists and a pull-through. She tugged on it. Barnes was right. That thing was strong and a handy skill to have in her back pocket. "I was just heading to the attic to get down some Christmas lights to use for tonight."

"I'll help."

She hadn't been hinting for help, but another pair of hands couldn't hurt. "Thank you. If you can untie a knot as good as you can tie one, you might come in handy with those strings of lights."

By the time Abby Ruth and Sera returned from their errands, Maggie and Deputy Barnes had the back yard strung with party lights, and the balloons flew above several chairs. Finally, something was going Maggie's way.

When Summer Haven's doorbell rang at five o'clock, Abby Ruth prayed she wouldn't open it to another box of cheap steaks.

When she answered the door, a cry of joy

broke from her lips, and she did a little cotton-eyed Joe right in the foyer. Jenny stood on the front porch holding Grayson's hand.

"You came!" She threw her arms around her daughter in a hug that could wrestle a gator to the ground. Grayson looked as if he might turn tail and run. She must've scared the bejeebies out of him. "Sorry there, sport. I'm just happy to see you two." And all it had taken was Maggie lying to Teague. If Abby Ruth had known it was that easy, she would've thrown her own damned birthday party long ago.

"Hi, Mom." As usual, Jenny was pulled together in some thick-looking slacks and high-heeled boots. Her hair was as dark as Abby Ruth's had been at her age. But Jenny kept hers long while Abby Ruth had always chopped hers short. When Jenny was little, her hair had usually been as knotted as a wild squirrel's nest. They'd had their share of battles—Abby Ruth screaming and Jenny crying—over that hair.

But as an adult, Jenny kept it ironed straight and sleek.

Damned pity that reckless little girl was gone.

Her daughter had taken after both her parents and was just a few inches shy of six feet. But even to a less-than-maternal mother like her, the girl looked too damned skinny. She'd need to take her to the Atlanta Highway Diner for a big mess of biscuits and gravy.

"What do you think of Georgia?" Abby Ruth bent down to catch her grandson's eye. He had the same dark hair and slim build shared by the Cady side of the family. But his eyes, they were his daddy's distinctively eerie green. Hopefully, that was all Grayson had inherited from that country-club weenie.

All those years ago when Jenny had called to say she was marrying a Boston native, Abby Ruth had come damned close to being overwhelmed by a case of the old-fashioned vapors. Because she'd known Jenny belonged with Teague.

Now, ten years later, her daughter could finally get back on the path she should've followed a decade ago.

"It's hotter than Boston," Grayson informed Abby Ruth.

After living in Houston for years, the fall temperatures in Georgia felt downright nippy to her at times. "It cools off at night."

"Do you have an Xbox?"

"Anything like a batter's box?" The look on the kid's face told her all she needed to know. "Summer Haven sits on over fifty acres, Gray. You don't need video games while you're here. Wouldn't even have time for them. There's a creek out back, a cool old car in the garage, and lots of trouble to get into."

His head angled to one side, and he considered her with those hundred-year-old eyes. "What do you do with a creek?"

"Well, you can fish or just muck around in it." Abby Ruth shot a look at her daughter. Sure, Jenny'd grown up in the city, but their neighborhood in Houston had been an older one with acre lots that backed up to some woods. The kids around there had ridden their bikes all over the place, explored the outdoors and generally run wild.

"Don't fish stink?" he asked.

"When you clean them," she said, grabbing one of the suitcases and ushering them inside. "But when you fry 'em up in a mess of cornmeal, they smell like heaven."

Grayson looked skeptical, but his eyes widened when he took in the gleaming wooden floors and antiques around him. "This might be bigger than Dad's new house." He ran a hand over the stair rail. "I mean, it's a lot older and everything, but this is kinda cool."

"High praise," Jenny said in a low voice.

There was more to the Daniel Northcutt story, and Abby Ruth would get it soon enough.

Maggie rushed into the foyer. "Hi, Jenny. Y'all made it! It's so good to meet you. I've got you all set up in the Azalea Room."

Abby Ruth put her hands on her hips. "You knew she was coming, and you didn't tell me."

"Oops. Did I keep a secret from you?" Maggie just grinned. "Grayson, you'll be staying in the Cherokee Rose Room."

"Cherokee? Like the Indians?" Grayson's eyes lit up.

"Just like that." Abby Ruth rustled his hair. Poor kid had no idea he would be surrounded by flowers. She pointed down the hallway. "Grayson, there are peanut butter cookies in the kitchen if you want to go on back."

Jenny gaped at her. "You baked cookies?"

"Those Boston winters are getting to you, girl." Abby Ruth elbowed her. "Sera made them. I had to beg her to use good old American peanut butter rather than cannabutter."

"Well, that's a relief," Jenny said, her tone as dry as a triple olive martini. "I'm trying to keep Grayson off marijuana until he's at least twelve."

"C'mon upstairs," she said to Jenny.

Jenny looked uncertain. "Mom, we could always go to a hotel. I don't want to be any trouble. I mean, this isn't even really your house."

That was like a double-tipped arrow to Abby Ruth's chest. Was it too much for her daughter to want to stay under the same roof with her? Because even if she didn't own Summer Haven, it had quickly become her home.

And wasn't that a kick in the ass? She'd left Texas, sold almost everything she had so she could travel. And yet here she was, settling down in a Georgia town the size of Angelina Broussard's skinny butt.

"Summer Haven has plenty of room for everyone." Maybe this wasn't the best time to mention they didn't exactly have bathroom facilities for everyone, though. Rather than risk Jenny making a break for it, Abby Ruth grabbed both bags and muscled them up the stairs. "Besides, you'd hurt Maggie's feelings something awful if you didn't stay."

"Mom, give me one of those damned things."

"I might be retired, but I'm sure as hell not an invalid."

"You're right." Jenny sighed. "You could

single-handedly carry the weight of the world on your back."

Abby Ruth made it to the landing and let the bags thump to the wooden floor. Jenny was right on her heels, like a spotter for a gymnast. "If you didn't want to come down here for my birthday, no one forced you."

Jenny slumped against the landing's floral wallpaper. "It's not that. I'm just a little out of sorts. All of Grayson's chatter about Daniel's new house and new wife. It's making me crazy."

"You're not sorry you divorced that schmuck, are you?"

"God, no." Jenny knocked the back of her head against the wall. "Sometimes it just sucks being a single parent. I make a good living, but rather than the Back Bay house where Grayson grew up, I now have him stuffed into a two-bedroom apartment. He has to stay in after-school care because I rarely leave the office before six o'clock. But when he goes to Daniel's house, he gets to swim in their new Olympic-sized pool. And the *good wife* doesn't work so there's no rushing here and there."

Abby Ruth's heart lurched. "You were a good wife, Jenny. A great wife."

"I know. I did as well as I could. She's just so...so perfect. And they buy him stuff. Too much stuff."

"Like the Xbox?"

"I told Daniel not to do it. But if he didn't listen to me when we were married, he sure doesn't listen to me now."

Abby Ruth, always awkward when it came to soothing hugs, wrapped her arms around her daughter. But she understood what Jenny was going through and tried to provide comfort. "Sometimes, being a single parent does suck."

"That's for sure." Jenny laughed, but it sounded too watery for Abby Ruth's liking. But when her daughter drew back, her eyes were dry. "Why did you do it, Mom?"

Abby Ruth knew her daughter's question wasn't as simple as it sounded. She was asking so many things. Why Abby Ruth had chosen to be an unmarried mother at a time when it hadn't been as acceptable as it was today. Why she'd been a career woman instead of a cookie-baking mom. Why she'd never told Jenny who her daddy was. "Because I wanted you. And because I loved you. Still love you more than I love another soul on this earth."

Jenny glanced away as though embarrassed by the conviction in Abby Ruth's voice. Is this what she'd created over the years—a daughter who didn't know how her own mom felt about her and when hit with the truth of those feelings, shied away from it?

Shame swarmed over Abby Ruth. This was her fault. Her doing.

To regain her equilibrium, Abby Ruth wheeled Grayson's bag into the room where he would stay for the next few days. None of the bedrooms at Summer Haven were particularly masculine, but Maggie had put Grayson in the one with dark, heavy furniture and a vivid green motif—as green as the leaves of the Cherokee rose, fitting since it was the Georgia state flower. Grayson would no doubt be disappointed when he realized there wasn't a single tomahawk or arrowhead in the space, though.

When Abby Ruth returned to the landing, Jenny had herself under control. She hustled into the Azalea Room. "Is this where I'm bunking?"

"For as long as you want."

"We're only here for the weekend, Mom."

This time. Abby Ruth could only hope. She sat on the edge of the bed. "Have you ever thought about leaving Boston? Wouldn't be such a bad thing to put some miles between you and the good wife."

"It's where my job is." Jenny placed her

bag on the luggage stand, but she made no move to unpack. "Even if Daniel would agree to let me move Grayson, Boston's the only home Grayson has ever known. Isn't it bad enough I've made him a child of divorce? It wouldn't be fair to uproot him from his friends too."

Abby Ruth noticed Jenny didn't claim her own life was there. "He's young and adaptable. And that kid has the ability to bloom where he's planted."

"I can't take him away from Daniel. A boy needs his dad."

Abby Ruth knew a man who would make Grayson a much better daddy, but she kept her mouth closed on that one. "He could see him on school holidays. If Daniel's still the man I knew, there's no way he's taking Grayson on every one of his visitation weekends."

Jenny sighed. "He picks him up every time, but it wasn't long after he remarried that Grayson started coming home talking about spending a good part of the weekend at Rogers Stadium."

"Wait a minute," Abby Ruth said. "That's where that new minor league baseball team plays."

"Exactly. The Miracles. Apparently, the good wife's dad *is* Rogers. He owns the team and the field."

"Son of a bitch." How in the world could Jenny—or Abby Ruth, for that matter— compete with owning a baseball team?

"They're actually nice people." Jenny rubbed her forehead as though fighting her own thoughts. "They don't have other grandkids, so they dote on Grayson."

"Far be it for me to point out that Grayson is *not* their grandson." This was ridiculous. Abby Ruth had to beg, borrow and steal to get Jenny to bring Grayson to visit. Damned if she wanted to play second fiddle to Daniel Northcutt's in-laws for Grayson's affection.

The boy needed to be introduced to the benefits of small-town living. Between Teague and her, they should be able to win Grayson over to the Mimi Abby Ruth team. "Teague will be at my birthday party tonight."

"Mom, don't start."

"Start what?" She projected all the innocence she could.

"That ship not only sailed a long time ago," Jenny said. "It sank to the bottom of the ocean."

"He's still looking good. Actually, if you ask me, he's better looking than ever."

Jenny groaned and dropped to sit on the

edge of the bed. "That's what I was afraid of."

"Don't you think it's time to get past his old mistakes?"

When Jenny's head came up, her dark eyes were blazing. "I loved him."

"Of course you did."

"And he hauled off and married another woman."

"Have you ever asked him to explain?"

"I shouldn't have to ask him to explain." She made a chopping gesture with her hand. If Teague had been standing in front of her, he'd now be split from the sternum down. "If he wanted my forgiveness, he should've crawled on his hands and knees. By the time he got to my door, his skin should've been raw and bleeding."

Abby Ruth tried to suppress her smile, but she loved it when Jenny's Cady side came out. "You're absolutely right."

"But has he ever come crawling? No, he hasn't. And if he thinks I'm going to make the first move, he's out of his ever-loving mind." Her hands were in tight balls. So tight that they'd taken on a white hue.

Abby Ruth leaned against the door jamb to keep from doing a celebratory electric slide. Regardless of Jenny's protests, she still had feelings—strong feelings—for Teague.

"Has it escaped your memory that you married someone else too?"

The look of hurt and betrayal on Jenny's face killed Abby Ruth's desire to line dance. "Only after he did."

"What are you saying?" Abby Ruth studied Jenny closely. "Did you marry Daniel to get back at Teague?"

"Of course not. I just...there was no reason for me to mope around. Teague was taken, and it was time to move on with my life. Besides, I wouldn't trade Grayson. He's everything to me. And no matter what a pain in my ass Daniel has been, I wouldn't have Grayson without him."

"Times have changed. You and Teague are both single now."

Jenny flopped back on the bed, arms and legs wide, like she used to when she was a moody teenager. "What does it matter? I live in Boston. And he lives here."

"That's just geography." Abby Ruth had a feeling Jenny wasn't as worried about the physical distance as much as the emotional one.

"About eleven hundred miles of geography in between," Jenny said, her tone flat. "Besides, I've never lived in a small town in my life. What do people even do here besides run around chasing small-time bad guys?"

"It's not as godawful boring as you think." Small-town living had some redeeming qualities. Otherwise, why would she still be here? "Did I mention that Maggie, Sera and I registered for an online dating site?"

That brought Jenny back to a ramrod sitting position. "You did what?"

"Yep. And Maggie's already had one very nice date." Didn't bear mentioning that the date was weird as all get-out and that Abby Ruth had already been kicked out of the game once. But she was back in the saddle now, by God.

"Is this a...senior dating site?"

"No. Maggie's pretty sure her beau is younger."

"Pretty sure? If she had a date with him, shouldn't she know?"

Damn, that was a stupid slip. "Well, you know how it is with men. If they take care of themselves, it's hard to tell. The bastards. But no...this isn't called OvertheHillDates.com. It's ThePerfectFit.com. In fact, Teague is registered on it too."

Jenny's mouth tightened. "What? Why would he do that? He doesn't need some online dating site to get a woman."

"Mmm-hmm. I ran across this profile

called LetsPlayBall, and there was his picture, big as Dallas. So, young lady, if you think the hunky Teague Castro is down here in Georgia burning a candle for you, you'd better think again."

"I don't. That would be silly. We haven't seen each other in years, and I barely think of him."

"I may have raised you to be a lot of not-so-nice things, Jensen Cady, but I did not raise you to be a liar." Abby Ruth shook a finger at her daughter. "So you may have been lying to yourself for a long time now, but that won't cut it with me. Here's God's own truth...if you want a second chance with Teague, you'd best get your fanny in gear."

Chapter Seventeen

By the time Teague made it to Summer Haven for Abby Ruth's birthday party, the circle drive was already crammed with cars. Truth be told, he'd been dressed thirty minutes early. But he'd been so nervous, he'd spilled half a pale ale on his pants. He couldn't see Jenny for the first time in ten years smelling like the inside of a beer can, so he'd pawed through his closet like a teenage girl. Most of the clothes he owned were now sprawled across his bed and his floor.

Good thing he had no intention of trying to lure Jenny back to his place. Not that he wouldn't love to, but tonight was a recon mission. He needed to feel her out, find out where they were with one another. Plus, her son was with her. Grayson created an entirely new layer of complication in rekindling his relationship with Jenny, but

238 Kelsey Browning and Nancy Naigle

one Teague was willing and ready to focus on.

Standing at the front door with three packages in his arms, he looked as though he was playing Santa Claus when Maggie walked up and intercepted him just as he was about to knock on the front door.

"Teague," she said, "there you are. Abby Ruth's been foaming at the mouth wondering where you were."

"With all these people here, I'm surprised she even missed me."

"Abby Ruth doesn't miss a trick." Maggie reached for his load. "Want me to put these on the gift table?"

He passed her the box wrapped in bandana print paper. "This one is for the birthday girl, but the others..."

Maggie eyed the bouquet of sunflowers and the bag with a supersized Nerf gun sticking out the top. "Are for Jenny and Grayson," she said with a soft smile.

Heat crawled up Teague's throat. "You think they're okay?"

With a pat to his cheek, Maggie said, "I think you're the sweetest thing around."

Was that supposed to make him feel better or just more of a bumbling idiot?

"By the way—" Maggie pointed toward a cluster of people gathered around a smoking chiminea, "—she's right over there." Then she squeezed his hand. "But who you really want is in the kitchen. Jenny is finishing up a special birthday cake for her momma. I swear she's used all the powdered sugar in Bartell County."

He knew that cake. Chocolate moon cake. His stomach let out an undignified yowl, causing Maggie to look down at his midsection.

She said, "And Abby Ruth will still be holding court outside when you get ready to see her."

"Can you give me a few minutes before you tell her I'm here?"

"You bet." Maggie wandered away with his gift for Abby Ruth.

Teague stepped inside the house and shrugged off his light jacket, but he wasn't quite ready to face his past yet so he closed his eyes and counted to ten.

"Do you have narcolepsy?" The question, asked in a young voice, yanked Teague out of his contemplative moment. Probably for the best since it was a little too close to Sera's meditation for his comfort. "Because I've heard old people do that sometimes. Just fall asleep for no reason."

Teague opened his eyes to find a dark-haired boy staring up at him. And in that second, he wanted to drop to his knees and grab the kid up in a hug. But that would probably scare the crap out of the boy. Have him screaming to his mom about some weird old guy. But it was damned hard to resist because that sharp chin, messy dark hair and superior attitude was vintage Jensen Cady, circa 1990.

"You're Grayson," Teague said.

The kid stepped back, suspicion clouding his face. "How do you know my name?"

It was easy to forget this kid was growing up differently from the young people in Summer Shoals. "I'm a special friend of your mimi's." And of your momma's.

Grayson's eyes, which were not warm brown like his mother's, opened to circles. "You're dating my mimi?"

Good Jesus. How had he gotten himself here? And what was he supposed to say? *I'm not that old.* All that would get him was a good ass-kicking from Abby Ruth. "No, I actually grew up in the house next door to your mimi and mom's house."

Now, Grayson's face went from horrified to speculative. "You're Mrs. Castro's son, the one who broke both his arms racing dirt bikes."

That memory should've been painful rather than prideful, but Teague was a guy, after all. "Yep, that's me."

"My mom said you were a self-involved daredevil your whole life."

Well, that wasn't much of an endorsement. "She said self-involved?"

Grayson rolled his eyes. "That sound like something an eight-year-old kid would make up?"

Teague was beginning to believe the boy was a forty-eight year old, especially since he was dressed in jeans and a button-up shirt too damn clean for the kid to have been having any fun at all.

"I miss Mrs. Castro," Grayson said on a sigh. "Since Mimi moved away from Houston, I don't get those swirly cookies anymore. And she used to play Go Fish with me."

His mom did love to play cards and bake. The thought of her *orejitas*—so flaky, sweet and buttery—made Teague homesick. "She visits me here sometimes. Maybe I could ask her to bring cookies next time."

"But I live in Boston."

For the time being anyway, but Teague would love to change that. "Maybe we could ask her to mail you some."

"Really? That would be sick."

Sick equaled *good* these days. Coaching Little League kept him up-to-date on the current lingo. "Have you been down to the creek yet?"

"Nuh-uh. Mimi says it's full of stinky fish."

"If you want, I could bring a couple fishing poles tomorrow and we could try to hook some of those stinky fish."

"Okay," Grayson agreed. "My mom shouldn't mind since she knows your mom."

He could only hope. "Hey, I heard from Maggie that your mom was making your mimi's birthday cake."

That got a fist pump from Grayson. "It looks like shi...uh...it looks bad, but it's the best tasting cake ever."

"Hard to go wrong with chocolate, pecans and a whole box of powdered sugar." Suddenly remembering the Nerf gun he was holding, Teague bobbled his armload of bribery. "Hey, I brought you something."

"No way!"

"Yes way." Teague handed over the bag with a rifle stock sticking out of it.

Grayson pulled out the gun and grinned, showcasing a missing incisor. "Sweet! Can I go outside and try it out?"

"As long as you don't shoot anyone."

"What's the fun in that?"

Exactly the question Grayson's mimi would've asked too. "How about as long as you don't shoot anyone in the head?"

"Got it." The kid hauled butt out the front door so fast he tripped over the threshold. Teague heard the rip of fabric and had to grin himself. Jenny probably wouldn't be too happy about whatever piece of clothing her son had just ruined, but it proved Grayson was the kind of kid who could fit right in around Summer Shoals, and that Nerf gun was the perfect starter kit.

"Did I hear Gray..."

Teague whirled around to find Jenny standing in the hallway wiping her hands on a kitchen towel. They both stood there, silently staring at each other.

Her hair was longer than the last time he'd seen her. She'd always been lean like her momma, but she was damned close to being downright skinny. A smudge of powdered sugar sat at the corner of her lips, making him want to lick it off. A few lines radiated from her eyes and mouth, proving that she didn't smile nearly enough.

God, he wanted to change that. He'd love to smudge that perfect layer of lipstick she was wearing too.

"Jenny," he said. Great, someone had put a bullfrog in his throat when he wasn't paying attention.

"Teague."

"At least we remember each other's names."

The quick flare in her gaze said she remembered a lot more than his name. Like those times they'd steamed up the windows of the Jeep he'd driven back then. "You're...you're looking...fit."

"Hard to chase down criminals when you've caught the fat."

Now, she scoped him out from the tips of his brown cowboy boots to his perfectly combed hair. "You sure haven't caught that."

He hooked his thumbs in his front pockets. "Grayson seems like a great kid."

"He is." Her smile was so open and genuine then, and Teague desperately wanted to be the reason for it.

Her eyes danced when she spoke of her son. "Smart, silly, and sometimes sweet."

"Well, you never want a guy to be sweet all the time."

Her expression hardened around the edges. "I'm pretty sure that's impossible. Most of them are more concerned with what they want than what the women in their lives want."

"What did Northcutt do to you, Jenny?"

"I wasn't talking about Daniel."

Her aim was as good as her momma's. The two women just used different weapons.

Not knowing how to bridge this long gap between them, Teague shoved the flowers at her instead. "These are for you."

It became immediately clear that the one thing he thought he'd done right, he'd done so incredibly wrong. Jenny's face went pale and slack as she stared at the sunflowers. Yes, she'd loved them when they were teenagers, but this was damned close to the same bouquet he'd given her their last date before he'd screwed up both their lives by marrying another woman.

He tried to pull them back, but Jenny was fast and snagged the paper-wrapped bundle from his hand. "Thanks for thinking of me, but I need to get back to Mom's cake." When she turned toward the kitchen, she let the flowers drop so their petals brushed the hardwood.

Teague was paralyzed. None of this had gone down the way he'd imagined it. He'd had this hope they would take one look at each other and the years they'd been apart would just crumble away, leaving them with a chance to start fresh. Yes, he'd known Jenny wasn't an easy woman. That she would expect an explanation and some major groveling. He'd just been trying to warm her up for the main event.

And if he didn't get his butt in gear, there

wouldn't be any event, main or otherwise. He lunged forward and caught her elbow. "Jenny, there's not a day in the year that I don't think of you."

Now, it was her turn to go still. But she kept her rigid back to him. "It's my mother's birthday. This really isn't the time to go into all this."

"When then?" Yeah, he knew it was out of line, but if he didn't push now, she'd see him as weak. And if there was one thing the Cady women couldn't stand, it was a weak man.

"I'm not sure there will ever be a time."

"That's bullshit." His words bulleted out. Too harsh, but he couldn't pull them back now.

When she turned, it was a slow and deliberate movement. "You don't get to decide what's bullshit and what's not. You lost that privilege about the time you married another woman."

"I want to explain everything to you now."

"You're assuming I want to hear your explanation."

Words weren't working, and he had to make her understand. So he pulled her in and kissed her. And God, didn't the combination of sweet powdered sugar and her even sweeter lips taste good? As kisses went, it was tamer than many they'd shared as teenagers, but it hit him like a billy club to the head, making him dizzy and disoriented.

How had he ever thought he could find someone on a dating site? Jenny Cady was his perfect fit. Always had been. Always would be.

Suddenly, she pulled back. Stood there panting with a hand to her mouth. "What was that?"

"Jenny, please."

"Please? Now you're the one begging, huh?" She laughed, but the sound was shrill and broken. "Because that's the same word I used when you called me with the news about your upcoming wedding."

"I didn't love her."

If he'd thought she was standoffish before, she now had a fifty-foot wall around her. "That's supposed to make me want to listen to you? Honestly, it makes me want to get Momma's AR-15 and pin your ass to a tree for a little target practice."

She jerked out of his hold, and Teague's heart felt as though she was dragging it along behind her.

"I didn't love her," he said to her retreating back, "because I've always been in love with you."

Chapter Eighteen

Lil had been standing in the phone line so long that her foot had fallen asleep, but she had to talk to Maggie. Martha was still in a mood after her niece's visit, and if Lil could just get a teensy update on how things were going on the search for OnceUponATom, it might calm Martha down. At least for a little while.

No one at Summer Haven answered, so Lil went to the library to look for some questions she could use in the mock interview sessions. She came across something called behavioral interviewing that looked promising. If she could impress the warden and the BOP representatives with tough questions and excellent inmate responses, she would be that much closer to her own goal.

Now, she was back in the cottage, doing

what she always did when she needed to think clearly...she cleaned. After thoroughly scrubbing her side of the room with a sponge and powdered cleanser, she unpacked her box of belongings and neatly tucked them away in the metal dresser. Bunking with Martha was a step up in housing, comforts and all, but she'd give anything to be back in her tiny space with Dixie. At least there, she'd been able to speak her mind without walking on eggshells.

Lil understood that Martha was worried about her niece, but goodness, that woman had mood swings that were higher than Tarzan's through the jungle. If the girls didn't come up with some solid information for Martha soon, there was no telling what she would do or say next.

A voice broke through Lil's ruminations. "Are you listening to me?"

She spun around to find Martha standing behind her. Clearly she hadn't been listening. By the scowl on Martha's face, she'd been standing there for a while.

"Sorry," Lil said. "I was daydreaming."

Martha's hands were on her hips, which always made her look bigger and more threatening. "Did you take my new nail polish?"

"No. Of course not. You know we don't wear the same colors." Lil wouldn't be caught dead in turquoise, yellow or bright orange nail polish. Those tones didn't go with her skin color, and a soft pink could take a gal anywhere.

"Well, it's missing and I doubt it grew legs and walked off by itself."

Lillian was growing tired of always having to put on the tough act with Martha. What she'd give for just one day in Summer Haven all by herself—for the peace and quiet. "Maybe one of your girls borrowed it. Goodness knows they parade through here day and night."

"Are you accusing my girls of dissing me?"

Lord, Lil couldn't win for losing. "I'm simply saying I don't know where your polish is."

A knock came at the door, and Martha yanked it open, admitting one of her girls. "You know better than to dis me, right, Bootsie?"

The girl looked up, her eyes the size of teacup saucers. "Don't nobody want on your bad side, Big Martha."

"If someone takes something without asking, don't you think she should replace it? Maybe run down to the commissary and even pick up something extra to say I'm sorry?"

"If the accused person *didn't* take your belongings," Lil interjected, "then she has no obligation to do a darned thing."

Martha stared her down for a long moment, but Lil didn't back down. She'd never back down.

Time to distract and defuse this situation.

"We need to finish the curriculum for Warden Proctor." Lil grabbed a legal pad from her drawer.

Meanwhile, Martha settled on her bed so Bootsie could give her a pedi. "I wanted turquoise toes," Martha complained.

Lil perched on the edge of a straight-backed chair, plucking at her tight waistband, and forged ahead. "So, I have a list of mock interview questions, but I'd like to fine-tune them." She tapped Martha's girl on the shoulder. "Bootsie, tell me about a time when you overcame a challenge."

"You mean like when I snuck that nose candy past airport security?"

Oh, Lord. Lil was in trouble. She shot a panicked look at Martha and handed her the clipboard. "The warden already selected the class, and somehow it ended up full of your girls."

"Imagine that." Martha scanned the list

and smiled. All sprawled out on her bed propped on the pillows, she looked like a beige version of Cleopatra.

"You have to help me prepare them. They have to be able to answer interview questions without mentioning their past...extracurricular activities."

"I'll see what I can do." Martha tapped her chin and stared at the ceiling. "But I've been thinking about something. Maybe we could *accidentally* dye all the uniforms in the Laundromat. I've got Bootsie and Phipps working in there. They could do that easily, then we could color up this place. Ditch all this gray-green-tan."

And tank Lillian's chances of impressing the BOP folks in a few days? No, thank you. Still, she said as sweetly as possible, "Although I think that sounds like a wonderful idea, I'm not sure we can get away with claiming it was an accident. The handbook is clear on penalties for intentionally misusing the machines, and any sort of dye is in direct violation."

Martha's lips pursed. "First, you take my polish, and now you shoot down a good idea. Miss H&M, you're not being much of a team player."

"Don't you think I'm thinking of the *team* by keeping us from getting shipped all over the nation? How would your niece feel about visiting you up in New Jersey?"

"No need to get your back up. I'm doing my part. I got the okay to thin out the plants on the back side of the camp so we can use them in the courtyard. My girls are working on that now."

Thank goodness. "I need to update the warden. Would you like to come with me?"

Martha pointed her toes, admiring the purple color the girl was painting them. "I wasn't invited."

"I just invited you."

"Yeah, yeah. Lots of crap ain't fair in this world. I know this ain't your fault." She waved off the girl who was hunched over her feet. "Lil, about that leg-breaker thing..."

Lil remained quiet. She wouldn't make this easy for Martha.

"You know I didn't mean that, right?"

She knew no such thing. "I know you're worried about your niece."

"I don't like feeling helpless. Makes me feel stupid and pissed."

Oh, Lil knew that feeling all too well. Because she had no control over anything happening with this tit-for-tat trade she and Martha were engaged in.

"I want you to keep your grannies on the job." Martha's jaw jutted out.

Lillian gave a silent prayer that Martha wasn't giving up yet.

"At least until I can talk my niece out of this whole online dating thing."

Please, please, please, God, let Martha's niece get suckered in for a while longer by this fairy tale paintball shooting man, but don't let anything bad happen to her. Amen.

Abby Ruth was standing in the gazebo watching Maggie set up paper plates and cups when Jenny marched across the lawn and slammed the cake down on the table. Now, the chocolate icing craters had craters.

"What's wrong?" She tugged Jenny aside and whispered, "Did you forget to put the sugar in my birthday cake?"

"That man," Jenny fumed. "He thinks he can just waltz in and have me swoon into his arms like some kind of silent movie heroine. Do you think he's been smoking some of the contraband the sheriff's department confiscates?"

"Excuse me." Maggie held the stack of plates up to her chest. "Are you talking about our Teague?"

Jenny lowered her eyes.

"I take it you two had a little chat," Abby Ruth said. Damn that Teague, what had he done?

"No, Mom. A chat is nice. You say polite things to each other, make small talk, and shake hands. Shoving a bouquet of sunflowers at you, kissing you blind and mouth-pooping a profession of love is not a chat."

Abby Ruth stumbled back and braced herself against the gazebo rail. The boy had moved even faster than she'd imagined. What the hell was he thinking? He had to know that Jenny was gun-shy.

"I'm sure he meant well." But it was clear she shouldn't have left Teague in charge of his first chance to see Jenny in years. Men should be required to enroll in some kind of relationship training before ever asking a woman for a date. Idiots.

Obviously, those bozos on ThePerfectFit.com needed the kind of training that would knock them upside the head with some damned sense because they were clueless about matching a woman with the right man too.

"Oh my," Maggie said. "That was awfully sudden. I mean he just got here. You just got here."

"Sudden?" Jenny wheeled on her. "That jackass was ten years too late."

Abby Ruth grabbed her daughter and pulled her away from Maggie. "Sugar, this isn't Maggie's fault. There's no reason for you to go on the attack."

Jenny swiped a hand—a trembling one—across her face. "I'm so sorry, Maggie."

"It's fine." Maggie busied herself with the plastic flatware. "Men can make us all crazy. And I know it's not my place to say so, but Teague is a good one."

Abby Ruth knew Maggie was thinking of that idiot Dan. A man who couldn't be bothered to use his own picture on his dating profile.

But Abby Ruth was ecstatic to see Jenny so off balance. She wasn't only not immune to Teague Castro, but she was likely so infected with the love bug that she'd succumb to it sooner or later. "Everyone's gathering for cake. Would you cut the cake, Jenny?"

"I don't mind—" Maggie started, but Abby Ruth threw her a glare. Cutting the cake would keep Jenny in one spot, which meant she couldn't get away from Teague, and that was the plan. Maggie quickly recovered by switching up her response, "—pouring cups of my special tea while Jenny takes care of the cake."

People, including Teague and Deputy Barnes, began to crowd into the gazebo. Sera skipped up the steps and said, "Anything I can help with here?"

"Actually," Jenny shoved the cake slicer in Sera's direction, "we need someone to serve cake."

Dammit. Her daughter was a wily one.

Sera fluttered her hands. "I'm not sure I have time for that. I'm supposed to meet my date in fifteen minutes."

It still chapped Abby Ruth's hide that both Maggie and Sera had gotten dates while she'd been kicked out of the whole system and had to sneak back in.

Teague stepped closer to the table, and Deputy Barnes followed. "Sera," Teague said, "I didn't realize you were seeing anyone. Someone local?"

"I'm not exactly sure," she told him.

Teague straightened at that. The boy had a suspicious streak a mile and a half wide. "He won't tell you where he lives?"

"It's not like that. This is just the first date, and the profiles don't—"

Maggie started waving as if she was swatting at a swarm of attacking mosquitoes.

"Maggie, are you having a hot flash?" Sera grabbed a paper plate and fanned Maggie.

"So," Abby Ruth put lots of cheer into her voice. "How 'bout them 'stros?"

The look Teague shot her was part you-can-do-better-than-that and part you-damn-well-know-the-Astros-aren't-in-the-World-Series. "What's all this about a profile?"

"Well, when you register with an online dating service, you have to fill out all these questions," Sera told him. "You know, and that's what the men look at to decide if they're interested."

A cup to his mouth, Deputy Barnes launched into a coughing fit. Teague whacked the poor guy on the back, but that only caused the deputy to tip his tea glass and dump liquid onto the table.

Jenny was as quick as ever, snatching the cake up in time to keep it from getting doused by the spillage or the liquid dribbling from the deputy's nose.

"Are you okay?" Maggie asked Barnes.

"Is..." Deputy Barnes wheezed. "Is this some kind of...hookup site for...liberals?"

"Not that I know of," Sera said, patting Barnes on the back. "Are you sure you're okay?"

"He'll live," Teague barked. "He's a cop, for God's sake. I want to know about the dating site. It wouldn't be ThePerfectFit.com, would it?"

"How do you know about that site?" Barnes asked. "I thought you'd already found your dream woman."

Teague shot a longing glance at Jenny, but she was staring down at the table, clenching that cake server like the killer in a horror movie. Oh yeah, she might still be mad at Teague, but she didn't want any other woman to get him, that was for sure. "Just doing a little research for work," he mumbled. His cell phone rang, and he fumbled in his belt to answer it. "Castro."

Abby Ruth could only hear a vague voice from the other end of the line, but Teague said, "Barnes is on call tonight. Why didn't you tag him? You couldn't reach him? He's standing right h—" Teague turned a complete circle, but Deputy Barnes was no longer there.

With a heavy sigh, Teague said, "Give me ten minutes and I'll be there. But keep trying Barnes. He's around somewhere."

Teague clicked off his phone and shook it toward the table, one shake directed at each of the women. "Don't think we're done here. Not by a long shot."

Chapter Nineteen

The next morning, Abby Ruth wandered toward the kitchen to the scent of already-brewed coffee. Smelled almost as good as hers. She passed through the doorway and discovered why.

Hunched over an iPad, Jenny sat at the farm table in the middle of the room nursing a cup liberally laced with cream and—Abby Ruth sniffed the air—Kahlua.

"You're up and at 'em early this morning," she said to her daughter. "Have trouble sleeping?"

Jenny jerked upright and bobbled her tablet. It flew end over end and crashed to the floor. "Dammit, Mom, that's brand new."

"Not my fault you were so involved in what you were doing that you didn't hear me walk in." Abby Ruth stooped down to pick up the tablet, but Jenny scrambled out of her seat and practically tackled her.

"I'll get that." Jenny grabbed for the tablet, but Abby Ruth was an excellent keep-away player, and she dodged her daughter.

She flipped the tablet over to find the screen intact. And what was on the screen made her smile stretch as far as the Rio Grande. Oh, this was better than the time she'd accidentally come across a handful of notes Jenny had written to a girlfriend about Teague. "The Perfect Fit, huh?"

"I'm just looking at it," Jenny huffed. "I have to watch out for your safety in your doddering old age."

"Doddering, my ass." Abby Ruth slid the tablet to the table and turned for the coffecmaker. "Checking out the dating site has nothing to do with your concern for me and everything to do with your jealousy over Teague."

Jenny flopped back down in her chair and held her head between her hands as though she was trying to keep her brain pressed inside. "He makes me crazy."

"All the best men do."

"I should be over him. I thought I was."

"A kiss can change your mind about those things right quick. But you don't have to register for that thing." She waved a hand toward the dating site pulled up on the tablet. "All you have to do is let him know how you feel."

"That's just the problem. I don't know how I feel."

"Hard to figure that out if you aren't willing to spend any time with the guy."

"This site is supposed to automatically match you with your perfect fit, right?"

"Well, it matches you with several potential perfect fits."

"Then if the system matches me with Teague, it's a sign I should at least think about giving him the time of day."

Abby Ruth blew on her coffee and sat down across from Jenny. Neither of them were big huggers or hand holders, but she reached across to squeeze Jenny's hand. "Sugar, that's about like shaking one of those Magic Eight Balls and expecting it to give you a straight answer. You giving Teague another chance is about what you feel in your heart, not about some computer—" what would Sera call it? "—algorithm."

"A computer program is way more objective than I am right now. And that's what I need, something with a clear head." With her fingertips, Jenny rubbed her temples. "Which neither of us have on this subject. You've never made it a secret that you thought my marriage to Daniel was a huge mistake."

"I wasn't trying to knock your choices, Jenny." Abby Ruth leaned back and sighed. "And I may not be much of a romantic myself, but I know true love when I see it. And, hon, that's what you and Teague had."

"Emphasis on the word *had,* Mom."

Abby Ruth waved at the iPad. "Fine. You want unbiased proof? Then waste your hundred bucks. Tell you what, I'll bet you another hundred that Teague is the first profile in your match list."

While Jenny typed away on the small screen, Abby Ruth drank her coffee and watched.

Jenny muttered, "If you could be any cartoon character, who would you be?" She glanced up at Abby Ruth. "Who writes this crap?"

My thought exactly.

Within ten minutes, Jenny was entering her credit card number. She took a deep breath and clicked the register button. "How long does it take?"

"Give the thing a few seconds to think." As soon as the words were out of Abby Ruth's mouth, the screen blinked and displayed several men's profile pictures. And that coffee turned to battery acid in her stomach. Because not only was Teague *not* Jenny's first match, but he wasn't anywhere in those pictures. Damn it all.

Jenny's mouth turned down, but she squared her shoulders and held out her hand. "You owe me a C-note."

Impossible. "I'll have to go get it from upstairs."

"Don't bother," Jenny said. "Because I'm going up right now to pack. It's time for me to take Grayson home to Boston."

Maggie carried a box and a stack of mail as she walked up the driveway toward Summer Haven. A tidy square glossy envelope embossed with a bumble bee wearing a crown, the Llewellyn Farm's logo, was addressed to her. Such a fun afternoon.

At least it had been at the time. Until she'd discovered Dan was a lying skunk.

She plopped into a rocking chair on the front porch, set the box beside her, and slid her finger under the envelope's flap sealed with beeswax.

The shiny honey-golden card held a picture of her with DanOfYourDreams in front of the bee hives. How could he have lied to her? He'd seemed so nice.

Tired of the whole mess, Maggie closed her eyes. It was actually easier to simply miss George and accept she'd be alone the rest of her life. Because that little taste of dating fun had only made her hungrier for more.

When she heard footsteps, Maggie shoved the envelope into her pocket. She didn't want the girls to see how hurt she was by the whole thing.

Sera plodded across the porch with a coffee cup in hand. Her skin didn't look quite as dewy as normal and the fine lines at her eyes were more pronounced. "Morning, glory."

"Your glory is look a little rough this morning," Maggie commented.

"I feel it. Too much wine."

"Gets you in trouble every time." Yeah, she probably shouldn't say anything seeing as she'd overindulged once and looked much worse than Sera the next morning.

"Can't help it. My kryptonite, but I'll sweat it out soon enough." Sera swung her arms around like windmill. "I stayed up too late on top of it all."

"But I thought your date cancelled."

"He did, but I was already so amped up about it that I found it hard to get to sleep. You had so much fun on your date. I guess I got kind of excited to see what might be in store for me."

"It was fun," Maggie admitted, even though she'd since found out Dan was undoubtedly a fraud.

"I checked my profile again this morning." Sera sighed, making Maggie feel a tad guilty about relishing a date with a phony. "Nothing else from him."

"It's been less than a day. He'll reschedule."

"Well, none of this was about dates. It was about finding this guy for Martha so we can get the septic fixed." Sera spotted the brown box next to Maggie's chair, squatted down to read the label. "It's to me."

"Then you should open it," Maggie said. "It'll make you feel better."

Sera picked at the tape and finally found a loose edge, then tugged it away from the cardboard. She peeled back the box flaps and let out a happy squeal.

"What is it?"

"Look, recyclable packing material." She held up a little geode-looking cardboard thing.

Maggie sighed. This woman would be happy with packing peanuts. "What's inside, Sera?"

She pulled some paper off of a rolled mat. "It's the prettiest purple yoga mat I've ever seen. There's more. Yoga Paws!" She slipped the gloves onto her hands and worked her feet into the things that looked like diving flippers except without the flipper part. Then she hopped around, springing into at least a dozen poses in as many seconds. "They're like having a mat that moves everywhere you do."

"Wow," Maggie said, but more about Sera's quick recovery than the weird paws. "What a perfect gift for you."

"I absolutely love them."

"Who sent them?"

Sera dug around in the box until she found a card and shoved it at Maggie. "You read it."

Maggie read it aloud.

> *Dear SunnyOutlook,*
> *Thank you for registering with ThePerfectFit.com. However, it has come to our attention that you do not fit our site's demographic so your profile is being disabled. If you should choose to try online dating again in the future, we would recommend a site better suited to your unique needs.*
>
> *Our best wishes in your search*

for love.
Sincerely,
ThePerfectFit.com

"I got the kiss-off too?"

Maggie shrugged, but a little kernel of pleasure warmed her heart. She was the only who'd gone on a date. And even Dan the Fraud couldn't crush her happiness at not being cast as the undesirable friend.

But it also meant they were down a woman, and they needed to get on the stick and find this guy for Martha. The inspection was barreling down on them.

Abby Ruth wandered out to the porch and flopped into another rocker, looking like she'd lost her last batch of rabbits.

"You drink too much wine last night too?" Sera asked.

"I wish," Abby Ruth grumbled and waved a hand toward the driveway. "Notice anything missing?"

Maggie's gaze swung immediately to the muck pit, but unfortunately, it hadn't disappeared overnight. "Noooo."

"Jenny's rental car."

"She left." Sera said.

"Teague spooked her something good last night." Abby Ruth tossed back whatever was in her glass and hissed like a cat backed into a corner. She was hitting the whiskey early today. "Then she registered on The Perfect Fit. When that damn thing didn't match her up with Teague, she decided they weren't meant to be. Who does that kind of thing?"

"Someone who doesn't trust herself to make her own decisions right now," Sera answered. "Give her a little time. If it's meant to be, they'll work it out."

"But speaking of The Perfect Fit," Maggie said, "we need to step up our investigation." Truth was, time was ticking away too darned fast. The big hole in the yard wasn't as soupy since they'd stopped using the toilets. But the weatherman was predicting rain, and to get Martha's septic guy out here, they needed to solve this mystery.

Abby Ruth brooded for several minutes, then finally said, "What if, instead of setting up female profiles, this time we set up one for a guy? That way, we could get access to some of the other women in the system. Message them to find out if they're getting scammed too."

"Isn't that a little unethical?" Sera asked.

"Do we care?" Abby Ruth asked. "It's not like we plan to dress up like men and take these gals out on the town. We'll tell them what we're doing, full disclosure. Believe me, they'll thank us for protecting the sisterhood from this whack-job."

Only Abby Ruth could say something like that and make her believe it. Maggie nodded. "I can see that working. Maybe we'll find someone who has actually dated OnceUponATom."

"True." Sera dropped to the porch to stretch. As limber as she was, she looked about twelve. "And we can ask them to help us by searching all of their matches for paintball and whatever else we know about OnceUponATom."

"Perfect. Let's register our guy and see what we can find out," Maggie said.

"We're running out of time, girls. You—" Abby Ruth pointed at Maggie, "—need to go out with DansTheMan again."

"It was DanOfYourDreams, and no thank you."

"You have to see him again and figure out what the deal is with these fake pictures."

"He's a liar." Maggie's chair was rocking so hard, she'd about rocked herself into the porch rail. "I don't like people who lie."

"This is *not* about you," Abby Ruth insisted. "It's about us. About Summer Haven. About a pot to piss in."

Literally, thought Maggie.

"Besides. We lied too."

"No." Maggie glared at Abby Ruth. "We

posted younger pictures of ourselves. We didn't grab pictures of strangers off the internet. Heck, I would've never even thought of doing that."

"So," Sera said cheerfully, in an obvious attempt to break the tension. "Who's our guy?"

They all looked at one another.

"I don't think a picture of George will snag anyone." Maggie glanced at the diamond chip-studded band on her finger. How she missed that man. "Even when we were in college he wasn't all that much of a looker. God bless his soul."

"You know what?" Sera raised a finger. "I have a picture we can use. Just a sec." She leapt from the porch to her feet and fluttered inside. In just a moment she was back with the laptop in her hands. "Okay. What should we name him?"

"Something romantic," Maggie said.

"Let's play to the paintball thing," Sera said. "How about RainbowShot?"

"Sounds like a gay pride NRA parade to me," Abby Ruth said. "Uh-uh. Too controversial. How about Shot2TheHeart?"

"Better," Sera said and began typing.

They spent the next thirty minutes brainstorming traits for the perfect man—loves to cook, enjoys the outdoors, plays the guitar. Maggie wished the guy they'd just made up was really a resident of Summer Shoals. She wouldn't mind having another date with a *nice* man.

"Here we go." Sera pressed ENTER.

Maggie was heading inside for more tea, when Sera's huff made her turn around. "What's the matter?"

"You won't believe this. In the "About You" section, the guys only have to fill out three things. Screen name, real name and billing address."

"Well, that's a bunch of bullcrap," Abby Ruth complained. "What about the medical records, birthday and all that? Hell, I figured we'd have to upload a blood sample for our profiles."

"Are you sure there's not another page?" Maggie asked.

Sera ran her finger along the screen leaving a dull smudge as she reviewed all the questions to be sure they'd populated each one with something. "I'm sure. Once I added Shot's minimal info, the system took me to the page that normally asks all those crazy questions, but look at this."

Abby Ruth scooted her chair closer to Sera and scowled. "What in the world? Those aren't crazy questions, and there are only four of them."

Maggie hovered over their shoulders and scanned the screen.

::What's your favorite sports team?

::What's your favorite type of beer?

::Are you looking to get married?

::Do you live with your mother?

"That last question is important," Sera commented.

"Not nearly as important as the first two," Abby Ruth said.

Sera clicked again, and the site took her immediately to the payment screen, and Maggie leaned closer to be sure she was seeing correctly. "Wait a minute. Did you say we were charged a hundred dollars for each profile?"

"Yep."

"And the men are only paying twenty?" she asked. "Something doesn't seem right about that."

"It sure looks like this whole thing favors

the guys."

"I don't like it," Abby Ruth said. "Something is rotten in Datingland."

"Well," Maggie mused, "it's certainly not fair, but it also doesn't get us any closer to finding out anything about OnceUponATom."

Sera sat back and did that spooky looking-off-into-the-distance thing she did when she was about to come out with something strangely insightful. "What if Martha's right—not only about her niece's guy, but the whole darn dating service?"

"What do you mean?" Maggie asked.

"I have the feeling this isn't just about a few guys pretending they're younger and more handsome than they really are," Sera said. "I think this site was set up specifically to scam women."

"Isn't there a way to find out who owns the darn thing?" Abby Ruth asked.

"Hang on a sec." Sera's fingers flew over the keyboard. After a couple of minutes, she said, "Should've known it."

"Did you find anything?"

"The registrar was one of those big domain registration places, but the person who bought it is protected by a private registration."

"Does that help us at all?" Maggie asked.

"Not really, but it's a start," Sera said.

Maggie sighed. "Regardless, I think it's time I went to the prison to give Lil an update."

Chapter Twenty

Although Jenny'd shot him down like a World War I fighter plane last night, Teague tried to be optimistic as he pulled into Summer Haven's driveway. He had a cooler with sodas, sandwiches and bait in it so he could take Grayson down to the creek for the kid's first fishing expedition. Today was about getting to know Jenny's son better.

If he just kept that in his mind, he wouldn't go crazy rolling all his mistakes over and over in his head.

Because by the time he'd made it out to Miller's Pass last night to check out someone supposedly cooking meth, only to discover Mrs. Miller was making up a batch of some noxious sauerkraut, it had been too late to return to Summer Haven. If Barnes hadn't been MIA for an hour, things might've turned out differently. But when the deputy had finally showed up at the supposed crime scene, he'd been pale and clammy, claiming food poisoning.

Maybe it had been for the best. Sometimes it didn't make sense to push a woman, especially one like Jenny.

Summer Haven's circle drive only held two cars—Maggie's small truck and Sera's van. Abby Ruth's dually and the compact he'd assumed was Jenny's rental car were missing.

Don't flip out, Castro. They're probably just running errands around town.

Still, he dashed up the stairs and jabbed the bell. When no one answered, he rang it again.

Sera answered the door with her hair pinned up with about a dozen pencils and a faraway look in her eyes. "Teague," she murmured. "Did you leave something last night?"

Yeah, he'd left his heart in Jenny's clenched fist. "I'm here to take Grayson fishing."

Her fuzzy look cleared, and she stood straighter, dislodging a couple of pencils and sending them tumbling to the floor. "Oh...hmm...well."

He pushed past her into the house

because, hell, it wasn't breaking and entering when she'd answered the door. "Where is everyone?"

"I was just doing something on the computer. Abby Ruth and Maggie went to visit L—"

He turned back to see Sera's mouth moving like a hungry guppy. Whatever lie she told this time might be a good one.

"—Love Lines."

"Love Lines?"

"Yes, it's an...uh...adult store."

He'd seen plenty of those kind of signs lined up down Interstate 75, interspersed with the church advertisements, but he'd never heard of Love Lines. "That a normal Saturday morning errand around here? Kinda like hitting the farmers market?"

Sera lifted her chin. "Women have needs too."

God, these women made him want to poke a skewer in his ear at least once a week. "I don't suppose Jenny and her needs went with them?"

"Teague, I don't want to hurt you."

Although his relationship with Sera had started out in very rocky territory, they'd become friends. So he didn't hesitate to touch her shoulder. "Sera, I'm a cop. I'm tough."

"No man is tough when it comes to the woman he loves."

"How did you know..." Of course. Women talked. Jenny had probably blabbed all about him spewing out his feelings like a runaway garden hose. He'd be humiliated if he hadn't meant every word he'd said.

"You have very expressive eyes," Sera said. "Every time you looked at her last night, they were full of emotion. The vibrant aura around—"

He held up a hand to stop her. "We have a deal on the aura talk."

"Right. Well...about Jenny..." Her eyes cast downward.

"She's gone, isn't she?"

Sera's nod was slow and somehow sad. "Apparently, she and Grayson left first thing this morning. Told her mom she was able to catch an early flight and that Grayson needed to get back to finish a school project he'd forgotten."

"She was lying, huh?"

"I wasn't there. I don't—"

"You're a good judge of people."

"Yes, she was probably lying." Sera didn't even try to soften it with a perky smile. He gave her points for not trying to pass it off as something unimportant. "Hey, we have some of Maggie's tea left over from last night. Why don't I pour you a glass?"

"A little early for that. Even under these circumstances. I'd planned to take Grayson fishing." And now going by himself seemed like the loneliest thing in the world. "I don't suppose you fish?"

She grimaced. "You know I'm not much of a meat eater."

"What if I promise we'll catch and release?"

"How about you fish and I'll keep you company?"

"Sure thing."

"Then I'll meet you outside," she said.

When Sera met him in the driveway, she had a thermos tucked under her arm. "Figured special tea could only make things better."

Or at least anesthetize them. "You up for a PB&J?" he asked her.

She bumped him with her hip. "You're already a better date than the guy I was supposed to meet last night."

"Whatever happened with that?"

"You'll be relieved to know he cancelled before I ever made it out of the house."

"He's obviously an idiot."

Her laughter was pleasant. "If you weren't twenty years too young and absolutely not my type, I might make a play for you, Teague."

He couldn't decide if that was a boon or a blow to his ego. "The first day I met you, I thought you *were* making a play for me."

That put a little spring in her step as they trooped through the pasture toward the creek. "Why in the world would you think that?"

"Because you were talking about my—" he twirled his finger in the general area of his crotch, "—sac thingie."

"Ah, your sacral chakra. Well, it was dammed up."

"Was?" God, what was he doing? He needed to know the state of his sex chakra about like he needed Jenny to have flown the coop this morning.

"Well, now it's flowing. But I'll be honest. It's on a sort of a loop. Normally, I'm a fan of recycling. But too much of that in the sacral chakra can eventually dissipate your sexual energy."

Great news just kept coming today. "I'll keep that in mind."

Dotted with a few remaining sprigs of grass, the creek bank was a gentle slope to the water. Within a couple of weeks, the grass would be brown and all the leaves that shaded the creek in the summer would have fallen. Autumn was pretty in Georgia in a stark sort of way. But it could be depressing if you let it.

He and Sera settled onto the ground, her with a thermos cup full of tea and him with a baited pole. They spent several companionable minutes with her sipping and him casting.

Finally, she asked, "What are you going to do about her?"

"Isn't that the million dollar question?"

"She's a mother. You can't just think about how you feel about her. You have to consider the little boy too. Children are such a gift, yet too many adults don't treat them that way."

"Last night was the first time I'd met Grayson. He hung out with my parents a few times before Abby Ruth packed up and left Houston. My mom thinks the kid hung the moon."

"Are you jealous of him?"

Teague cast in a jerky motion, and the whole thing became a tangled mess of line. "Not the way you think." He pulled the line in, tried to sift through it, but his fingers were a fumbling mess. "It eats at my gut that Jenny's kid isn't my kid. That was the way it was supposed to be, the two of us with a family. The way we'd always promised each other it would be."

"You've loved her for a long time."

"Since I was ten years old."

"But you hurt her."

"It was one of those situations where I was damned either way."

"I don't expect you to tell me the story. That's between you and Jenny. But just remember, if you're mourning what should have been, she is too."

He glanced over from untangling the fishing line to see Sera propped up on her elbows staring at the clouds. Her normally cheerful expression was nowhere to be seen. Instead, her mouth was a downward curve and cheeks were hollow. "You sound like you know something about that," he said.

"Oh, Teague," she said, her words piggybacking on a sigh. "We all know something about what it feels like to make the wrong choices."

When Maggie and Abby Ruth sat down at the table with Lil, darned if Martha wasn't with her again. Maggie supposed she should be glad Martha was there so they could seal the septic deal, but next time she got some alone time with her best friend, she would tell Lil how she felt about it.

Then again, maybe Lil felt the same way about Abby Ruth. Lil smiled her polite smile toward Abby Ruth but focused primarily on Maggie, as if poor Abby Ruth didn't exist. That felt a bit familiar.

"How are you doing, Lil?" Maggie asked. "Sorry I missed your call last night. Things have been hectic, but we've made some good progress."

"I'm fine." Lil waved off the question. "I'm not going anywhere...yet."

"Did you get some good news?" Hope percolated inside Maggie. When Lil returned to Summer Haven, it would be so nice to rebuild their old relationship.

"No. No word on an early release, but we can hope." Lil smiled at Martha, but her lips trembled. "Martha and I are working on another project for the warden. Hopefully, these favors are adding up."

Martha snapped her fingers twice. "We're short on time. Do you have something for me or not?"

Maggie's heart rate picked up speed, and her shoulder muscles tightened. This woman would make a man of the cloth contemplate breaking one of the Ten Commandments. A very specific one.

Lil flashed Maggie a pleading smile.

"Yes." Maggie forced the word from her tight throat. "Something weird is going on with that website. This is bigger than

Martha's worry about OnceUponATom. First off, not everyone is getting dates. Maybe that's not so odd, but as Sera and I looked over all the men we were matched with and you won't believe what we found."

Abby Ruth cut in, "Basically, a lot of those guys are lying. Their profile pictures aren't really them. They're photos these guys scammed from the internet.

Maggie let out an exasperated breath. "I'm telling her."

"I know, but at this rate we'll have to do it in episodes. This ain't no Lifetime movie."

Lil clasped her hands together and leaned toward Maggie. "So are you telling me these men are lying about who they are?"

Maggie shrugged. "Well, they're definitely lying about what they look like. Then, there's this." She shoved the honey-golden card across the table to Lil.

"What is this?"

"*Who* is it?" Martha asked.

"Me," Maggie told them. "It's a picture of me on my date with DanOfYourDreams."

Martha let out a snort, and Abby Ruth grinned wide. She was having so much trouble containing her enjoyment that her leg was moving, her roach-killer boot bonking Maggie in the shin with every swing.

"What's so funny?" Maggie slapped Abby Ruth's knee to stop the assault on her leg.

"Beekeeping?" Martha let out a hearty laugh and then pushed the picture back over to Lil. "Seriously. Now, that's a first. I thought paintball was bad."

"It's a nice picture," Lil soothed. "Too bad we can't see your face."

Maggie lifted a brow. "You should've seen my hair before they stuck that safari hat on my head. Sera fixed me all up in a pretty sleek 'do."

"Wait a second." Martha pulled the picture back. "You couldn't see his face?"

"Nope, but I'd seen his profile. He was the right height and build. I guess he could have favored the picture, but the photo was of some model from a stock site."

"That's it. The connection," Martha exclaimed. "I bet your guy is my niece's guy."

"Why would you think that?"

"Because Tom kept his face hidden too."

Maggie's mouth dropped. "But my guy was DanOfYourDreams and hers was OnceUponATom."

"And she had a picture from her date too." Martha's mouth twisted up. "You've found him."

"Well, I don't really have his address or anything yet. I mean..."

"I need you to find this guy. Now," Martha demanded. "I just thought he was a tool, but what if he's using this site to troll for pretty young victims?"

"Has your niece received any gifts from The Perfect Fit?"

"No, but she said Tom sent her flowers."

"She get a note with that?" Abby Ruth asked.

"Didn't mention one. Why?"

Maggie leaned forward. "Because both Sera and Abby Ruth have gotten the kiss-off from the dating site."

"It was not a kiss-off," Abby Ruth said through gritted teeth and a forced smile.

"Whatever you call it," Maggie said, waving her fingers in front of Abby Ruth's scowling face. "Regardless, some women are getting kicked out of the site. They're sent a form letter that, strangely enough, comes with a gift."

"Isn't that nice?" Lillian angled her head and raised her eyebrows. "What'd you get?" she asked Abby Ruth.

"Cube steak." When Martha snickered, Abby Ruth raised a finger and locked eyes with her. "Not a word."

Martha's nostrils swelled as she held back a grin, then she shifted her focus back to Maggie. "What else you got?"

Kelsey Browning and Nancy Naigle

"We decided to register as a man," Maggie told her, "and the process is totally different for them. Fewer personal questions and fewer profile questions. Plus, they have the ability to search through all the women's profiles."

"So?" Martha asked. "The world ain't exactly a fair place."

"Sera is convinced this means whoever owns the site is trying to dupe women. So it's bigger than just your niece."

"I'm not in this for other women," Martha said. "They can take care of their own selves. I just want you to track down this Tom guy. How hard can that be?"

Maggie wanted to reach across the table and shake the woman, but she buried her hands in her lap instead. "Believe me, we've been trying."

"Sera even dug around to find out who owns the URL," Abby Ruth added, "but it has one of those privacy things on it."

Martha looked up at the ceiling as though they were trying her patience. "Plenty of people do that. Would you want your address and phone number splashed all over the internet for any nut-job to call you up or pay you a visit?"

The more Martha discounted what they'd found, the more Maggie felt like digging in.

"No, but this isn't just about your niece anymore so you have to give us more time. Sera has a lead." Maggie wasn't about to admit she didn't have an idea in the world about how they might use it. "She found the hosting company."

Martha raised an eyebrow and scoffed. "That doesn't tell you anything. The site could be hosted in Timbuktu, but that doesn't mean the person behind it is there."

"Oh." Maggie felt herself shrink in her chair. And here she'd thought they'd made some real progress. "Well, I'm sure Sera will find out more."

"Yeah, that's not gonna happen through a Whois search," Martha said.

"Why not? We've proven we're smart and resourceful. And Sera's getting darned good on the computer."

"What you need to do is get inside that dating site database to figure out exactly who Tom is."

"Well, if you're so smart," Maggie demanded, "why don't you tell us how to do that."

"All it'll take," Martha said with a sharp smile, "is something illegal."

Chapter Twenty-One

After Maggie and Abby Ruth left, Lil and Martha stalked out of the visiting room. Or rather Martha stalked at a fast clip, and Lil did a hop-skip-jog to keep up with her.

"I don't like what we just heard," Lil said.

"Your girls better get the lead out before that creep decides to dump Maggie and boot her out of the system too."

"Maybe this guy really likes her and has no plans to break up with her." Wishful thinking, but Lil was grasping at straws.

Martha shot a raised-brow look at Lil and kept trucking. "Maggie's nice and all that, but she's no spring chicken."

"Being seventy-something doesn't keep a woman from deserving companionship and even love. But this doesn't sound like one rogue Romeo anymore. I don't want my girls to be in danger, and this is starting to feel dangerous."

"What are you saying?" Martha stopped, and Lillian ran a few steps past her before slowing down. "You saying you're slithering out of our deal? What about your shitters?"

"You should really work on your language."

Martha flipped her hand in an unconcerned gesture and started walking again. "We're not in etiquette class right now. Besides, your language has gotten a little salty over the past few months."

"But Summer Haven's toilets aren't a valid reason for putting Maggie and the others in jeopardy."

"They haven't been hurt so far." Finally, they arrived in the courtyard, and Martha's attention was only partially on their conversation. Instead, she was inspecting the progress made on the camp's beautification.

"Weren't you the one worried he was a serial killer when he went out with your niece?"

"Hey, I don't really care if they bring down a whole scam," Martha said. "But they still haven't found Tom, and that's what I'm really after. I get that, and your girls can flush again."

Martha studied the women hunched over new flowerbeds, and Lillian followed her gaze. "Oh, no."

"Hell's bells," Martha snapped.

The perennials they were planting were obviously the ones thinned out from the other side of the camp. Only problem was they were drooping as if they'd been allowed to stay out of the ground too long. The indigestion Lillian had been battling recently came roaring into her chest like a bonfire doused with gasoline.

Martha growled, "Hang on a second." She strode toward a blonde girl kneeling near a batch of anemic asters.

Here Lillian was, trying so hard to get out of this place so she could get back to Summer Haven, but she was being thwarted at every turn. And really, was her family home worth putting Maggie and the others at risk?

For a while, their sleuthing had seemed daring and romantic. But now, she remembered how scared she'd been at times. Maybe she just wasn't cut out for a life of crime or crime fighting.

By the time Martha returned to her side, Lil had made a decision. As much as she wanted to impress those BOP folks, she had to put her own girls first. "I want to pull the plug on this dating site nonsense."

"Those girls, not a plant lover in the bunch," Martha grumbled. "They'd probably kill a cactus."

"Did you hear me?" Lil upped her volume to pull Martha out of her HGTV *Gardening by the Yard* fantasy. "Maggie and the others are done with digging into your niece's love life."

That snagged Martha's attention, and she rounded on Lillian. "Would you think it was nonsense if Maggie was head over heels for a guy who won't show his face?"

"Inmate Fairview!" someone called.

Lillian looked over to find the warden striding toward them. By the smile on her face and the pep in her step, she had another fabulous idea.

"Yes, Warden Proctor?"

She clasped her hands in front of her chest. "I just found out the BOP representatives will be visiting us in the evening instead of during the day. And I thought..."

Here it comes.

"...that we could whip up a little Southern style dinner for them while they're here. Show off the kitchen's cooking skills and give them a little down-home hospitality."

Lillian's knees ached, and she would have

collapsed to the ground if she'd had time. But she pasted a hopefully pleasant expression on her face. "That's nice."

"However, I don't trust the kitchen manager not to slap some limp pasta and a meatball on a plate and call it good. So I want you to work on the menu, vet the recipes and oversee the waitstaff."

Waitstaff? The cafeteria was set up buffet style. It wasn't as if their meals were white-cloth affairs. A little throb behind Lillian's right eye pulsed in time to the ache in her knees. "And you expect me to put all this together by Tuesday?"

"For someone like you, Lillian, I'm sure this will be a piece of cake." The warden waved a careless hand. "Maybe Martha can even help in some way."

Once the warden was out of earshot, Martha jabbed Lil with her elbow. "Are you kidding me? What next, a dinner show? Maybe she wants us to tap-dance or juggle too."

"Don't say that too loudly or she'll turn right around and assign it to us."

"What do you know about running a prison kitchen?"

"Not a darned thing. I do, however, know a thing or two about throwing dinner parties. But I'll need a full inventory of the freezer and pantry and some suggestions on who I can trust to serve the BOP without throwing us under the bus."

"Only if your grannies hold up their end of our deal."

Lil was out of options. Too much pressure and too little time. "Fine."

By the time she and Abby Ruth made it back to Summer Haven, Maggie felt as though she had a ten-penny nail pounded into her temple. Martha only cared about one thing. But to get the information on Tom, Maggie and the others would have to make even more progress.

Abby Ruth glanced over. "You're thinking so hard over there, it's making my head hurt. Let's get inside and see if Sera's made any more progress. If not, then you can torture yourself."

"Fine."

They walked into the kitchen to find a slightly sunburned Sera enjoying a glass of wine. She lifted it and toasted them both.

"What's got you all happy?" Abby Ruth asked.

"I spent the afternoon with a handsome man and—"

"You got a date?" Maggie rushed to her side. "Was it Tom or Dan?"

"—I found some fabulous information. And no date. I spent the afternoon fishing with Teague."

Abby Ruth winced. "Was he upset?"

"He tried not to show it—" Sera pulled her feet up into the chair, "—but he was brokenhearted that Jenny and Grayson were gone."

"I should go over and—"

Sera caught Abby Ruth's arm before she could stomp out the back door and handed her the wine glass. "I don't think that's what he needs right now. Sometimes people just need time to lick their wounds."

Maggie agreed. "As sorry as I am about all this trouble Teague and Jenny seem to be having, we have bigger fish to broil right now."

"Fry," Abby Ruth muttered into the glass. "And damned if I wouldn't like a big old mess of fried catfish about now."

"We have more important things to do than eat," Sera said. "After you left, I did a little research and read about something called a trace route."

"And?" Maggie asked.

"So I ran one and I have some very good news." Sera bounced in her chair and clapped. "I was able to trace the IP address to Summer Shoals Telephone Company."

"Does that mean whoever's behind this works there?"

"I doubt it. But if we can talk to the people at SSTC, then—"

Just when Maggie'd begun to get her hopes up for some real progress. "The telephone company isn't open on the weekends."

"Um...and there's another thing," Abby Ruth said. "Do you remember what Martha said about doing something illegal? The telephone company won't tell us where that ISP address goes unless we have a subpoena or warrant. And unless Sera is hiding one of those two things in her tight yoga pants, then we're shit outta luck."

Maggie sagged against the kitchen counter. "There has to be some way around all this. What's the point of living in a small town if you can't find out things about your neighbors?"

"If you two Nellie Naysayers would just be quiet and listen to me," Sera said, her voice surprisingly tart. "I do have an idea."

Maggie just nodded.

"Billy Parr comes to my yoga class every Wednesday, and I happen to know he works for the phone company."

"That doesn't get us around the fact that it's Saturday night, and I doubt Billy's at

298 Kelsey Browning and Nancy Naigle

work."

"You're right. He told me he goes to a meditation session this time each week. If we can just find that, then—"

Abby Ruth snorted. "Meditation? Is that what he called it? More like medication—the liquid kind."

"What do you mean?"

"Billy is a Saturday night regular down at Earlene's Drinkery. Maybe he considers the way he becomes one with his barstool a form of meditation."

"That man," Sera fumed. "Lying brings bad karma. He has to know that."

"I think he's more concerned with his Johnnie Walker than his karma," Abby Ruth said. "But the good news is we know exactly where to find him and what to ply him with. Maggie, do we still have any of that birthday cake left over?"

"Only because I stashed a couple of pieces."

"Wrap 'em up because we're going fishing."

Earlene's Drinkery was dark and loud on a Saturday night. The TVs were broadcasting sporting events at ear-bleeding levels and the crash of billiard balls came from the back room. But Maggie, Sera and Abby Ruth homed directly in on a forty-something man with a receding hairline at the end of the bar.

They ringed around his barstool, effectively caging him in.

"Hi, there, Billy," Sera said, her tone as sweet as peach preserves.

He glanced up and did a double-take. "Oh, hey...uh...hi, Sera. Funny meeting you here."

"Isn't it? Your meditation session must've already wrapped up for the evening."

"My medit...oh, yeah, yeah. It was...uh...cancelled tonight."

Abby Ruth knocked on the bar twice with her knuckles to get the bartender's attention. "I need four shots down here." When the young guy strolled over, Abby Ruth leaned in and said in a low tone, "Cheapest you've got."

Holy moly. Maggie leaned over and whispered, "I don't drink whiskey straight."

"Don't worry," she whispered back. "They're not for you."

"Ladies, I'd offer you a seat but..." Billy gestured to the occupied stools to his right and left.

"Oh, don't worry—" Abby Ruth smiled and it reminded Maggie of one of those Trigger Fish with the pointy teeth, "—we won't be here that long."

The bartender carefully placed four shot

glasses on the bar. "That'll be five dollars." Lordy, at a dollar and a quarter a piece, those glasses probably held drain cleaner.

"Put it on my tab," Abby Ruth told him. Then she turned to Maggie. "Didn't you bring something for Billy?"

"Oh, yes." Maggie pulled a plastic fork and a hunk of foil-wrapped chocolate cake from her purse. "We thought you might enjoy some of Abby Ruth's birthday cake. It's a special family recipe."

He unwrapped it and grabbed the fork.

"Before you eat that," Abby Ruth said, nudging a shot glass toward his hand, "let's drink to it."

They clinked glasses and tossed back the whiskey. Just the smell of it made Maggie's eyes water.

Billy dove into the cake, shoveling in bite after bite. "This shtuff is delishush."

Abby Ruth leaned toward Maggie. "If I'd realized he was such a cake fan, we could've just doused it in liquor."

Within the next fifteen minutes, Abby Ruth and Billy had done the first four shots, and Abby Ruth had ordered another setup. Thank goodness the man on Billy's right finally abandoned his stool because all this drinking was making Maggie woozy. She perched on the stool and braced her elbow on the bar.

"So, Billy," Sera said, moving in to lightly brush against his arm. What she and Abby Ruth needed with Maggie, who knew? Between them, they had temptation down pat. "I'd love to hear more about your work at the telephone company."

He scraped up one last bite of icing with the side of his fork. "Not much to tell. Pretty boring. I just work in accounts."

Abby Ruth gave a fist pump near her hip.

"I've always admired men who can work with numbers," Sera cooed.

Lord have mercy. If it got any deeper in here, Maggie would have to get out her septic system slogging boots.

Billy puffed out his chest. "Well, I guess when you think about it, it *is* impressive."

"Do you know I've never seen the inside of a telephone company?" Sera draped herself on the bar, apparently trying to drum up some cleavage for Billy to ogle. That's what they should've left to Maggie. She could provide enough cleavage for all three of them. "I'd love a tour. A private one."

Billy swallowed. "That's...uh...kinda against company policy."

"Oh," Sera pouted. "That's too bad. I always feel so free when I try new things."

"And," Abby Ruth drawled, "Sera's been

known to get naked when she feels free."

He pushed away from the bar and shot off his stool so fast that he bumped Maggie's still-sore foot. Not that he realized it even though she sucked in a pained breath and grabbed her throbbing foot. "I suppose a short tour couldn't hurt anything."

Sera looped her arm through his and squeezed his biceps. "I do love a man who's not afraid of breaking a few rules for a good time."

Billy led her toward the door, and Sera shot a look over her shoulder, mouthing *follow me.*

Once Sera and Billy pulled out of the bar's parking lot, Abby Ruth eased out behind them but left a good distance between the cars.

"Shouldn't you get closer?" Maggie asked.

"We know where they're going."

"What if Sera needs help?"

"She's a big girl, and we'll be parked right outside."

Not fifteen minutes later, Maggie received a text from Sera. *Need backup. Meet me at the front door.*

She and Abby Ruth hustled out of the truck toward the twin glass doors fronting the phone company. Sera pushed it open and stuck her head out. "He passed out."

"Before or after?" Abby Ruth asked.

"After," Sera said.

"Sera," Maggie gasped, "you didn't..."

"No! Of course not, but I need help. He'll get fired if anyone finds him like this." Sera led them to a cubicle behind the reception desk. And sure enough, Billy was sprawled out on the indoor-outdoor carpet, shirt unbuttoned and snoring like a freight train. "He might've gotten a little enthusiastic, but he's obviously not one of those men who can drink and drive, if you know what I mean."

Abby Ruth gave a belly-busting laugh and hauled Billy up by one arm. "Y'all get the other side."

Once they had Billy stashed in his backseat to sleep it off, Maggie asked Sera, "So where is this database thingie?"

"According to Billy's records, Dogwood Ridge Assisted Living."

Chapter Twenty-Two

Standing in front of Dogwood Ridge Assisted Living the next day, Maggie toyed with the macaroni necklace around her neck. The gift that would gain her, Sera and Abby Ruth access to Warner Talley and, in turn, a reason to snoop around the facility for the person behind this whole dating site farce.

She swallowed, trying to dislodge the lump in her throat she got every time she reflected on the day Warner had given her the necklace, certain she was his wife, Melba. Alzheimer's was a wicked disease. One that Maggie never wanted to experience firsthand.

She hadn't been able to bear throwing away the red and gold painted necklace, even after it got wet and stuck to one of her favorite appliquéd shirts, completely ruining the cute pink cow stitched near the neckline.

Now, she was extra glad she hadn't tossed it because it would make her visit to Warner all the more believable. Hopefully, the piece of makeshift jewelry would comfort him and bring back good memories of his deceased wife. That would make Maggie feel slightly less guilty about using the old guy to gain access to the information they needed.

Before she could ring the buzzer, the front door swung open and out walked Deputy Barnes' handsome young nephew.

"Hey there, James," Sera said brightly. "Visiting someone?"

"I volunteer in the rec room once a week," he said with a smile. "What about you?"

"Stopping by to see Warner Talley."

James' smile dimmed a watt or two. "You realize he doesn't remember the people who come see him, right?"

"It's all about cheering him up in the present," Maggie broke in. "And speaking of, we'd better get to it."

Maggie, Sera and Abby Ruth filed inside, their footsteps squeaking down the sterile linoleum hallway. Sera approached the nurses' station desk and signed each of their names on the register.

The blonde nurse with the ponytail smiled when she saw they were visiting Warner. "He'll be delighted to have visitors.

He's been a little restless now that his son is...unable to visit. The transition from seeing Nash several times a week to not at all has been hard on Mr. Talley."

"I'm sure," Maggie murmured.

"He doesn't understand."

Abby Ruth said, "We'll try to be better about coming more often."

Where heck had that come from? Was Abby Ruth softening up?

Abby Ruth leaned her elbows on the counter. "You know, I was wondering if you had a layout of the facility."

Maggie winced. Nothing subtle about Abby Ruth.

"My older sister needs a place like this," Abby Ruth continued, "and I think having her close by would be nice."

The nurse nodded. "Oh, yes. Being near loved ones is so important." She pulled out a brochure. "Here's the information about Dogwood Ridge and a little map showing the number of rooms in the facility is printed on the back." She drew four stars atop some of the units. "These are vacant right now."

Abby Ruth held the brochure at arm's length and waved it in a circle encompassing the other end of the hallway. "What's in that section of the building?"

"Mainly our administrative offices and

equipment. Mr. Talley's room is the last patient room on this floor."

"Hmm...I was hoping for a first floor room for my sister, but it sounds like you don't have many." Abby Ruth tucked the brochure into her back pocket. "I'll think it over."

"The residents here not only get excellent care, but we also offer a shuttle for shopping and a number of enrichment activities. I'm sure your sister would be very happy here. Please let me know if you'd like to set up a tour for her."

"I'll be sure to do that if she shows the slightest interest," Abby Ruth said.

"Y'all can go on down to Mr. Talley's room." She motioned toward the end of the hall. "I know he's awake because I poked my head in not five minutes ago."

The nurse busied herself behind the desk, and the three of them walked down the hall. "That was easy," Abby Ruth said from the side of her mouth.

From Warner's room, muffled dialogue from the television echoed into the hall. Maggie paused for a few seconds, just to get her courage up. What they were doing felt so sneaky, but it was for a good cause. Plus, she really would be visiting him. That was her job in this mission. She gave a double-knock on his door. "Yoo-hoo. Warner?"

The old man was sitting in front of the screen watching *Family Feud,* where Steve Harvey was teasing two ladies with their hands held over the buzzers. Warner looked up as Maggie and the others flooded into his small room. His stare was initially blank, but when it landed on Maggie, his eyes brightened and he reached for her hand. "Melba. You've come back. It's been so long. Did I do something wrong?"

Sera nudged Maggie forward, so she clasped his hand and leaned in to give him a hug. "You? Do something wrong? Never. It hasn't been that long," she tried to reassure him.

He touched her necklace. "So pretty. So pretty. As pretty as you. I'm glad you're wearing it and like it too."

"I love it." She took a seat in the chair next to his. The man was still talking in rhyme. That sure seemed like a lot of work. "How have you been?"

"I'm fine. A bit tired. It's been nice to see Nash. I worry about him. Does he have enough cash?"

"You raised him right, Warner." That was a bit of hogwash, but no harm, no foul. "I'm sure he's fine."

"We did it together. We raised him right,"

Warner chanted. "You in the day and me by night."

"Right." Maggie figured the best thing she could do is play along with whatever fairy tale was playing in the theater in Warner's mind. "Have you and Nash had nice visits?"

"We surely did. Oh, yes indeed. And he even brought a present to me."

"A present?"

Warner nodded. "A surprise, I suppose, because he tucked it away. I found it when he left the other day." His joints creaked as he rose from his chair and shuffled across the room to the armoire. Reaching above his head, he grasped a small black box and carried it back. "At first, I thought it was a game. But look, it's a picture frame."

He opened the picture frame. Only it wasn't a picture frame at all. Maggie recognized what it was right away. One side was a keyboard and the other a screen. It was a miniature laptop.

"You're saying Nash brought you this?" Maggie shot a look at Sera and Abby Ruth, who were standing like statues near the door. Obviously, they were both happy to let her take the lead on chitchatting with Warner. He had to be mistaken about a visit from his son, since that was impossible. But then again, Warner thought she was Melba, so there was no telling who'd actually given him this little computer.

"I suppose he'll bring pictures to tuck inside. Wouldn't it wonderful to see him with a bride?"

Yeah, not likely to happen anytime soon. Warner handed her the computer, and she balanced it in her lap. In better times Warner had probably used it for email and other Talley Funeral Home business. "What a thoughtful gift, Warner." She passed the laptop back to him. "We do have a good boy. He loves you so much."

The man beamed with pride. He returned the treasure to its place, then shuffled his way back to his chair. A groan escaped as lowered himself. "I'm very tired today. Can you stay?"

Abby Ruth shot Maggie a thumbs-up. "We're gonna just skedaddle, Mags. You cover us. Got it?"

"Go on," she said. "I'm not going anywhere."

"You'll text if anyone comes in his room, right?" Sera asked.

Maggie pulled her phone from her pocket. "All I have to do is hit send."

"Let's hit it," Abby Ruth said to Sera.

Within minutes after they left, Maggie watched Warner's facial skin begin to sag.

His eyes looked as if they'd slip down his face if it weren't for all the folds holding them up. His shaky hands found comfort in the threadbare spot on the arm of his chair.

"Yes, my friend," she told him. "Rest. I'll be right here." But she doubted he'd remember if she'd been there or not when he awoke.

His eyes slowly drooped and he was mumbling in a state of dreamland in just moments.

Maybe his low, nonsensical conversations were how he coped with the loss of his son's regular visits. Maggie didn't see her own daughter, Pam, nearly enough. In fact, it had been two weeks since their last phone call, and that was too long.

Suddenly, Maggie missed Pam like she'd missed her the first time she'd gone off to Girl Scout camp. *I miss my baby girl and my baby girl's babies. We're due for a visit. Overdue.*

Out in the hallway, Abby cast a quick glance at the nurse's station to find it mercifully empty. Sera was a better good luck charm than a hundred rabbit's feet. "Who would've thought an old folks' home could be such a hotbed of criminal activity?" she said to Sera. "If we trace one more baddie to this place, I'm gonna suspect the mob."

"Summer Shoals seems awfully small for organized crime."

"In here." Abby Ruth waved Sera toward a door marked with a sign that said Server Room.

"Oh, hi there," Sera said brightly.

Abby Ruth spotted the object of Sera's cheer, a man with messy, gray-white hair wearing jeans, paisley print suspenders and a bow tie stamped with...computer mice sporting thin black tails.

Dammit. The plan had been to snoop first and confront only if necessary. If they continued to track down bad guys, flexibility would fast become a critical skill.

The man smiled, which took him from fashion-challenged geek to geekily handsome. "You must've made a wrong turn. This is the IT area. Believe me, no one comes in here by choice. In fact, the only time people enter that door is when something's wrong."

"We're in the right place," Abby Ruth told him.

"Having trouble with the wireless in one of the rooms?" He sprang from his chair and hustled for the door. "If you'll show me the spot, I'll have you fixed up in a jif—"

Without completely thinking it through, Abby Ruth drew her 9mm from the holster at her back.

"Whoa, whoa, whoa. This stuff might look valuable—" the man waved an arm at the small stash of humming boxes and monitors, "—but most of it's at least five years old. If you're hoping to pawn something, you'd be better off stealing hubcaps from the parking lot."

"Abby Ruth!" Sera scolded. "There's no need for that."

"I find ammo talks faster than words," she said. "Besides, a Glock is one of the safest weapons in the world."

"I'm sorry about my friend's impulse-control problem." Sera patted the man's arm and gently led him back to his chair. "But we need you to stay here."

"Why are you treating him with kid gloves?" Abby Ruth demanded. "We've found our guy."

"Haven't you ever heard innocent until proven guilty?"

"You know," the man interjected, "usually trials happen at the courthouse. And that's only *after* the person's been arrested for doing something wrong. Which I absolutely haven't done. By the way, do either of you have ID? I didn't realize Sheriff Castro had added seniors to his citizen's arrest program."

Abby Ruth speared Sera with a glare. "I should shoot him for that alone."

"It's hard to get information from a dead man," Sera said with a smile.

For the first time, the computer guy looked alarmed, with his hands gripping his chair arms. "I...I have grandchildren. They love their poppy and would be very sad if he was gunned down in his own office."

"I won't shoot you unless you do something stupid." Abby Ruth hooked a rolling chair with her boot toe. She pulled it toward her and sprawled into it. "Besides, in this tiny enclosed space, a gunshot would echo like a bitch. Sera, since he seems to like you, why don't you try to get the truth out of him?"

Sera smiled her charm-grown-men-into-trying-yoga smile which encouraged IT Guy to focus on her. "What can you tell us about ThePerfectFit.com?"

"Um...that it sounds like a shoe sales website?"

Abby Ruth pushed off, rolling her chair forward to ram his. "Don't play stupid with us. You're obviously a smart guy if you work on all this stuff." She waved a hand at the wall-to-wall racks. "The longer you deny you're involved, the more likely my finger is to sweat. The more my finger sweats, the more likely it is to slip."

"Thought you said the noise would be too loud," he said.

"But I didn't mention I have ear plug implants."

He turned to Sera. "Is she for real?"

"I'd like to say no, but she's unpredictable." Sera patted him on the shoulder. "Usually, I can keep her under control. But we really need you to tell us about the website."

"Forget the site," Abby Ruth snapped. "We want to know why you're stringing women along with these paintball and beekeeping dates."

The guy dropped his chin toward his chest and looked at Abby Ruth with an I-was-taking-you-seriously-until-now stare. "Beekeeping?"

"Yeah," Abby Ruth said. "You look like that type."

"I'll have you know I'm allergic to all stinging insects. You'd no more find me waltzing around in a bunch of bees than you'd find me letting someone else defrag my hard drive."

"Sounds kinda kinky," Sera said, looking him up and down as though considering his bedroom skills.

"Besides," he said, "I was married for over thirty-five years. My wife passed away a couple of years ago, and I haven't been interested in jumping back into the dating pool. No matter how much my kids have encouraged me. In fact, that's one reason I work at Dogwood Ridge part-time, to avoid their hovering."

"Then why did we trace the IP address for ThePerfectFit.com to here?"

"Excuse me?"

"That's right," Abby Ruth said. "Someone in this building is the one behind that site. How many men work here?"

"Well, we have a few nurses, janitors, two doctors who come in to check on their own patients. You're sure you're looking for a man?"

Abby Ruth shot a look at Sera. Sera lifted a shoulder. "Don't ask me. Los Angeles is home to some of the prettiest transvestites in the world. Could be one reason to cover his...or her...face."

For whatever reason, Abby Ruth believed IT Guy. Really, if he couldn't be bothered to match his suspenders to his tie, it was unlikely he'd go to all the trouble to dress up in costumes for his dates. She leaned forward and holstered her gun.

"But," he said, "I don't like this one bit. These computers are my domain. If someone's messing with my equipment, I should know about it. Now that I'm not looking down a barrel, do you mind if I check for anything out of place?"

"Be my guest," Abby Ruth told him.

He hopped up, sending his rolling chair careening into Abby Ruth's knees. He *hmmed* his way through an inspection of every piece of equipment in the office.

Lord, Abby Ruth hoped Maggie was keeping Warner occupied and the nurses out of his room. The last thing Abby Ruth and Sera needed was for someone to come looking for them.

"Nothing is out of order here, but..."

"But what?"

"It's not unheard of for someone to piggyback off a wireless network," he explained. "It's easy enough to set up a web server. All you'd need is a small computer and—"

"How small?" Sera asked. "Like a desktop?"

"Yep, or even one of those slick netbooks."

Sera and Abby Ruth locked gazes. "Warner."

"That's just silly," Sera protested. "He can

barely shuffle across the room, much less wage a paintball war."

"Are you saying you saw a computer in Warner Talley's room?" IT Guy asked. "Some of the other residents have their own computers, but Warner does video visitations with his son in the common room."

Hmm...she'd have to mention that to Maggie. Skyping Lillian sure would save a lot of time and gas money.

"Let's go." Abby Ruth grabbed IT Guy and yanked him out the door. Half a dozen strides later and the three of them were in Warner's room, where they found Maggie sitting next to the old guy. He was asleep in his chair, and she was perched on the love seat holding his hand, a sad expression on her face.

"Mags, where's that little computer Warner pulled down earlier?"

"Right there in the armoire."

Abby Ruth snatched it out of the piece of furniture and thrust it into IT Guy's hands. "Do your thing. We need to know what's on this."

He settled onto the love seat next to Maggie, and the butt-shot cushions cratered, sending him sliding into her side. IT Guy put his arm out to catch himself. From Abby

Ruth's vantage point, the whole thing looked like one of those yawn-to-get-your-arm-around-the-girl schticks guys pulled back in her day.

Maggie and IT Guy made eye contact, then scrambled away from each other to their respective sides of the couch.

"What's going on?" Maggie asked while IT Guy bent over the little computer.

"We're following up on a hunch," Abby Ruth told her. "IT Guy here...what is your name, anyway?"

"Bruce Shellenberger," he mumbled.

"Old Bruce here said it would be a snap for someone to steal onto Dogwood Ridge's network."

He glanced up, lasered his gaze onto Abby Ruth. "Not a snap. I said it could be done. You make it sound like I sit around watching cat videos instead of doing my job. I'm diligent about the security here."

"I'm sure you are," she soothed, then turned back to Maggie. "So apparently a superhero mastermind could use his security-busting powers to finagle his way onto the network here."

"I'm in," Bruce declared, squinting at the screen. "You little son-of-a..." He glanced up and flashed Maggie a sheepish smile, "...biscuit-eater."

"That sounds like you found something good."

"An IIS and a MySQL database."

Whatever the hell those were. "And?"

"We need to find out what's in that database," Sera said. "That has to be the backend of the dating site."

Maybe they needed to invest some resources into Sera. A few classes and she'd be a whiz at this stuff.

"If the person has half a brain," Bruce said, "the database will be password protected."

"Ain't nothing for a stepper," Abby Ruth said.

Bruce typed, frowned, mumbled a couple of modified oaths. "Definitely has a password, and he closed the backdoor, so I can't create another admin account."

Damn. So close and yet so far.

"But," he said, "we have another option. Gimme a sec to download SQLMap."

"What's that?" Sera asked.

"Utility to hack vulnerable databases."

"Oh," Maggie leaned closer to Bruce, "that sounds fascinating."

Abby Ruth shot her a narrow look. Maggie had no more idea what the hell that meant than she did.

Bruce's fingers flew across the keyboard.

"Gotcha, you little bas—" His face reddened, and Abby Ruth could almost see possible cuss words scrolling across his forehead. "Basket weaver?"

Sera bounced on her tiptoes and clapped. "Bruce saves the day."

The guy blushed from his bow tie up to his moderately receding hairline. "Well, I don't know about that."

"Do you mind?" Sera nudged him over to wiggle her skinny behind onto the love seat, forcing Bruce almost into Maggie's lap. "I need to look at the records."

"Well, this is interesting," she said after only a minute or two of scrolling.

"We don't need interesting," Abby Ruth said. "We need answers."

Sera said, "I can tell you that about fifty of the male profiles in this thing are using the same email address, including Tom, Dan, and the guy who asked me out and cancelled."

"What does that mean?" Maggie asked.

"It means," Sera announced, "that our guy has been stacking ThePerfectFit deck."

Chapter Twenty-Three

Maggie sat in the back seat on the short ride to Summer Haven, staring out the window at the passing scenery while Abby Ruth and Sera uttered not a word from the front seat. It was as though they were all shell-shocked by what they'd discovered. DanOfYourDreams and OnceUponATom were the same man.

One bad apple was one thing.

But most of this orchard was rotten.

And Maggie felt as if she'd been duped most of all. What the heck was that guy up to? He'd made her feel special.

And now to find out he was probably doing the same with lots of other women in his database harem? Wrong, wrong, wrong.

If it weren't for all that stinkin' septic mess, she'd love to turn her back and pretend this whole online dating fiasco had never happened. But to put their potty problem to rest, they needed Martha's septic guy. And that meant they had to tie up loose ends and bring down DanTom.

"Big Martha's bad feeling about this guy was spot-on, but I don't think she'll be satisfied with what we know so far," Maggie finally said. "She'll want to know exactly who her niece is involved with."

Abby Ruth parked, and they all trooped up to the front porch. Sera immediately dropped cross-legged in front of two rockers.

"If we have to find out who The Perfect Fit guy is, then Maggie has to be the bait." Abby Ruth settled into one of the chairs, and Maggie followed suit.

"Why me?"

"Because you're the one he likes."

"Me, Martha's niece, and maybe a hundred others," Maggie said, because who knew how many other women that guy had boondoggled? "Why he didn't show up for a date with Sera is beyond me."

Abby Ruth frowned and finger-drummed the rocker's arms.

"Or you, for that matter," Maggie quickly added. "But the important thing now is to figure out how we get this guy to show his face."

"He's been awfully careful," Sera said, pulling her knees up in front of her and hugging them. "What's that hanging from your shirt?"

Maggie tugged at the open hemline of her shirt. "Oh?" She tugged on the plastic holder that still hung from the placket. "I guess I forgot to turn in my visitor pass when we visited Lil earlier. Great, I'll probably be on some blacklist for doing that."

"I'll put it in a safe place." Sera held out her hand for the badge. "That way, we can concentrate on what's important right now. Like you asking DanOfYourDreams out on a date."

Maggie felt the blood drain from her face. "I...I've never done that in my life."

"All you have to do is private message him on the site. I'll help you."

"Say I do that," Maggie said, "but what kind of date?"

"Obviously has to be something where he can hide his face," Abby Ruth said.

"Motorcycle riding?" Sera suggested.

Abby Ruth busted out laughing. "I can't see Maggie doing that."

Maggie glared at her. Why didn't this woman believe Maggie had an adventurous bone in her body? "I'll have you know I rode a mini bike once when I was twelve."

"Not the same thing."

"Fencing?" Maggie brightened. "I took

fencing in college. I was actually quite good."

Sera clapped. "That could work, and those outfits are so cute. I've always wanted to try that." She leapt to her feet and struck an *en garde* stance.

"Nice form, but what's that rattling in your pocket?" Maggie asked.

Sera looked as if she'd been caught stealing, her shoulders hunched and her gaze averted.

"Sera?"

"Fine," she finally said. "We've known each other this long. I can't hide it any longer."

Oh, no. Maggie couldn't take any more surprises or bad news today.

Sera slipped her hand into her pocket and pulled out a bright green box. Mike and Ike's? What was so bad about candy? "You've been hiding chewy fruit bites?"

"They're full of sugar," Sera said, her tone apologetic.

"Yes," Abby Ruth said, "that's normally how candy's made."

But it wasn't the kind of vice Maggie expected from Sera.

"Maybe I wouldn't feel so bad about it if I shared them. Hold out your hands." Sera shook generous portions of the colorful candies into their palms.

Maggie popped a red one into her mouth. Cherry. Oh, yes, *she* was already feeling better.

Unsurprisingly, Abby Ruth chowed down on a handful, swallowed and finally said. "So back to this fencing thing. Where in God's name could you go fencing in Summer Shoals, Georgia?"

"Good point." Maggie carefully selected a lemon flavored piece that created a pleasant puckering sensation in her mouth. She said to Sera, "I can't believe you've been holding out on us with these."

"Sorry. I can't help myself. When I was a kid, I'd change costumes and trick-or-treat multiple times to build a stash that would last for months. All year, I looked forward to Halloween."

"That's it!" Maggie held out her hand for another hit of candy. "Halloween. We'll invite him to the masquerade party. I can invite DanOfYourDreams. It'll fit his M.O."

Abby Ruth cleared her throat. "That party is at the bus barn, isn't it? We'll never be able to control the situation there, and we can't have another party here. Portable potties for my party was one thing, but we can't have half the town here and keep that mess in the front yard a secret."

"True. Where can we have it?"

"The ball field?" Sera asked.

"The Ruritan Club?" Maggie offered.

"Nope. We need a spot where we can corner him," Abby Ruth said. "Both of those places are wide open. He'd get away."

"Angelina's house," Sera said. "She has that big fence around both the B&B's and her backyard all the way down to the river. One way in and one way out."

A party at Angelina's? Oh yeah, that idea would go over like a hot air balloon filled with cinder blocks. "That's a horrible idea. You do remember that Angelina isn't our biggest fan, right?"

"What some might see as a challenge," Sera said, "I see as an opportunity."

Abby Ruth rubbed her chin with one finger. "The idea has some real merit. A party at Angelina's could work in our favor. She'd stay busy with decorations and whatnot while Martha's guy fixes this damn septic system."

Dang it, they were right. "Sera's best at persuading people to do things."

"Thank you, Maggie," Sera said. "But what we need here are negotiating skills and maybe a slice of humble pie. I think Abby Ruth should be the one to talk her into it...well, we'll make her think it's all her idea."

"You really are a sneak," Maggie said.

"What?" Abby Ruth squawked. "You want *me* to talk to her? You do remember she thinks I tried to kidnap her kid, right?"

"Sometimes," Sera told her with a smile, "catching people off guard is a very good way to get exactly what you want. She'll see the request as a peace offering, or she'll want to steal your thunder. Either way, we win."

"Which could not only help us catch DanTom," Maggie said, "but would also soften up Angelina for the inspection."

"You're both crazier than Cooter Brown with two jugs of moonshine," Abby Ruth said. "Besides how do we get people to come to our party instead of the one they go to every year?"

Maggie pulled a wrench out of her back pocket. "I think I can handle it, with a little help from my friend."

"I don't even want to know what you're going to do, Mags." Abby Ruth pinned them with her trademark stare. "And Sera, don't think I won't remember this the next time I want something from you."

"After Maggie and I lure DanTom to the party—" Sera gave Abby Ruth an exaggerated wink, "—sugar, you'll be thanking me."

Abby Ruth sat in her truck, parked on Pecan Orchard Street, looking down at the layer cake in her passenger seat. *Happy retirement, Sully.* Too damn bad for him that someone had forgotten to pick up his cake yesterday. But she'd scored it at half price from the grocery store a few minutes ago.

Offering any kind of gift, aka *bribe,* to Angelina still got Abby Ruth's hackles up. But if buttercream frosting would butter up that uptight woman, then it would be worth the $12.63 Abby Ruth had paid for the damned cake.

She scooped up the round plastic container and jumped down from the truck. Unfortunately, she landed in a pothole and tightened her grip on the cake holder in her struggle to find her footing. Well, apparently her barely-big-enough-for-the-Panini-press breasts were good for something. Because they'd squashed Sully's good tidings into an unreadable smear of blue frosting. Even better.

The Broussards lived in a Victorian house that matched the one beside it. The only difference was the house was painted in pink and trimmed in blue, while the bed and breakfast Angelina owned was just the opposite.

Reminded Abby Ruth of twins whose mother had the annoying habit of dressing her kids alike.

She prayed Angelina wouldn't answer the door. Maybe she'd taken Booger to the batting cage, and that would be the end of this plan.

Abby Ruth stomped up the stairs and pressed the doorbell. A few minutes later, little Ben—aka Booger—came to the door. When he saw her, his skinny little face lit up. "Please tell me you're here to take me to the batting cages."

If only. "Not today. I'm actually here to see your mom."

"Damn."

She felt sure that word wasn't on Angelina's approved list, but she sure wasn't going to ding the kid for it. After all, he'd used it in perfect context.

"Booger," Angelina called from somewhere else in the house, "I'm not hearing the piano. Why is that?"

"C'mon in," he said to Abby Ruth, a full-on sulk clear in his voice. Then he hollered, "Mom, company's here."

"I wasn't expecting..." Angelina, wearing leggings and a purple tunic-type top, swung into view on the stair landing on the second floor. "Abby Ruth?" Her face was tight, suspicious, as she descended the stairs. "Booger, you need to get back to your practice."

"But, Mo-o-om, Miz Abby Ruth has cake."

"Those show tunes won't learn themselves."

It took every bit of Abby Ruth's mental stamina to keep her eyes from rolling back in her head like two marbles. As soon as they had this masquerade and DanOfYourDreams stuff settled, she would call her financial advisor in Houston and have a custodial account set up for Ben Broussard. Five thousand probably wouldn't be enough for the amount of counseling the kid would need, but that was all she could transfer out of her retirement fund without getting dinged by penalties.

He plodded out of the room, then the sound of multiple piano keys being flattened simultaneously bonged through the foyer.

Angelina looked Abby Ruth up and down as though calculating the odds that she'd shake like a wet dog and ruin the silvery wallpaper and spindly side table by the front door. "This is certainly a surprise visit."

Abby Ruth shoved the cake into Angelina's arms. "This is for you."

"I didn't know you baked..." She glanced

down at the mangled mess of frosting now clinging to the plastic top. "Well, I suppose you want coffee with this."

She sure could go for a stiff shot of Jameson in that coffee, but she forced herself to say, "That would be great."

Angelina's kitchen was actually a warm space with painted cabinets and a center island surrounded by barstools. "Make yourself at home," she said.

While Abby Ruth settled on a stool, Angelina fiddled with one of those single-brew coffeemakers. Maybe they needed one of those out at Summer Haven. Sure would make those afternoon pick-me-ups convenient.

"How do you like yours?"

"To go" was what she wanted to say, but she pasted a demure smile on her face and said, "Black."

A few minutes later, Angelina carried two mugs to the island and handed one to Abby Ruth. Rather than taking a stool, however, she stood studying Abby Ruth over the rim of her cup. "I wouldn't have pegged you for the cake and coffee kind."

Abby Ruth flicked a quick look at the cake that Angelina had placed on the countertop across the room. A big piece of that sure would make the crow she was about to eat go down a little sweeter. But then again, she wasn't one to fiddle-faddle around. "Did you hear about the bus barn?"

"Um..." Angelina's eyes widened and her gaze darted all over the kitchen. She wanted to say yes, Abby Ruth knew it, but she couldn't have heard about something Maggie was likely setting into motion right this minute.

"The PTO has to cancel tomorrow night's Halloween party. Someone left the water on and the whole place is a flooded mess. Shame of it is so many kids already had their costumes." Abby Ruth shook her head, using every bit of her college dramatic training to convince Angelina she was heartbroken too. "Don't you agree that's a crying shame?"

"Booger looks forward to it every year."

Abby Ruth gazed up at the ceiling and snapped her fingers as though she was counting through the many ideas in her head and had just hit upon something perfect. "What if we put together a masquerade party? And not just for the kids, but a shindig the adults would enjoy."

Angelina sipped once, then set down her cup. "You want to put together a party for the entire town in one day? That's impossible."

"From what I've heard, they've pulled off

last-minute events at Summer Haven a number of times, what with Lillian being Summer Shoals' hostess with the mostest."

"I thought you said she was on an extended vacation."

"That's just the thing. Since the town's social director is out of pocket and time is short, we were wondering if you'd be willing to do some of the behind the scenes work."

Angelina stiffened. "You want me to serve as some kind of...of...flunky for a party hosted at Summer Haven?"

"Well, we sure wouldn't want to disappoint Booger and the other kids, now would it?"

By now, Angelina's hand was clenching around her coffee cup like one of those robot claw toys Grayson loved. "I think Summer Haven gets more than its share of the limelight around here. And it seems a little ambitious for y'all to host something like that so close to inspection time." She sniffed and tossed her hair. "But I'm not the party police."

No, just the historic register Gestapo. "Great. So I can tell Maggie and Sera you're on board?"

"Absolutely not," Angelina snapped. "If I'm hosting an event, it will happen in the B&B's backyard. With the landscaping and the river flowing at the property line, it's the perfect place for a party."

That had been way easier than Abby Ruth had expected. Angelina had taken the cake ball bait like a hungry catfish. "True, but only if think you can handle such a big event on such a short timeframe."

"Oh, I can handle it," Angelina said. "But if you want this party so darned bad, then I expect you to help me."

Abby Ruth stood and dusted at the seat of her pants. "I can ask Maggie and Sera—"

"No, Abby Ruth," Angelina said with a smile that would make angels curl up and bawl, "if I'm hosting this party, then I want *you* to help me."

And what in three hells did she know about throwing a party? Sure, she could do a ballgame get-together with beer and peanuts any day of the week. But people at these things expected food made to look like eyeballs and guts and crap.

She might not care one way or another if Summer Haven was on that Christmas house tour, but she'd come to love the estate. And if this was what she had to do for Summer Haven, she'd suck it up and pitch in. "I'm not much of a party planner."

"Oh, I'll take care of all that," Angelina assured her. "But I'll need your help setting up tomorrow."

That didn't sound too bad. "Deal." Abby Ruth pushed off the stool, figuring they were done.

Before she could take a step, Angelina said, "But I do have one stipulation."

Abby Ruth's bowels froze into a Popsicle.

"Booger's all-time favorite movie happens to be *The Wizard of Oz*."

Even as a grown-up, Abby Ruth found that film a little creepy, but hell, the kid did live with Angelina, so it probably looked like a pleasant fairy tale to him. "You don't say."

"A few years ago, I bought a costume, but it's much too long for me." Angelina stepped back and sized Abby Ruth up from head to toe. "But I think it would fit you just right."

Maggie watched over Sera's shoulder as she typed in the URL for ThePerfectFit.com and clicked through the links to Maggie's profile. Sera stood and gestured for Maggie to take her seat.

Maggie plopped into the chair. "What do I do now?"

Sera pointed to the screen. "Click on this private message button and type in his screen name. It works just like Facebook messaging."

"I've never done that. Pam always

messages me and I just respond."

"It's easy, Maggie. You can do this."

Her hands hovering over the keyboard, Maggie drew in a breath, then let it out.

Sera laid a hand on her shoulder. "It's not that big a deal."

To her. But to Maggie, this felt like jaywalking across Main Street in the altogether. "What if he doesn't answer?"

"He'll answer."

"You don't know that."

"Type." She didn't pat Maggie's shoulder. She squeezed. And Sera had very strong hands. *Ow.*

Maggie sat there for a minute. "It's like peeing. I can't do this if you're standing there watching me."

"Want me to turn on the kitchen sink?"

"I'm serious, Sera." Maggie looked up at her friend. "I need to do this by myself."

Sera's nod was slow and considering. "I'll be right outside the room if you need me."

Once she was gone, Maggie tried to formulate sentences in her mind, but they were all a jumble of words and letters.

Just type something. Anything.

Finally, she began clicking the keys. Slowly, but she was typing.

Dear DanOfYourDreams,

I recently received the souvenir picture from our date at Llewellyn Farm, and it made me realize I never followed up to tell you how much I enjoyed myself.

I'd love to see you again. A masquerade party is being held here in Summer Shoals tomorrow - on Halloween. Would you consider going as my date?
DIYDarling

Maggie reread the note twice and then sent it out to the universe. Well, wherever emails went. She doubted he'd even respond, but if he didn't, she had no idea what Plan B would be.

She pushed away from the desk to head outside. Surely she could find something around here to fix. That would make her feel in control again. But as she walked out of the room, she heard a *ping* from the computer. Her heart caught. Could he have answered that quickly?

She peered around the corner into the kitchen like a detective checking for an all-clear. There on the computer screen was a big envelope pop-up thingie.

That meant mail, right? She had mail.

From him.

"Come quick," Maggie called to Sera, then stood frozen, staring at the screen.

"What's the matter?" Sera raced back into the room. "Are you okay?"

Maggie pointed.

Sera slid into the chair, then looked back at Maggie with a mile-wide grin. "You rock, girl. Let's see what he said."

Maggie held her breath, and Sera began to read aloud.

> *"Dear DIYDarling,*
> *I enjoyed our date too. I've never seen a woman look so pretty in beekeeper's coveralls.*
>
> *I'd love to join you at the masquerade party, but let's make it even more fun by keeping it between the two of us. Just let me know the time and place.*
>
> *I'll come as Friar Tuck. What will you be wearing?*
>
> *With all my affection,*
> *DanOfYourDreams"*

Sera turned and gave Maggie a high five.

"He went for it! Only now I'm worried he's really sweet on you."

Abby Ruth clomped into the room. "Who's sweet on who?"

"Dan's already returned Maggie's message and said yes to the masquerade."

"Good work, Mags," Abby Ruth said. "We have this guy where we want him."

Not exactly, because Maggie had wanted him to be real. But he wasn't. He was just a liar. "I need a costume."

"How about a zombie?" Abby Ruth offered. "I love the ones with hatchets stuck in their heads."

"You would," Sera said. "But Maggie's not going as a corpse. She needs to be pretty."

But Maggie knew she wouldn't ever feel pretty around Dan again because he sure wasn't *her* DanOfYourDreams.

"What's he dressing as?" Abby Ruth asked.

"Friar Tuck," Maggie told her.

"A priest? That's just wrong for a date," Abby Ruth said.

"I know." Sera hopped up and twirled, stretching out her arms as though holding a full skirt. "You can be Maid Marian. You'll be lovely!"

Chapter Twenty-Four

Maggie gazed into the mirror at the long curls Sera had fashioned with a curling iron and some industrial-strength hairspray. Maybe Laura from *Little House on the Prairie* or Maid Marian, it could go either way.

And although Maggie now knew her DanOfYourDreams wasn't the man of her dreams, she was still a little nervous about the date.

Probably because Sera had insisted Maggie wear this flowing velvet skirt and a white peasant blouse cinched with one of those bustier things. It squeezed her ribcage and lifted the girls until they were in danger of spilling over into Maggie's lap.

"Are you sure we don't have time to stitch some lace onto this shirt?" she asked Sera.

"We want Friar Tuck distracted by your...assets," Sera said, glancing down at

Maggie's cleavage. "That way, we can take him down when he's least suspecting it."

"I thought friars were supposed to be celibate."

"I'm not even trying to second-guess this guy anymore." Sera shoved a frilly handkerchief between Maggie's boobs.

"Hey, I can tuck that in and—"

"Distraction, Mags. It's all about kicking the guy where he's weakest. One look at that little hanky and the only thing he'll be thinking of is diving headfirst into your bosom."

Lordy, why had she ever agreed to this? Any man who wanted to dive into Maggie's girls needed not only a good eye exam but a thorough head check too. "Why do you get to go as a ninja?"

"Because I'm not trying to catch a man." Sera smiled and brushed a hand down her skintight black outfit. "Besides, this costume might come in handy tonight."

"Do you think Abby Ruth has killed Angelina yet?"

"Guess we'll know if there's fresh dirt under the B&B's rose bushes."

"She really came through for Summer Haven." Maggie turned so she didn't have to look at herself in the mirror anymore. "I know kowtowing to Angelina is a huge stretch for her."

"Doesn't hurt for any of us to eat a little humble pie every once in a while." Sera smiled and pinned a couple of curls on the crown of Maggie's head. "You really are beautiful, you know that, right?"

Maggie ducked her head and mumbled a few sounds that didn't even make words.

"You did notice the way Bruce looked at you yesterday, didn't you?"

"Bruce?" Maggie's head popped back up. "The IT guy at Dogwood Ridge?"

"I spotted stars in his eyes."

"Oh, go on."

"I'm completely serious."

"Do you think he'll be at the party tonight?" Maybe the evening would be about more than taking down the man who'd raised Maggie's hopes.

"On a magic night like this," Sera said with a wink, "I'd say anything could happen."

In the prison kitchen, Lillian reviewed the menu with the staff one last time. From mini ham biscuit appetizers to the banana pudding, this menu had pure Southern written all over it. If the way to a man's heart was his stomach, this menu would have that Bureau of Prisons team wanting to honeymoon at Walter Stiles Prison Camp. They'd practiced these dishes to darn near perfection. The final garnish tweaks they'd discussed put the crumble on the cobbler. She prayed the meal would be flawless.

Martha strolled over with a clipboard in her arms. "Shipshape," she reported. "Chef Ramsay would drool to work in our kitchen."

A few months ago, Lillian would've had no idea who the potty-mouth Englishman was, but the inmates here had a thing for reality TV, and *Hell's Kitchen* and *Kitchen Nightmares* were favorites. Lillian had to admit that, aside from the bleeping words he wielded as effectively as his knives, he was nothing short of amazing.

"I guess we're as ready as we're going to be. I pray those women don't burn the meal. I don't know how those Broadway actors do it. There's no way they can practice as much as we have...and we're still about a mile from perfection."

Martha looked like she was biting the inside of her cheek. "I'd thank you to be a little more respectful to my girls. They're doing the best they can and doing it for me. Not you."

Lil felt the verbal knife in her back. She hoped like heck Martha wasn't going to do anything to sabotage the day. Dixie's feral cat comment kept popping up in her mind.

It was time to give the kitty a bright ball of yarn. Anything to keep her from sinking her claws into Lil. "I chatted with Maggie earlier."

Her face lighting up, Martha stepped closer. "They found Creeping Tom."

"Not exactly, but they've arranged for another date, which means it's only a matter of time."

"Well, that's the kind of news I like to hear." Martha looped her arm through Lil's as if they were besties rather than off-again-on-again frenemies. "They're wrapping up their end of the deal, which means we can concentrate on impressing the hell out of the BOP."

"We've got our work cut out for us, but if I don't tee-totally mess up the mock interviews, we should be in good shape." She tried to infuse her words with confidence rather than the anxiety bubbling inside her. *Exhausting* was the only way she could describe the efforts she'd put into making sure WSPC and Warden Nell Proctor came out of this review with a glowing report. One that Lillian prayed would strike the prison from the closures list and launch her back to Summer Haven in record time.

"Let's go." Lillian and Martha strolled out

of the cafeteria together. "We have just enough time to get everything in the classroom set up, then we can get ready." Lillian led the way, not waiting for Martha to answer. Usually she'd let the woman act like she was running the show, but today she was driving.

One of the guards stepped onto the sidewalk in front of them. "Martha, you have a visitor."

Martha looked at Lil and shrugged. "I wasn't expecting anyone today."

"It's your niece," the guard said.

"I'm on my way." Martha turned to Lil, her color paling to the same shade as her faded khaki shirt. "Something's wrong. Her visits are never this close together."

"Calm down. You don't know that."

Martha sucked in a breath and shook her head.

"Go on," Lil said. "I'll set up the room and meet you later."

"No. You're coming with me." She took Lil by the hand and started marching toward the visiting area.

"Hold on a second." Lillian stumbled over her own feet as Martha nearly dragged her along. "We've worked too hard on this plan to let anything slip now, and the clock is ticking. I can't be late."

Martha never broke stride. "You've got half an hour to spare. We're in this together, you and me. We'll just be sure everything is okay and then we'll get back on schedule."

A fifty-yard dash later, Martha was huffing like a woman giving birth. When they arrived in the visitors' room, she did a hip whip move like a Roller Derby girl, landing her and Lil in the chairs across from her niece. "Is everything okay?"

Martha's niece smiled, then burst into tears. "You were right. OnceUponATom was some kind of kook. Look." She held out a small florist envelope.

Martha grabbed it and tugged out the card.

Dear WannaBeAMomma,

Thank you for registering with ThePerfectFit.com. However, it has come to our attention that you do not fit our site's demographic so your profile is being disabled. If you should choose to try online dating again in the future, we would recommend a site better suited to your unique needs.

Our best wishes in your search for love.
Sincerely,
ThePerfectFit.com

Martha sighed. "I hate to say I told you so, but that paintball had trouble written all over it. When did you get this?"

"Apparently a while ago. I expected him to contact me after he sent me the flowers. When I didn't hear from him by the next day, I tried to go online and thank him. But my account had been locked out. I thought it was just some kind of technical glitch. Then, as the flowers wilted—"

"You didn't get the Davilo green thumb."

"'Fraid not." She sniffed back the tears. "Anyway, when the flowers died, I saw the envelope tucked in the leaves."

"You should be glad it's over. This guy is a complete d-bag." Martha flopped back in her chair and glared at her niece. "That'll teach you to try to find a man online."

"Then how am I supposed to meet anyone?"

"Maybe try the old-fashioned way like going to bars."

"Or church," Lil added. "You'll meet someone nice one day." Her stomach clenched knowing that this meant the whole cure to her septic problems had just taken a giant flush. Martha was an eye-for-an eye kind of gal, and she had no reason in the world to call in that favor from her septic guy now.

"I didn't mean to worry you, Aunt Martha. I just thought I'd better—"

"Martha, if I don't leave here right now," Lil said, "I won't have enough time to set up for the interviewing class. Feel free to stay and chat with your niece, but I have to—"

"Not on your life, Miss H&M. If you're going, I'm going too."

They said hurried goodbyes to Martha's niece and hustled out of the visitors' room.

"Thank goodness." Martha's breath was heavy as they jogged through the courtyard. "Now that's completely behind us, we can focus on this little project."

"What about OnceUponATom?"

"I could care less who that wacko is now or who he dates as long as it isn't my niece."

Lillian didn't know why the words stung so much. She'd known that was what Martha would say. "I have to call Maggie immediately. Now that your niece is out of harm's way, I don't want my girls hunting Tom down and getting themselves into any trouble—or worse, putting themselves in danger."

"I'm sure he's harmless," Martha said.

Lillian stopped dead in her tracks. "Just stop that. This is not all about you anymore." She turned and walked to the main hall to make that call, leaving Martha standing there with her mouth open.

After waiting in line for nearly ten precious minutes that she should have used preparing for the BOP, Lillian finally got her turn at the phone. Three tries to the house phone, and she got nothing but the answering machine. No one could sleep through that many rings. She left a third message. "Mags, in case you didn't get the other two messages, stop chasing down that dating-site guy. The deal with Martha is off. We need to go to plan B on the septic system. I'm so sorry I didn't trust you to begin with. I'll find a way to get the money."

Lillian swallowed hard.

She'd been so busy telling Martha that she thought everything was always about her that she hadn't even taken inventory of her own behavior. Why was she putting Summer Haven at the top of every list? That house wasn't Maggie's priority, but darned if she hadn't stepped to the plate like she was family. It was high time Lil readjusted her own priorities.

But how on earth would she get the

money to get the care and feeding of the monster estate under control?

Selling dribs and drabs of furniture was not even a bandage to the problem.

There was only one thing, besides the estate itself, that might be worth enough to make a difference. She prayed that Tucker Torpedo was really worth what Abby Ruth Cady had said it was, because she was getting ready to break that promise to Daddy.

She was left with absolutely no other choice. *Daddy, I have a feeling you'd have told me to do this a long time ago.*

Maggie and Sera decided to leave for the masquerade party early for two reasons. One, they wanted to be there before the friar arrived and two, Abby Ruth probably needed moral support.

When they arrived, a few cars were lined on either side of the street, but it was clear the hordes hadn't yet arrived. Sera parked behind Abby Ruth's truck.

Maggie opened the door and scooped her heavy skirt over her arm. Lord, the insides of her thighs were sweating, and the extra air flow was welcome.

Angelina gave an elbow-wrist wave from the B&B's front porch. She was dressed as

Glinda the Good Witch, and her white dress sparkled with enough glitter to make a unicorn jealous.

Maggie and Sera waved back and headed for the B&B's backyard. They were stepping through the arbor when the whine of a golf cart came from behind them.

"Move it or lose it," the driver hollered.

They each jumped to the side to let the cart barrel through the opening.

"Is that Abby Ruth...?" Maggie choked out.

"It's her voice," Sera said.

The Wicked Witch of the West was driving that golf cart as if she were competing in a rally car race instead of puttering around a neighborhood party. Her broom was bungee-strapped to the roof, and the straw end fluttered as she zoomed away.

"That's a little extreme," Maggie said, "even for Abby Ruth."

"Did you notice something sitting on her shoulder?"

"She was moving too fast for me to see."

Sera grabbed Maggie's hand. "I know we're here to catch a creep, but I will kick myself forever if we don't tease Abby Ruth first."

They power-walked across the lawn and finally caught up with the golf cart, parked next to what looked like a cattle trough full of water and apples. The Wicked Witch of the West was dumping another bag of Gala apples into the tub.

"Damned woman," she was muttering to herself. "How many people does she think will stick their heads in here for a piece of fruit? Hell, none when there are popcorn balls and caramel apples on the treat table."

"Abby Ruth?" Maggie said, her voice low as though she were approaching a mountain lion with a thorn in each paw.

The witch spun around, almost dislodging the fake animal clinging to her left shoulder.

Sera clapped a palm over her gaping mouth. "It *is* you."

The view had been enjoyable from the back, but the front? Well, it was a masterpiece. Abby Ruth not only wore the sweeping black cloak and pointy hat, but her makeup was perfectly applied. A layer of green covered her from her hairline all the way down her neck. But it was the hooked nose and the raised mole on her chin that really did the trick.

Sera dug around in her skintight ninja suit and pulled out a phone. The camera function whirred and the flash blipped.

Abby Ruth lifted her chin and pointed a

green finger in Sera's face. "If I find that on Facebook later with my profile tagged, I just want you to remember that I know where you sleep."

"You can't blame me for wanting to save this for posterity."

Suddenly, the stuffed winged monkey perched on Abby Ruth's shoulder started chattering, and Maggie jumped back. "That thing's alive."

"God, don't I know it," Abby Ruth said, her voice a tired drawl.

"Where in the world did you get it?"

"Same place all this—" she swept a hand down her Wicked Witch of the West get-up, "—came from. I'll give you two guesses."

"Angelina," Sera said.

"You got it in one."

Oh, Maggie had only believed she knew the extent of Abby Ruth's sacrifice for her and Summer Haven. Abby Ruth might be maddening at times, but she was as true a friend as Sera.

The monkey reached under Abby Ruth's hat, tilting it to one side, and began picking through her hair. Every so often, he brought his hand to his mouth as if he were eating what he'd found.

"I can't convince him I don't have fleas."

"He's certainly attentive," Sera said.

"He's also incontinent," Abby Ruth remarked.

Fluurp. A sludgy mess of brown goo oozed down Abby Ruth's shoulder.

A nervous chuckle worked its way up Maggie's throat. There was absolutely nothing right about this scenario, so she yanked the hanky from its secure place between the girls and dabbed at Abby Ruth's shoulder. At close range, she and the monkey did have a gamey smell about them.

"Where did he come from?" Sera asked.

"Apparently, Angelina is on the board at the zoo. She wrangled some rent-a-monkey deal with her connections at a wildlife place near Atlanta. You wouldn't believe the forms I had to sign to take possession of this flea-obsessed, Depends-needing chimp."

Maggie tried not to smile, but this was the best thing that was likely to happen tonight. "I guess this was Angelina's way of getting a little something out of this deal."

"Oh, I wouldn't be surprised to find she has a Chinese water station and thumb screws in the basement of her house. That woman has a flair," Abby Ruth said, then waved a hand. "But Angelina was just a cog in a bigger plan tonight. Have y'all come across Friar Tuck yet?"

"Darn," Maggie said. "We were hoping

you'd spotted him."

"I have a feeling he'll wait until closer to sundown, when more people are here and he has a better opportunity for camouflage."

"Until then, can we help you with anything?" Sera asked.

"How are you with setting up tie the tail on the donkey?"

"How hard can it be? And I think it's *pin* the tail on the donkey."

Abby Ruth pinned them with a this-is-the-seventh-circle-of-hell stare. "Oh, no. It's tie because Angelina insisted we play with live donkeys."

Chapter Twenty-Five

An hour later, twilight had fallen and the B&B's backyard was a wild crush of kids brandishing glow sticks and adults enjoying Halloween punch. The costumes ranged from uninspired—one guy draped in a white sheet—to incredible—a woman dressed as Carmen Miranda, complete with fresh fruit piled on her head.

Maggie nursed a tiny cup of punch because she needed her wits about her, but Sera had insisted a tad of alcohol would calm Maggie's crackling nerves.

She was watching Hollis Dooley bob for apples. He'd almost fallen in once, but had insisted on a second chance. Now, Abby Ruth was fishing his false teeth out of the water with her broomstick.

"Maid Marian, you're looking lovely tonight," a male voice said from behind Maggie, and she whirled around to find a hooded, not-at-all-rotund Friar Tuck making a low bow.

This is it. I'll finally see his face.

But when Tuck untucked from his bow, Maggie was disappointed to find he was wearing one of those rubber masks. She had to give him kudos for finding one with that funky fringe of brown hair, though. "Friar Tuck, you're looking very...brown...this evening."

It was hard to find a decent compliment for a man wearing a burlap robe and rope belt.

"Brought you something," he said.

"You did?" Maybe he really did like her. I mean, she'd fudged her picture, so maybe he'd been afraid to use his real one.

He extended his hand. "Give me your wrist."

A niggle of self-preservation made her hesitate. She glanced around, praying Sera was nearby, then raised her arm toward him.

He tucked a hand into his robe and pulled out a lovely purple length of rope tied into one of those pretty heart knots, like the ones he'd used to secure the legs of his beekeeping outfit.

"It's beautiful."

"Tied it myself," he said, wrapping the homemade bracelet around her wrist. In a few tugs and twists, he had it secured.

She held it up to admire his handiwork. "I love it. Thank you." Her heart was filling with second doubts about him. She wished she could just tell him to run, so that she might be able to pursue more little moments like this with him.

Maggie scanned the landscape, looking for either Sera or Abby Ruth. But Abby Ruth was no longer by the apple trough. She'd probably had to take the monkey for a potty break.

"Would you like some punch?" DanTomTuck asked her.

She surreptitiously dropped the plastic cup she'd been holding behind her back. *I'll make up for it by doing trash duty later.* "I'd love some, but please let me come with you." That would give her an opportunity to find her girls.

"Maggie?"

She turned to see Bruce Shellenberger, the IT guy, standing there all dressed up as a geek, although it wasn't much of a stretch except for the black glasses with the tape on them. "Hi, Bruce."

Friar Tuck stopped and looked at her, then toward Bruce. How did you introduce two men when you're on a date? This was a first for her.

"IT Guy meet Friar Tuck." That would have to do for now. "We were just going to get some punch," she said to Bruce.

"Well...have fun. I just wanted to say hello." He backed away, looking uncomfortable, making guilt crawl over Maggie. He was such a nice guy, and she'd just blown him off.

"Let's get that punch," DanOfYourDreams said.

Maggie was following her "date" to the refreshments table when a handsome cowboy reached out from another group of people and grabbed her arm. "Maggie?"

What was it with men tonight? Everywhere she turned, they were pursuing her. And the last man she wanted following her was Teague. That man showed up at the most inconvenient times. As if he had a nose for trouble or something.

"Well, don't you look like a real Texan?" she said cheerfully.

"And you...you're a..."

"You might be looking for the word *wench*."

He averted his gaze from the expanse of her cleavage. "You want to introduce me to your friend here?"

And Lord, Friar Tuck began fidgeting as though he'd swallowed a cistern full of water, and there wasn't a rest stop for miles.

"Teague, this is...Friar Tuck."

Teague reached across to shake the man's hand, but before he could make contact, the friar turned tail and took off in a dead run.

"What the hell?" Teague asked.

"He's kind of shy," Maggie improvised. Where oh where were her girls when she needed them?

Abby Ruth pushed through the crowd, her monkey clinging with both hairy arms around her neck. "Did I just see Friar Tuck make a break for it? We've got to catch him. C'mon." She grabbed Maggie's hand and pulled her in the opposite direction from Tuck's flight.

"He went the other way."

"The wheels are this way, though." Abby Ruth swung into the golf cart's driver's seat, and Maggie gathered her skirt and dove into the other side.

Teague dashed up. "What the hell is going on here?"

"No time to talk, Tadpole." Abby Ruth gunned the accelerator and clipped Teague before he could jump out of the way.

"What if he's hurt?" Maggie asked.

"That boy is tough. In fact, I probably should've hit him right on. That would've put him out of the action for sure."

"Pretty sure that might've also put you behind bars for assaulting a police officer."

Sera came running toward the golf cart. Like the physically talented woman she was, she grabbed the pole that held up the cart's roof and swung herself onto the back where the golf bags were normally stored. "I spotted him. He took off across the Broussards' lawn."

Oh, no. Their plan to keep him contained wasn't working.

Abby Ruth put on the lead foot and tore right through a prickly hedge. When they came out the other side, Sera was hanging on by her fingernails, but she was grinning wide.

"There he is," Maggie yelled. "On the other side of the rose garden."

No skirting the edges of the concrete-edged flowerbed for Abby Ruth. The tires hit the barrier at a slight angle, and the cart went airborne by at least a foot. When they hit the ground again, the monkey let out a high-pitched squeak. Abby Ruth barreled on, flattening what Maggie was pretty sure was a rare hooligan rose.

She started calculating reparations in her head.

Oh, forget reparations. Once Angelina learned they were responsible for murdering her flowers, there wouldn't be enough money in the world to guarantee that Summer Haven would pass her inspection.

"Shoot," Sera hollered from her vantage point of peering over the cart's roof. "He just scaled the fence."

Angelina had a dainty white picket fence separating her yard from the neighbor's.

"Hang on, gals." Elbows out, Abby Ruth gripped the steering wheel, and Maggie grasped the cupholder with two hands to keep from tumbling out of the cart.

No angling involved this time. The cart careened into the pickets head-on and took out a good six feet.

"Duck, Sera," Maggie called.

Sure enough, the pickets slid up the plastic windshield and flew over the top of the cart. When they cleared into the next yard, Friar Tuck looked as though he was having a little trouble with his own skirt, stumbling and staggering as he tried to head toward the river.

Abby Ruth adjusted the cart's trajectory to cut off the guy. He juked left, which was his fatal mistake. His foot caught in his long hem, and his arms windmilled as he tried to catch himself. Unfortunately for him, Angelina's neighbors had installed an oval-shaped koi pond.

Sploosh. In he went, face first.

Abby Ruth stomped on the brake, locking it down to the floor and stopping the cart on a dime.

Maggie and the others poured out to surround the flailing friar.

"We need to get him while he's down," Abby Ruth ordered.

"I'm on it," Sera scrambled into the water with him. Maggie waded in after her.

Shoot, they needed to assemble some kind of bad guy takedown emergency kit for these occasions. Then again, what else did a girl need other than her own duct tape and a crazy Texan with a big black gun?

Abby Ruth was locked into her make-my-day stance, her pistol trained on their guy. Maggie and Sera yanked at his sopping robe while he flapped his arms and finally flopped over to face them. His mask was pushed up just enough so his eyes weren't aligned with the eye holes.

With a quick yank, Sera pulled off his rope belt and held it out to Maggie. "Want to do the honors? You're kind of an expert at tying up the baddies."

She was, wasn't she?

Maggie squatted down in the water while Sera held his hands in her strong grip. With a few deft moves—unders, overs and crosses—Maggie tied him up in a perfect stevedore knot.

"I didn't mean anyone any harm." His words were muffled by the rubber mask.

Maggie's heart ached for the guy. He seemed so sad and sincere, but darn it, he had hurt someone. Her. If only her pride.

The sound of footfalls came from behind Maggie, and Teague drew up short beside her, followed by Bruce and a few other people in costume.

Teague pushed his cowboy hat back on his head a bit. "Just when I think you gals aren't stirring up trouble anymore, I find you with a man of the cloth hog-tied in a fish pond. Ladies, what in hell is this all about?"

Teague might have come to the party as a Texas Ranger but the last thing he'd planned or wanted to do was work. These women thought they could just run all over his county doing whatever the hell they pleased.

"You should cuff him," Abby Ruth said, standing over the guy in the pond, her gun never wavering from the friar's forehead.

"That might be a little dicey," Teague said, "since I have no idea who he is or what he did."

"We don't know who he is either," Sera said. "But it's probably about time we found out."

About time? That insinuated these ladies had been chasing this guy for a while now. *Shit.*

Teague leaned over to check out the guy's hands. They'd tied him up something good. So well that he wasn't worried the guy could get loose.

Sera reached down to grab the guy's mask, and Teague had a Scooby-Doo *déjà vu* moment. *If it weren't for those meddling kids...*

She yanked it up his face to reveal...

"Deputy Barnes!" the three women said in perfect tandem.

Good Lord, these three women were a massive stitch in his side. He reached over to pull his deputy out of the water.

"I wouldn't do that, Tadpole."

"Aunt Bibi, this is Barnes. I know the three of y'all like to think you're some crime-fighting trio, but this man is an officer of the law. You'll be lucky if he doesn't press charges against you." He shot her a hard look. "Speaking of, I could do the same."

"Starting talking, lover boy," Abby Ruth demanded, raising her chin and giving Barnes her raised eyebrow look.

Barnes exercised his right to remain silent.

"You heard me." Abby Ruth kicked at Barnes' sandal. "You owe us a hell of an explanation."

"Can you blame a man for wanting to find the love of his life?" Barnes asked, casting a longing glance at Maggie.

Maggie's expression closed up, became almost as mean as Abby Ruth's. "I thought you liked me, but you're nothing but a liar."

Oh, God. Were they gunning for Barnes because he had a thing for Maggie? No, it wasn't exactly normal, but a May-December romance wasn't illegal.

"Maggie, you have to understand—" Barnes reached out with his tied-up hands, but Maggie stepped back.

"All I have to understand," Maggie said, "is that you're a fraud. Probably committed fraud too."

Teague's ears went supersonic at that. "What's she talking about, Barnes?"

"Ole Barnes here started a dating site called The Perfect Fit," Abby Ruth said, "and created tons of male profiles trying to troll for women."

Oh, hell. Teague had hoped this was just a case of overactive hot flashes. But seeing as he'd been poking around on that site himself, there was obviously something to the grannies' takedown.

"Charged a hundred dollars a pop for women to register," Sera added.

"I only paid twenty," Teague blurted before he thought better of it. By Abby Ruth's evil grin, she'd already been aware of that little fact.

"And then," Abby Ruth said, "he had the nerve to boot people off the site."

"I can explain." Barnes shook his head. "I made sure every penny went back to the ladies by way of the money spent on the date or gifts. Those I didn't take on a date got big gifts. Just ask Sera and Abby Ruth."

Abby Ruth twirled a whoop-dee-doo finger in the air. "I got cube steak. Trust me, I'd've rather had the money." She glanced over at Teague. "Come to find out, he was putting up fake pictures and false information. He was behind over fifty of the profiles in that database. Ain't that right, Deputy?"

Teague wasn't an expert on fraud, but this dating thing was hinky all around, what with those fake charges on Sue Ellen's credit card.

"Jesus, Barnes, what have you done?" Teague asked his deputy. Likely his former deputy now.

"I never meant for anyone to get hurt."

Yeah, tons of criminals said that. "I didn't

know you were such a computer whiz."

"I'm not," Barnes admitted. "My nephew James was working on website design for a computer science project in school. I talked him into setting it up for me."

"And then you ran the whole thing?"

"No way. I'm not that smart," Barnes said. "But please don't make trouble for James. He has a real chance at a scholarship to UGA when he graduates next year."

What a holy mess. "What do you know about extra credit card charges to people who registered on that site?"

Barnes' head came up, and he stared openmouthed at Teague. "Huh?"

"Yeah," Abby Ruth said, "Jenny's card was run up by a couple hundred bucks."

Teague swung around to goggle at Abby Ruth. "Jenny's registered on The Perfect Fit?"

"Not anymore," she muttered.

"Teague, you gotta understand," Barnes pleaded. "I wanted to find someone special. Dating's hard in a town this size, and figured I might have more luck if I broadened my search. The online dating thing is so hot right now, but I knew I couldn't compete against some of those other guys. Ones that make more money and are better-looking."

It was damned hard to fault the man for

searching for the woman of his dreams. Teague didn't have to search. He knew who his dream woman was, but right now, Jenny seemed as far away as Barnes' perfect woman.

Still, he reached for his phone and called in. "I need a transport to the county jail at 555 Pecan Orchard Street, and I need someone to go round up James Barnes."

Angelina came barreling into her neighbor's yard, waving at the destruction behind her. Although she was dressed like the Good Witch, she was wailing like a wicked one out of control. "What on heaven's earth have y'all done to my yard? Who is going to pay for my fence?" She spun around to Abby Ruth. "You are nothing but a walking disaster."

"Excuse me, Angelina." Teague yanked Barnes out of the pond and frog-marched him to the front yard. The grannies trailed along behind them. Within minutes, one of his other deputies pulled up, and Teague escorted Barnes to the patrol car's backseat. He said to his deputy, "Don't ask. I'll be right behind you to process him."

He turned back to the grannies, finally registering that something furry was hunkered down on Aunt Bibi's shoulder. Could this night get any more surreal?

"His name is Peter," she said and stepped over to put her non-monkey-bearing arm around Teague. "I'm really sorry about all this."

"Me too. Barnes has always been a good guy. But if he was defrauding folks, he needed to be stopped." He smiled at the three women, but his mouth muscles felt fatigued. This was bad enough, but it was clear Barnes or his nephew James were behind those fraudulent charges on Sue Ellen's credit card too. Plus, three others had come forward with small charges on their cards recently. All for little things like candy, flowers, cheap jewelry, books, and services less than one hundred dollars each. No. Things didn't look good for Barnes. "Y'all done good. But next time, do you think you could bring me in on things a little earlier?"

Abby Ruth bumped him with her hip, sending her monkey swaying. The critter steadied himself by grabbing onto Teague's cowboy hat. "Well, I figure you're gonna need another deputy now. And I know just the woman for the job."

God help Bartell County if he ever let Abby Ruth loose on them.

Chapter Twenty-Six

Lil watched from the kitchen pass-thru as the Federal Bureau of Prisons team enjoyed the dinner she'd planned. The girls would have made even the best chef in the world proud today. Not only had they provided a five-star presentation, but the smiles and nods coming from the white-clothed cafeteria table were nothing short of a standing ovation.

Now, all she had to do was get through the mock interviews, and they were home free.

Janisse, one of Martha's loyal posse, stopped and showed Lillian the tray of desserts before they were presented to their visitors.

Lillian raised a hand to her chest. "Simply lovely." Although she needed to hustle across the building to set up the classroom, she watched for long enough to gauge the group's response to the banana pudding. If their closed eyes and moans were anything to go on, they'd passed this part of the test.

Once in the classroom, she placed a lesson plan sheet in each seat, as she always did. The back row seats held a booklet outlining the entire etiquette curriculum for the BOP folks.

And although most of the women in the upcoming session were in Martha's hip pocket, Lil just couldn't relax. Martha no longer needed Lil to solve her problem, which meant Martha could have her girls turn on Lil.

Warden Proctor walked into the classroom with the parade of people following her, including Martha. Lillian glanced up at the clock. Right on schedule. The inmates would be here in exactly eight minutes.

Everything was going according to plan.

The warden led the BOP group to the special seats in the back of the room and motioned for Lillian.

Suddenly, anxiety choked Lil. Ridiculous. She'd been in social situations her entire life. She just needed to pretend this was a library fundraiser or something of the sort.

Kelsey Browning and Nancy Naigle

Martha leaned in and said, "You've got this, Miss H&M."

"Come with me." She and Martha walked down the aisle toward the guests of honor.

"Ladies and gentlemen," the warden began, "this is Inmate Fairview and Inmate Davilo. They organized your meal this evening. Inmate Fairview has started an extensive etiquette series here at Walter Stiles. The classes have been instrumental in changing both the behavior and the mindset of many of our women. As their social skills have improved, altercation rates have gone down, and we're discovering our new releases are getting better jobs. But we didn't want to stop there, so Inmate Fairview has put together a special session on dressing for success and interviewing effectively."

Beside Lil, Martha shifted her weight from side to side. Which meant she was waiting for her helping of praise.

The warden said, "Inmate Fairview, why don't you tell our guests a little about tonight's class."

Looked like she'd have to be the one to pat Martha on the back. "Thank you, Warden," she said. "The booklets I placed in your seats include the lesson plans from the inception of this project until tonight's session. You'll see we've covered everything from proper hygiene and posture to table etiquette. If you have any questions about previous lessons or how we've tracked progress, I'd be happy to discuss that with you." She smiled and paused for effect. "Now, for today, I'm very excited to bring you one of the most important sessions we've put together. Martha—" Lillian pulled her forward, "—and I have worked closely on this session. The etiquette classes will certainly help our inmates develop a sense of confidence and assist them in social situations that may not have been commonplace prior to their stay at Walter Stiles. However, we all know job placement is one of the most important hurdles those exiting the program contend with. Martha, why don't you tell them a little about what we have planned for this evening?"

Martha stood straight and made eye contact with the group. She even gave them a professional smile. "Tonight, we'll be taking these inmates through a mock interview process in their chosen fields, which I think you'll find is a great way to prepare them for a real interview." She glanced toward the warden. "May I bring our job candidates in?"

"Please do," the warden said.

The BOP team watched intently. There

wasn't a smile or look of encouragement from the bunch.

Lillian walked back to the desk at the front of the room and glanced down at her notes. She picked up the stack of folders she'd prepared and when she looked up, they slipped from her grasp and hit the floor. Papers slid every which way and she squatted down and scooped them toward her. When she stood, she blinked several times, but the scene in front of her didn't improve.

Not a drop of khaki—any of the three shades the prison seemed to think were appropriate for mix-and-match—in the entire bunch. What might've made her happy under any other circumstance heated her face and chilled her hands.

Her face a little paler than normal, Martha walked up to join Lillian.

Was this Martha's way of getting back at her?

Lillian turned as if to put some folders back on the table and hissed close to Martha's ear. "What have you done?"

"I didn't do this," Martha said, her voice high and tight. "I swear."

Lord, Lil would give anything to just run right out of the room and never stop running. Maybe run all the way back home to Summer Haven.

Each of the twenty ladies had transformed her uniform into business attire. One in a black dyed "suit" she'd fashioned from a long-sleeved top, cut down the center and refastened with what appeared to be foil-covered buttons, and a skirt made from a pair of cutoff pants with the center seams ripped out and resewn. Frankly, the hem work was excellent and the buttons were smooth, not a wrinkle anywhere in the foil. Another wore a green sleeveless top with hemmed arm holes and a very short skirt that Lil was relieved to see had little shorts underneath.

One of the Bureau of Prisons team members stood, and Lillian swore she heard the warden suck air. "This is a violation of even our minimum uniform regulations," the BOP woman said.

Hand over her mouth, Martha shook her head, and by the greenish-khaki hue of Warden Proctor's face, she was about to lose the lovely dinner the girls had so carefully cooked and served.

Remember, Lil, you can hold your head up among even the hoitiest of the toities. You will convince these people to give you what you want.

Which meant pretending this was

business as usual and conducting her class.

Lillian held up her hand for forestall more comments. "This is a controlled experiment, and I hope you'll bear with us. We've found that our inmates have responded quite nicely to these creative types of..." Her legs were like rapidly melting butter. She'd lost her train of thought and quite frankly if God would just strike her dead right now, it would be a blessing. Lillian turned around and took a sip of water. "How could you do this to me?" she whispered to Martha.

Martha dropped her hand from her face and stared at Lil as though she'd just told her to jump on the table, strip naked and put on a show. "You sure don't think much of me, do you?" She elbowed her way around Lil and said, "You should know the inmates created their business attire by using a stack of old uniforms. We thought it would be the perfect way to show how the prisoners here can recycle resources which have otherwise been written off by the BOP. I think you'll agree it's creative and cost effective."

Clearly proud of their accomplishment, the inmates nodded and smiled.

"The old uniforms were faded, but they were better made than the ones we wear now." Martha motioned to the inmate in the first seat. "Step up here for me, so we can show off your handiwork."

The woman wearing the suit walked—with perfect posture—to the front of the classroom.

Martha strolled around her. "Nice. Black business suit with silver buttons. Tell us about your...briefcase."

"Louis Vuitton," the girl said, lifting the makeshift purse made from a library book covered in brown fabric and embellished with what appeared to be gold glitter paint, "ish."

Lillian opened her folder and began to play along. "I'm pleased you ladies have taken this opportunity so seriously. We know how important appearances and first impressions are, so putting your best foot forward can be what helps you get the job you want. And you'll be interviewing for the lead sales associate here at Chic Boutique today, correct?" she said to the inmate.

"Yes, ma'am," the inmate responded.

"Please have a seat—" she indicated a small table with two chairs, "—and we'll begin."

Before sitting, the inmate held out her hand and said, "Hello, my name is Janisse, and I'm here to interview for the sales associate position. It's a pleasure to meet you."

Lil's heart swelled. What she was doing here was making a difference. "Lillian Summer Fairview. The pleasure is all mine." They both sat, and Lillian asked, "Tell me a little about yourself."

"I've worked in retail on and off for the past ten years. You'll see on my resume—" the woman pulled a sheet of paper from her Louis Vuitton-ish bag and handed it to Lillian, "—I've held positions in both large department stores and small boutiques. Although I enjoyed all my jobs, I like the specialty boutique environment better."

Lil could've reached across the table and snatched this gal up in a hug, but she forced herself to limit her reaction to a smile. "Why is that?"

"Uh..." Janisse's gaze darted from Lil to Martha to the warden and back again. "Because..."

You can do it, Janisse. Lil gave her an encouraging smile. "Maybe something to do with the customers?"

"Oh, yeah. I mean, yes. In a small store, there's more opportunity to get to know your clients and help them choose clothes they not only like, but look and feel good in."

"Why are you the best candidate for sales associate at Chic Boutique?"

"I'm mature enough to know retail is my chosen profession instead of a less experienced teenager who works in a store for spending money. I don't mind working weekends and you can count on me to show up on time, ready to work."

Lil shot a quick glance Martha's way to catch her doing a little fist pump down by her hip. Then she turned back to the inmate. "Thank you so much for coming by today. We'll be making our choice later this week."

The inmate stood and held out her hand again. "I look forward to hearing from you."

After the retail candidate, the girl in the skort came forward and did a bang-up job interviewing for a scheduling position at a golf and tennis club.

Lillian glanced at the clock. They'd used fifty-five minutes of their allotted sixty. "Our guests will be leaving in just a few moments, so now I'd like to give them a chance to ask a few questions." She walked to the back of the room and stood with her hands lightly clasped behind her back. Even if these people dragged her over hot coals, she wouldn't change a thing about this evening's class. The girls had been amazing.

The woman who'd complained about the so-called uniforms spoke up again. "You've destroyed federal property by altering those inmate uniforms. Do you feel that stealing and vandalism is setting a good example for these women?"

Lord have mercy. Some people were just born into the world to make trouble, and it appeared this woman was one of them. "You have to give these inmates points for creativity and taste. They took uniforms that otherwise would've been surplussed and altered them to make for a more realistic mock-interview situation. I don't believe they should be faulted for that. Besides, all these skills, creative thinking included, will allow them to go back out and rebuild productive ties to their communities."

Martha chimed in, "Of course, not everyone wants to be a sales associate or a golf pro, so we did work with each inmate on realistic opportunities. You can't deny we have some excellent chefs in the making."

The BOP team looked at each other and nodded, the one woman reluctantly, but she was moving her head in the right direction.

Lillian continued, "This curriculum could be easily replicated across other camps and low-level security facilities with high success. I'd be happy to share my lesson plans. In addition, reusing old uniforms for other creative projects could be a morale booster and a cost saver."

"Upcycling is huge right now," Martha added. "Doing something like this shows the world the BOP is innovative, yet money smart.

"Exactly," Lillian said. "Reusing older uniforms could help balance your squeezed budgets without shortchanging the re-skilling programs that this type of facility offers. You can thank Martha for the beautification program. She was quite innovative in finding ways to put the inmates to work keeping the place looking nice by upcycling things already in use here in that way too."

Heads were nodding around the room, and Martha was grinning.

Maybe Martha'd forgive her yet for not finding out what she needed about her niece's kooky admirer.

"Ladies, before our guests leave," Lil said, "I'd like to ask you to stand and let our esteemed visitors have another look at your outfits."

The inmates stood. Good posture. Pleasant smiles. They were as fresh and shiny as first graders with their new lunch boxes. Lillian had never felt prouder.

The warden stood and the BOP walked toward the door, the warden falling in step at the very back of the line.

Warden Proctor stopped and shook Martha's hand and thanked her, and then leaned into Lil and whispered. "I have a letter to write." She leaned back. "Thank you."

The door clicked behind them and the inmates sat quietly until they heard the buzz of the next two doors, indicating their guests were out of earshot.

The inmates hooted and hollered and danced around Martha and Lillian.

"Were you surprised?" the women asked.

"Like you wouldn't believe," Martha said.

Lillian hugged Martha. "I thought I was so SOL. You really didn't know anything about this?"

"Not a thing." Martha laughed, and pointed to a girl's turquoise pinstriped suit. "I know where my nail polish went, though."

"Thank you for stepping in and saving me earlier when I couldn't think of a thing to say. I want you to know I'm sorry Maggie and the others weren't able to get that dating site information when you needed it. Regardless, I'm happy your niece is out of harm's way. Even if I didn't get my half of the deal."

"Miss H&M, you did your part. I called my guy yesterday. He's already put you on his schedule to get out to your house."

"You did?"

"Of course. I'm a woman of my word. I thought everyone knew that."

Lil had to admit that was true. But usually Martha was good to her word on threats, not favors. Maybe they were all learning some lessons here at Walter Stiles Prison Camp.

Maggie watched the Mrs. Potts Pots truck trundle off, its flatbed loaded with the hot pink portable potties as planned this morning. They were the last distraction at the otherwise spic-and-span Summer Haven.

Martha had come through with her septic guy. They must've showed up right after Maggie and Sera left for the party. When they'd gotten home, the guys were still working under floodlights. She and the other gals had been so tired after all that Deputy Barnes brouhaha, they hadn't even cared about the septic ruckus. Lo and behold, not only had Martha's people fixed the potty problem, but they'd even sumped out the hole and laid sod over the spot.

Maggie deadheaded a few of the huge cushion mums in the flower bed, trying to burn off energy in anticipation of the inspection. Angelina and her merry band of men would be here any minute.

Maggie couldn't help wondering if things might have been different with Deputy Barnes had he and James not concocted that whole website together. The different registration fees and Barnes' multiple profiles, they might've gotten away with. But those fraudulent credit cards charges Teague had mentioned...those would be harder to duck. Abby Ruth was inside checking her account right now.

Apparently, James had been the mastermind who'd stashed the little computer in Warner Talley's room at Dogwood Ridge. So much for those volunteer hours going on James' college applications.

"They're here." Sera came bounding down the front stairs. "They just turned in the drive. I saw them from the landing."

"Here goes nothing." Maggie glanced at the bright-purple heart rope bracelet Barnes had tied around her wrist last night. Even though he'd turned out not to be the man of her dreams, he'd truly wanted a second date. Plus, he'd given her a little something. Something she didn't know was even still inside her. The hope of sharing some of her golden years with someone.

Abby Ruth strolled out of the house.

"Nothing on my credit card that's not supposed to be there," she reported.

"Thank goodness," Maggie said.

"Yeah," Abby Ruth agreed. "Guess I'll make myself scarce. Kids are practicing on the back forty again. Need me for anything?"

Maggie shook her head. "Just keep your fingers crossed or whatever Texans do for luck."

Darrell Holloway was in the driver seat of the white SUV with Hollis Dooley riding shotgun. Darned if Angelina didn't look as if she was being chauffeured. Probably the way she'd planned it. He pulled the truck to a stop just a few feet short of the spot that only yesterday could have held a battleship.

Angelina waited until Darrell opened the door for her, then slid out of the back seat, her shiny pumps hitting the ground in a one-two click.

As usual she was glittering from head to toe. A scarf with shiny metallic thread halved and tugged around her neck made her look a little like a turtle.

Darrell lagged behind while Hollis Dooley, his old hound dog at his side, plodded forward with his walker one slow step at a time.

"Where do you want to start?" Maggie asked Angelina.

388   Kelsey Browning and Nancy Naigle

"Upstairs, I suppose." She pushed forward, knocking on the porch posts and taking a second glance at the front door jamb as she did. At the stairway, Angelina pushed and pulled on the wooden railing, as she took each step in an overly cautious way.

"The stairs are safe," Maggie said.

"She's dramatic sometimes," Darrell said as he walked by.

"Sometimes?"

Hollis parked himself and his dog in the parlor. "Mind if I sit down?"

"Not at all," Maggie said. "Tea?"

"I'd love some."

After fetching Hollis a glass, Maggie paced the first floor, going over all the problems in the house in her head and hoping that Angelina wouldn't find something she'd missed.

She could hear Angelina ordering Darrell to go into the attic. Seriously? She was just determined to find something. Maggie didn't know why she'd worked so hard. The sound of every door opening and closing reverberated through the house. Then finally, there was a flush.

Maggie held her breath.

Not a gurgle or burp followed. Thank goodness.

Angelina came down the stairs without

using the handrail. She tapped her pen on the clipboard, then whisked right by Maggie without a word.

In less than five minutes, she and Darrell were back outside, mumbling on the front porch. Hollis might have well stayed home. He hadn't done anything but sip tea with Sera, but if he got a vote, Maggie felt certain they had his.

Hollis finally joined the other two members of the Historic Preservation Committee on the porch, then he and Angelina headed for the truck.

"Are they leaving?" Sera asked Maggie.

But before Maggie could muster a response, Darrell strolled back inside.

"Congratulations, Maggie." Darrell extended his hand. "You've passed your inspection, and here's your invitation to the annual Christmas Candlelight Tour of Homes."

Sera clapped and hugged Maggie.

"Thank you!"

"I didn't say anything to Angelina, but that tree close to the house is a definite problem. I know you have had it on your radar, please take care of it soon. I'd hate for something to happen."

"I will," Maggie said. "I promise."

"And come on by the store, and I'll set

you up with some new lights for the holiday tour decorations. Wouldn't even mind lending you a hand stringing them, if you need it."

Sera elbowed Maggie.

"Thank you, Darrell. I'll stop by next week."

He raised a hand in a wave and walked outside.

Maggie and Sera watched him all the way to his truck. "He's kind of good-looking," Sera said. "And he's totally sweet on you."

He had seemed interested. "It's probably just the hardware connection." Or maybe that little beekeeping date had re-pollinated her in some sweet kind of way.

"Whatever." Sera grabbed her hand and dragged her back inside. "Let's have a glass of wine to celebrate."

"Perfect."

Sera grabbed a bottle from the kitchen counter and went to work on the cork.

The front door slammed.

"Uh-oh," Sera said.

Maggie peeked down the hall. "That's just Abby Ruth coming in."

"Not that." Sera frantically opened drawers and cabinet doors. "Your visitor badge from the prison camp. I put it in the silverware drawer, and now it's gone."

Maggie raced to Sera's side. "When did you last see it?"

"This morning," Sera said, panic clear in her voice.

Maggie shoved things around. Lifting the trivets and refolding the dish towels. But no badge. She turned to Sera. "If that's fallen into the wrong hands, and people find out about Lil..."

"She'll be—" Abby Ruth's voice boomed like God from the heavens, and there wasn't a smile line in sight, "—fit to be tied."

THE END...
of this adventure

What's Next?
Book Three – IN HIGH COTTON (2015)
and for our romance readers ~ special set of novellas ~
The Teague and Jenny Romance

Acknowledgements

Thank you to all the fabulous folks who make us (and the Grannies) look good.

Thanks to Michelle Preast for giving our vision of the Grannies life in the form of caricatures and for creating a fabulous cover template. Lillian, Maggie, Sera, Abby Ruth and Teague wouldn't be who they are today without you!

And a huge shout-out to Deb Nemeth. You make every story stronger while helping us hang onto what makes these women special. We're grateful.

Major Oxford-comma appreciation to Kim Cannon. You help us dot all our i's and cross all our t's.

Oodles of love and thanks to our fabulous street team, the Dangerous Darlings. We couldn't get the word out to the world about these stories without your help and support. Big Southern girl hugs to each and every one of you!

To Pam Dougherty, big thanks for doing such a bang-up job on the audiobook of *In For a Penny*. You made us laugh at our own words, which was such a treat. We hope we'll be able to continue to bring the Grannies to life in audio.

Much appreciation to Keith Sarna for tweaking this cover so the entire series will groove, yet each book will have its own personality.

And thanks to Miss Bettie, Tech Guy, and Smarty Boy for understanding when we lock ourselves away for days at a time to work on these stories and for not panicking when you hear loud and crazy laughter from the other room. An extra hug and smooch to Tech Guy for teaching us the difference between a whois search and a trace route. We promise Nan *is* real!

And finally, thank you to all the wonderful readers who have contacted us about The Granny Series asking for the second book. You're the reason we get up every day, put on our moose pajamas, and get to work.

About the Authors

Kelsey Browning writes sass kickin' love stories and co-authors Southern cozy mysteries. She's also a co-founder of Romance University blog, one of Writer's Digest 101 Best Websites for Writers. Originally from a Texas town smaller than the ones she writes about, Kelsey has also lived in the Middle East and Los Angeles, proving she's either adventurous or downright nuts. These days, she hangs out in northeast Georgia with Tech Guy, Smarty Boy, Bad Dog and Pharaoh, a (fingers crossed) future therapy dog. For info on her upcoming single title releases, drop by www.KelseyBrowning.com.

Nancy Naigle writes love stories from the crossroad of small town and suspense. Born and raised in Virginia Beach, Nancy now calls North Carolina home. She's currently at work on the next book in The Granny Series, and a new women's fiction novel. Stay in touch with Nancy on Facebook, twitter or subscribe to her newsletter on her website ~ www.NancyNaigle.com.

STAY UP TO DATE ON RELEASE INFORMATION ABOUT
THE GRANNIES AT
www.TheGrannySeries.com

Also by Kelsey Browning::
TEXAS ★ NIGHTS Series
Book 1:: Personal Assets
Book 2:: Running the Red Light
Book 3:: Problems in Paradise
Book 4:: Designed For Love

Also by Nancy Naigle::
The Adams Grove Series
Book 1:: Sweet Tea and Secrets
Book 2:: Wedding Cake and Big Mistakes
Book 3:: Out of Focus
Book 4:: Pecan Pie and Deadly Lies
Book 5:: Mint Juleps and Justice
Book 6:: Barbecue and Bad News

Young Adult Mystery
inkBLOT – co-written with Phyllis Johnson

Made in the USA
Lexington, KY
04 May 2018